Praise for A.H. Cunningham

"*Out of Office* is a romance for the moment, a lushly penned tale of finding true love and building a life to meet it. Exquisitely sensual and deeply heartfelt— and so, so gorgeously grown-up. Five stars!"

—Sierra Simone, author of *Misadventures of a Curvy Girl* and *Priest*

"As sexy and sultry as a hot Panamanian night, Genevieve and Adrián's romance will leave you breathless. I devoured their story."

—Farrah Rochon, *New York Times* and *USA TODAY* bestselling author, on *Out of Office*

Also by A.H. Cunningham

Out of Office

Visit ahcunninghamauthor.com or the Author Profile
page at Harlequin.com for more titles.

Ms. V's Hot Girl Summer

A.H. CUNNINGHAM

HARLEQUIN

afterglow
BOOKS

Recycling programs
for this product may
not exist in your area.

ISBN-13: 978-1-335-57497-8

Ms. V's Hot Girl Summer

Copyright © 2025 by A.H. Cunningham

Harlequin Enterprises ULC
22 Adelaide St. West, 41st Floor
Toronto, Ontario M5H 4E3, Canada
www.Harlequin.com

Printed in U.S.A.

Para mis amigas del alma:
Anilena, Desiree, Itza Maylen, Lauri, Lili, Taika y Yarenis.
To the next adventure, our forties!

The following story has a brief mention of the death of a parent that happened off the pages, conversations about divorce, as well as the lived experience of a character caretaking a parent with bipolar disorder.

I hope that I have handled these topics with care.

A.H.

One

Trinidad

The candle I left burning on my desk had never worked as hard as I asked it to today. The invocations had been plentiful and dramatic while I packed the picnic basket before I left home. Pleas to God, my ancestors, Tía Patricia, que en paz descanse, and the spirits were my only thoughts as I walked toward Williamsburg Park to meet Milton.

Lord, let this be the last time I have to date.

My prayers were very warranted, and no, I didn't think I sounded desperate. Being a single mom and filing the thirty-five and above category in all documents quickly got old. My path to love had started early and had been tumultuous and eventful, leaving me with two fifteen-year-old children and a co-parent who usually got a C in the *co* part of parenting. As long as the ancestors, Tia Patricia, God, and the spirits forgot about the consequent wild years after my divorce, I should get my prayers answered today. Right?

"So I told Greg, listen, man, give me a couple of hours, and I promise you'll also fall in love with golf. I think he's gonna take my offer, so it's me and one of the top executives having one-on-one time. I'm telling you, Trinidad, I can feel it. This is my year. This is my year."

Milton, dear man, had given me a soliloquy of all the reasons why he was going to make partner this year in his accounting firm. It had been an hour-long picnic, and he barely paused for breath. Now we were strolling down the park, people-watching, holding hands. The pleasant breeze carried away the occasional sigh that escaped me.

During my wild years, I would have never entertained such a career-driven...*steady* individual, but now? I felt like I'd won the lottery. Not quite the Powerball, but the local scratch off at least. And that was good, Milton was good. A good man. A caring, respectable man. And I loved everything about those characteristics. It's what I had envisioned and failed to get in my first marriage, no matter how hard I tried. But now this was my time. It was our time.

If only Milton could get with the program.

"Oh yeah, amor, I can see how that would really put you in the right place at the right time," I mumbled. Would I have been better served using this Saturday without the kids to catch up on my latest reality love show? Or maybe I should have gotten acquainted with my newest toy... Demarquis the III. I'd been playing Goldilocks these past few months while testing a new spot in my dildo rotation. I might have become a staid sports mom, but that didn't mean the wildness had completely left me behind. My weekends on my own could get pretty rowdy…just me and my collection having a good time.

"Right?! That's exactly what I thought." His face lit up with excitement, and he closed his eyes. And maybe, just maybe, this time with Milton was better than those single mom plans. The rays of the afternoon sun hit his mahogany skin, long eyelashes, and lush lips, and weak flutters grew in my stomach. My lips stretched on their own accord as I admired how handsome Milton was when he had his guard down.

Milton might be…composed, but standing at six feet, burly physique, deep brown skin, and a smile that could kill, I truly had lucked out. The one thing I'd change was his willingness to drag along this casual, no-strings-attached thing we had going on. Milton, coming out of a hard relationship, had decided he wanted to date casually and see other people. I'd known two dates in that we could build a life together. Ten months later, the candle and the prayers became an emergency solution.

My best friend hated the fact that I was still waiting. "Investment in the future" is what I told Miranda when she scoffed at Milton's request to casually date after five outings and a few sleepovers when the twins were with their father.

"Girl, you don't need to remarry! What you need is good dick and enjoy your life. Maybe someone that loves you and you love and wants to go with the flow with you. With this libido we have right now? You should be getting it in regularly and with enthusiasm. Forget chasing big goals and a family; you got that girl; we are in our 'living in the moment era.'" That advice activated all my annoyance. Wanting to be in a stable marriage so that my boys and I could have the type of family we deserved wasn't something to scoff at. There were things that Brandon and Brian needed that I couldn't give them, no matter how much I portrayed the strong Black mother role.

The reality was that I was tired of doing it all by myself. Exhausted.

The park faded back into my periphery, the greens morphing into beige, brown, and stone. Our surroundings transformed into brownstones, children and parents walking their dogs, and the bustle of the never-sleeping Brooklyn. Milton's warm hand held mine, the safety and security as addictive as a bowl of popcorn during a good movie. If I could only get more of this… If only he had given me some type of signal to move things to the serious stage.

"So, I was wondering if you and the boys should have some type of outing—" My words trailed off as a gorgeous South Asian woman walked past us, her laughter loud enough to surpass the three kids screaming on the opposite sidewalk while playing with a Portuguese water puppy. Her white dress cape flapped in the breeze and, for a second, all time suspended.

The woman extended her hand toward another woman, laughter coloring her aura in beautiful tones of happiness. The other woman wore a white suit with plunging cleavage. She was beautifully brown skinned with pink braids and her gaze told the story of a deep comfortable love. To have someone to love you so completely and unapologetically…the mere idea took my breath away. They both took my breath away.

The woman wearing the suit took the South Asian woman's hand and kissed it. As they separated, the shine of a ring flashed, bringing things back to normal speed.

"Hey... I lost you there for a second. You good? What were you gonna ask?" Milton's worried face appeared in front of me as the women's giddy laughter faded away into the melee of the afternoon.

"I... I don't even know what was on my mind." I trailed off, incapable of hiding my wistfulness. The South Asian woman was now dancing on the street while her new wife gazed at her adoringly.

When was the last time I smiled like that? When was the last time I felt like dancing on the street because my joy was so damn filling I couldn't but move my body?

There were so many ways that Milton made me feel content, but *happiness*?

"They look so happy, don't they? Good for them. Life is ethereal; you gotta take those risks," Milton said, and all my nerves saluted in alertness. His eyes met mine, and I let it show—the interest for more—the yearning that had settled in the pit of my stomach and refused to depart.

"Yes, risk-taking...an important part of life, wouldn't you think?" I asked. Damn right, my candles had worked. *Gracias, Tía Patricia. I knew you had my back, girl.* A quick sign of the cross wouldn't hurt anyone right now either, so I did one, hoping to hide it from Milton.

"Yes...yes, I would think. Listen... I—I wasn't planning to ask yet, but you've been so supportive of me, and our dates these past ten months have been the highlight of my romantic life, so…" Milton shifted from one foot to the other, his loafers and crisp jeans flexing with the movement. "I never thought I'd be courting again at forty-two, but here I am… I want to…formally court you if that would be okay with you… I want us to…take things more seriously, you and I. I mean, maybe not exclusive yet, I would have to end a couple of casual dating situations I have, but we can chat about that…"

Yeah, let's chat about those right the fuck now. One of his situationships had reached out to me via my business IG page, woman to woman. Miranda had been livid, ready to slay dragons for me via DM. I in turn recognized myself in the woman. She was also a divorcee, but with no children. She worked in finance in some lofty firm—Miranda had become better than Jarvis and found everything there was to know about that woman. Everything she put in her DM told me she thought *she* was the main one in Milton's life, only agreeing to the polyamory lifestyle because she was already forty and thought this was her last chance.

This woman *was* me.

I explained to her that I had no control over Milton's actions and that she should speak with him.

Two days later Milton called me assuring me that woman wouldn't bother me again.

"She was a little confused about our arrangement, and to be honest, if I ever went monogamous again it wouldn't be with her…" Milton had a way of dangling monogamy like the end prize. And he knew I wanted that prize bad.

Suddenly, that pretty smile of his loomed too close. I took a tentative step back from Milton, attempting to calm down the hairs on the back of my neck. Nothing around us should have caused the foreboding sensation that ran through me. I glanced around. Same kids, same families, nothing odd. Same pretty dog. Same summer green everywhere, same cars beeping and honking. Where could the threat be? Milton called my attention again.

"I should have waited. Sorry for asking this in the middle of the street. I'm just excited to ask because I've got this trip to the Poconos, and I want you to come with me for the holiday weekend."

The hairs all calmed down as my mind focused away from whatever momentary threat was around us, and flashes of a romantic getaway captured my attention: tub and all. Milton and I had already been intimate enough for me to know all his special moves, but maybe with this weekend away, we could further align our desires and find that sweet spot for both of us. And maybe I should bring my toys in case we didn't find that elusive sweet spot. Like any other damn time we had tried.

"We've never had a romantic trip yet...that would be so good." I grabbed his hand, and again that solid, dependable quality hit me in my chest—until Milton grimaced, his thick lips pursing.

"Oh well, it won't be fully romantic...it's well, it's a non-compulsory workretreat for couples. Only people in relationships get invited, but I thought if you and...well, you and I get along so well, it seems it was all destined to happen right now, you know, like it was meant to be?"

Oh...

"Oh..."

Oh…maybe playing Goldilocks would have been a better use of my time. But here I was, getting the question I hoped to get today, and giving a one-syllable answer back.

Story of my life.

Two

Orlando

The mailbox key barely pushing into the slot told me everything I needed. The small mail room smelled of newspaper and cardboard, a bunch of Amazon packages piled high in a corner. Testament to the tight-knit community we had in this building that the packages didn't disappear daily. The unspoken rule was: run down by 6:00 p.m. to get your package after all the major deliveries happened, and you're good. It's a free game from eight in the morning till midday when the deliveries start again. That's why I was in the mail room, getting my latest package before the sun went down. I didn't intend to check my packages until next Monday. Pretending things wouldn't change was the main reason for my delay.

Pushing all the air out of my lungs, I pulled the key out of the slot and stared at the apartment number I shared with my mom and my two younger brothers. The offending mailbox stared back at me. How can an innate object carry so much judgment about my bravery?

"Nah, son, if I open you, it's a warp. Then I have to read what's inside there, and I ain't ready."

"Does talking to the mailbox help decrease the amount of bills? Because if it does, I might try that approach." Fast on my feet, I whirled to find Mrs. Barranco's wrinkly face and mischievous smile.

"Damn, Seño B, you almost gave me a heart attack." I pressed my hand on my chest and stumbled back for a bit of drama.

"Ay por favor. You're nowhere close to having a heart attack when your mama just finished wiping your butt a year ago."

Kissing my teeth after an octogenarian said something would be considered rude and disrespectful, so I didn't go that route. But clearly, between Sra. Barranco and me, the comedian was her, because my mother hadn't ever been that attentive, and I had to learn really early how to take care of her, myself, and my siblings. Shit, I was probably wiping when I was three years old.

"Now, Seño B, you well know I'm the most mature twenty-five-year-old you've ever met."

"Hmm." Sra. Barranco's smirk didn't faze me. She'd said that shit to me plenty of times when she saw and heard Mom in one of her episodes, after I'd calmed her down. Or when she saw me making sure the boys had what they needed for school.

"Nah, don't hurt my feelings now." I rubbed my hands together and gave her a little twinkle-twinkle for extra humph.

"Oh please, did you decide when to go to Ofele Town? Did you make the plans?"

And just like that, my chest was tight again. First, the mailbox awaiting to dictate my faith, and now Sra. Barranco reminds me of my impending fatherhood.

I guess it wasn't impending when my child was already three years old and living in Ofele Town in Florida. But I hadn't known of the existence of said child until Ms. B here decided to share the news a few weeks ago. Maria, her grandchild, and her parents had decided against telling me. Fuck knows why. I was good to Maria. Yeah, we weren't sweethearts or anything, but I'd never abandon her and my child if I'd known. Co-parenting would have worked for us.

"Yeah, you know they have carnival over there? I'm going with my friends in a few weeks." My smart watch vibrated, reminding me of said friends waiting for me in our favorite coffee shop. "Damn, sorry, Seño B, I gotta run." I ignored the judging stares of both Sra. Barranco and the inanimate object behind me and power walked toward the exit.

"Do you…so you're not gonna check those admission letters then?" Sra. B's question stopped me cold.

"How you know?"

"Tú mama is very proud. First, you finish your degree in three years and get that great job finding the kids who fiddle with those funny-looking cartoons in la computadora. I mean, if they wanna pay you all that money to find people who doodle, that sounds like a good investment of your three years, okay?"

Yo! I'd never heard my job described like that. Forget my

job description under Animation Talent Expert. I should have used what Seño B said. Now, the rest about Ma, yeah, I was gonna sidestep the hell out of that landmine.

"Cool, well then, you know I can check it later, maybe Monday. I did early submissions, so there is time to accept."

"Mm–hmm. Alright then, see you around. But if you wanna talk…you know you got people that truly see you, right?"

Yeah, Ms. B was definitely the better comedian out of the two of us 'cause she had jokes for days.

"Damn, son, why you took so long?" Franco's loud ass greeted me the moment I entered our favorite spot. Franco sat in a corner, charming smile on full display as he attempted to make eye contact with two ladies at the next table. He kept stroking his chin, and what he thought was a beard, but what we all knew was fuzz. He was lucky his mother gave him some good looks, good melanin, and the best cooking skills 'cause his game was weak otherwise.

"Damn, chill; we didn't set an exact time."

"But we did, ugh. I sent it in the group chat. Why am I best friends with guys only?" Grace, our Black pixie queen, lamented next to Franco.

"See, he didn't accept the invite to the new group chat, babe," Desmond, my third best friend, said, lounging in the booth, observing Franco's failed attempts and Grace's growing exasperation.

"I'm not your babe." Grace gritted her teeth.

"Not anymore…" Franco and I whispered and guffawed when we realized we said the same thing.

"You'll always be my babe. Stop playin'." Desmond winked at Grace, deploying his Dominican and Jamaican charm. The reason why Grace no longer allowed him to call her *babe* after a year of dating. She should have known better, though.

"If you don't stop, I'll leave." Grace shrugged in her cute summer dress that was probably driving Desmond wild. Served him right. Grace was a gift, and he squandered that shit with his lack of communication—to the point he had her believing they were in a nonmonogamous relationship, but he kept getting mad when she was dating other people. She grew tired of all the mixed messages and dropped him. If only he'd been upfront with her…and what he really wanted…shit would have been different.

Now, Grace was dating a nice girl from Manhattan who took her to raves on Fridays and farmer's markets on Sundays and brought her backpack when she spent the night. And shorty was okay with Grace dating other people, for real. I had never seen Grace happier. Low-key, I was jealous of her, living her life and doing the things she wanted unencumbered by other responsibilities.

Hell, all my friends were living their best lives.

"Quédate, please. I'll behave," Desmond said, contrite.

"Good," Grace said. "Now look at the table that Franco keeps drooling at; that is Gina Star."

"Oh shit!" I plopped next to Desmond, his grumble loud as I made him scoot.

"Grace, that's why you mah my main one. I've been trying

to reach her via social media with no success. She's mad talented. I really think she would be a good fit at my company."

"That's great! Then go ahead and talk to her."

"Nah, I don't want to seem like a creep."

After much cajoling from Grace and getting heat from Desmond and Franco, I approached Gina Star. Gina was an illustrator I'd found on IG with mad potential to make it big. I wanted to bring her to my company and hopefully get her a great contract. After exchanging info, I ambled back to our table when I realized I wouldn't be at my company long enough to get her a contract if I accepted the admission to law school.

Fuck.

The instant gut punch at the thought of law school took the air out of me.

No use focusing on that pain though; law school was the path to ensure me and mine would be good, regardless of how I felt about it. There was no gain in overthinking it. No gain in trying to figure out other ways.

Sitting back down, I caught the new topic of conversation, attempting to rally after the reminders of what was coming my way.

"So, I booked us all in the hotel that is the closest to the grounds where they do the carnival, and I finished the last deposit for our band spot and costumes, so we ready for Ofele!" Grace explained.

"Oh... I meant to tell you, Grace, I got a house rental instead, so don't worry about a room for me in the hotel; I... I want to get there early and do some sightseeing."

"What the fuck for? The town is small and quaint unless it is Caribbean carnival weekend." Desmond looked at me sideways.

"You know he an old man in a young man body, probably gonna do some of their walking tours and shit," Franco said between cackles.

"Don't listen to them. I think it's nice that you want to go and explore the town and learn more about its history. I've always been fascinated with Ofele and its story. How our Black people there kept it a secret from the white Floridians who were displacing any major Black towns back in the Reconstruction era. And they kept their beaches? Impressive."

"Yeah…yeah remember Maria? Yeah, she told me about the town. She loved the history behind it too…" Which explained why she found refuge there. I debated saying something to them about how important this trip had become to me. The last fun before law school. The potential of meeting my child.

But the debate was a wasted effort when I already knew the decision. Opening up to these children cosplaying as adults wouldn't be any type of solution. I was a man who looked for results and didn't dwell on anything but facts.

Having an extra perspective on my impending meeting with my daughter would be ideal, and Grace would probably be a great sounding board, but it would also bring judgment and outside thoughts I wasn't ready to deal with. Parenthood was the scariest thing on my horizon, but I could handle it. I had plenty experience with parenting people.

"Oh, boring! Fuck that! I'm going to whine and wuk somebody's daughter. Dats it." Franco interrupted my thoughts.

Desmond dabbed him up, and they both started making noises to get the attention of the other table with the ladies.

For a second, I really thought I'd be able to talk to them and tell them all my worries, but that's not the time we were on. That's not the time *they* were on. Not even Grace, honestly. She was busy videocalling her girl and planning her next move.

Yeah…better I kept that shit to myself. Better to enjoy the trip and have the best time ever. A stolen moment where I get to be my age for only a few days.

That's all I needed. Nothing more.

Three

Trinidad

My last call with my client took everything out of me. The company had hired me to plan their incentive trip to Mexico, and what started with a million-dollar budget for three hundred top sellers had become a $500K trip for five hundred top sellers. If I'd known they'd slash the budget, I wouldn't have taken the contract. At this point in my life, multitasking was my middle, last, and married name, but there was no need to be on the struggle bus while doing it.

Frustrated, I left my living room and working area and went to my bedroom. My hormones were my other enemy today. Since I woke up, I could not for the life of me calm my horniness down. I'd done two rounds with my rose, and still, I could go all day.

My phone calendar reminded me it was ovulation week.

Great.

The moment I hit thirty, I thought something was wrong. I still remember feeling slightly feral in the libido department. But I was not ready for what happened at thirty-five. Honestly, I now understood castration belts more than ever.

Not even getting it on the regular with Milton helped. His libido didn't always match mine, and he joked around that I needed a young guy to date on the days I wasn't with him. I never laughed at those jokes because I wasn't trying to date him casually, and I didn't want to encourage those thoughts. And two, there was this young guy in my life right now that made my hormones react even more unhinged than usual. Probably why I was about to change my underwear for the third time in a day.

Because I was going to see Orlando Wiggins.

In need of distraction, I called Miranda, my voice of… reason.

"Miranda, I'm dying. Girl, I need a medicine that lowers this shit because why am I always in heat now?"

"Well, good afternoon to you too, darlin'. School was lovely today. Only two of my kids cheated on their math test, so I'm gonna take that as a win. Also, I have no tutoring this afternoon, so I'm already leaving this place."

"Oh damn, I was gonna ask if you could drop off the after their mentor session twins. They are about to be home 'cause you know them and food…but after that they were gonna go to the school's basketball court to meet with…him. I was hoping you were finishing tutoring around the same time they were done."

"You can't even say that man's name."

"He's not a man, he is a boy."

"Beg to differ, but listen, I have no time for the back and forth; I have a date tonight, so it sucks to be you and your hormones."

"I truly can't stand you, girl."

"You a whole lie." Miranda laughed as I heard her jingling keys. "Were you really not gonna pick up the twins? This is the highlight of your week, girl. If you don't go, what material will you use for your shower sessions next week?"

"I should have never told you that. And that is not what I fantasize about, okay? I think of my man only."

"Girl...that man is your man and every other women's man. You need an upgrade."

Not wanting to argue with Miranda, I changed the subject, and by the time the twins walked into the apartment, my belly hurt from so much laughing.

"Ma, what's so funny?" Brian asked, walking straight to the kitchen and opening my pot of rice.

"Well hola, mi cielo, how are you?" The urge to roll my eyes at how inconsequential I had become lately to these two boys, the flesh of my flesh, was tempting, but I refrained.

After all, I was their example. The only one they had for a while because their father was barely around when they needed him. They needed constant guidance and love, mentorship, and someone to talk to on how to be a Black man and Latino in this country, and I couldn't give them that.

My parents, may they rest in peace, had been such a good example for them and for me of how a family should be. But now they were gone, and I was doing this all by myself. And

with these men out here trying to date and hit it only, I didn't
bring men to the apartment. Milton was the only one I had
introduced to the twins, and they had a lukewarm understanding at best. Desperate to give them what they needed, I signed
them up for a mentorship program at school for young Black
men, and that is how Orlando Wiggins came into our lives.

"I'm alright, Ma, but we gotta eat and hit the road again
to meet Orlando on time. He told us not to keep him waiting, and we don't wanna do that," Brian said as Brandon approached our sitting area and bent to give me a kiss on the
cheek.

"Hola, Ma, tas bien? How was work today?"

"Hola, mi Brandon. And yes, I did cook you arroz con
pollo. So no need for all the buttering up."

"Thanks, Mommy," Brandon singsonged, and Brian
laughed from the kitchen island.

"One, sit down to eat and get a plate! How often do I have
to ask you not to eat from the paila?" You would think they
were wolf cubs eating straight from the pot. Brandon pulled
two plates, and soon they were both sitting atour dining room
table, eating with their phones out.

"I'm gonna take a shower; please lock when you leave, alright?"

Grunts were the only answer, so I knew I was again rele-
gated to the back of their minds. My sons loved me and protected me at all costs, but attention to detail wasn't their strong
suit. And that was okay.

With thoughts of Orlando Wiggins, I went to take my
shower. This was the place where magic happened. I had

planned PTA meetings, major concerts, and a couple of executive meetings for CEOs you usually see on TV in this shower. This is where I did my best thinking. And my filthiest too.

Demarquis III waited for me, looking all innocent with its dark brown veins attached to my shower wall. The shower's steam rose quickly as I removed my T-shirt and sweatpants and hopped inside the tiled area. The fact that Demarquis was a very similar color to Orlando's smooth, dark skin was a coincidence that would not be further explored.

My lavender steam bag scented the air with calming vibes, but nothing calmed the throbbing between my legs, not the water or anything else, as I remembered last Friday when I saw Orlando.

He'd come out smiling while talking to Brian and Brandon. His clear interest in what they had to say was alluring. He wore that fitted that went with him everywhere and a baggy T-shirt and jeans.

Honestly, the kid was a bit scrawny, not enough meat on the bones as I liked my men, but there was something about how he carried himself… His head held high, knowing that many people wished people like him, like us, didn't carry themselves with so much pride. His shoulders were wide, and he seemed capable of carrying…heavy things. The veins on his arms were exposed under his sleeves, suggesting there was some definition hidden under the shirt. And his *stride*.

Whatever meat did not go on the bones went elsewhere, which was noticeable by his walk. I was ashamed to even think of the dreams I'd had, figuring out if I was right about my theory or not. Honestly, the fact that I was lusting after a man ten years my junior was something that caused me shame every Friday.

But every Friday, I took a shower, made sure I smelled real good, put on a cute dress or top, and made my way to the school to pick up Brian and Brandon. I thought I had left my harlot behavior behind, but Orlando had a way of reminding me of my old days.

There was no need for lubrication, but I still squirted some on because of comfort. I pushed my ass back, and Demarquis, the third, stepped up to bat. The slide-in was smooth, and I threw my behind back over and over, enjoying the fullness and rightness of the size.

"Oh yes…." The urge to say a name—and it wasn't Milton— tried to escape, but I refrained from it. This wouldn't take long. The water cascaded over my chest and breasts, making my nipples stand in attention. Demarquis and I clearly had a good thing going on, and soon, my bottom lip was bruised by all the biting.

So close to my fourth orgasm of the day, Orlando materialized behind me, the right-but-latex feel to Demarquis transforming into warm, hard flesh.

"Right there, right, there…" My fingers did the dance of their ancestors, exactly enough to make my legs shake.

"So close…"

"Ma!" I jumped off Demarquis the III so hard the suction gave up, and the dildo splashed on the shower floor. My heart was right next to it, still beating a million beats per hour.

"Yes, Brian, what is it?"

I must not want to murder my children. I must not want to murder my children.

"Oh, nothin', just letting you know we leaving. See you in an hour and a half!"

"See you, boys."

And see you soon, Orlando Wiggins.

You think you're used to something, that you know a routine down pat, that you plan events and execute them with your eyes closed, that you *got this.*

But today I didn't have it. All poise deserted me while I waited in my car and pulled up to the sidewalk by the basketball court entrance. Orlando walked out with the twins, and the three of them were shirtless. It was getting much warmer, so it made sense. They'd been playing for a good hour and some. But I wasn't ready for Orlando.

First, tattoos. Tattoos everywhere. They were well hidden. But they were there. One on his chest, another on his upper left arm, and one on his inner upper right arm. Another one on his right side. It was still too far to admire their intricacies, but they were sexy, and I didn't want to know that.

The other thing I wasn't used to was the definition. Yes, Orlando was lean. Yes, Orlando was cut. Yes, Orlando was strong. Yes, Orlando. And then he clapped Brian's shoulder and from where I sat in the car, I could see his plump lips moving. *"I'm proud of you."*

Oops. Fifth orgasm…here we come.

Scrambling out of my car took me seconds. Maybe standing, I wouldn't feel all the sensations between my legs and in my chest. And why my chest? What was happening? This was a kid; he just graduated from college. He was twenty-five years old and carefree. He had no responsibilities in life. He had a cute little animation job or whatever and was probably successful, but still, a kid.

Good, this was working. Things calmed down south, and when Orlando flashed that cute smile of his, I was ready for it.

"Good afternoon, Ms. Velasquez; you doing fine?"

Not as fine as you.

He is twenty-five!!

"I'm alright, how're you, son? Good to see you today."

Orlando grimaced, the expression disappearing like a single drop in a pool of water. Trying to hide it, he played with the diamond stud with his index and thumb, rolling the jewelry over and over, and a twinge of regret hit me in my stomach.

"Come on, Ms. V. I've asked you not to call me son, please. You're not *that* old."

Touché, Orlando.

"You're right. I'm not that old; it's you that is a little younger and untried. But you're correct; I should respect your wishes. It's good to see you, hope you have a wonderful weekend. Alright?"

"Oh, he will, he going to that new club that recently opened closer to Dad's apartment? Everybody talking about it."

"People still go to clubs?" I asked. I was sure I'd read an article lately about how clubs were closing left and right because the new generation didn't like going out to dance anymore. Shame on them—if I was young…well, I did all the things when I was young after I divorced, but still. Sometimes it felt like I was missing some shenanigans, but that was just young Trinidad trying to pop out from where I buried her when I decided to grow the fuck up and fix my romantic life.

"I mean it's not a club…" Orlando flashed an annoyed glance at Brandon, and for a second, they looked more like older and younger brothers than mentor and mentee.

Oh God, and I tried to come on a dildo thinking of this man-child. Help.

"It's a bar. A Caribbean bar, they hosting a fete."

Now fetes I knew, but respectable women like me should not be going out to wuk on no man or woman. So, I didn't partake in them anymore. But damn, did my waistline and hips try to remind me of how much I loved going out whenever one of my favorite soca songs would come up on my random playlists.

"Oh, I remember my younger days, when I used to—"

"Ma, Orlando ain't care about you being mad loose when you were younger. Come on now."

"Who said I was loose? Más respeto!" I gave him The Stare.

Brian must have a death wish right now 'cause he didn't just expose my business in front of this man-child.

Said man-child's eyes shined with an interest I had noticed sometimes in the past and had gotten real good at ignoring.

"You're right, Ma, my apologies—that was out of bounds. We believe in women's empowerment and the right to be as sexual or not sexual as they like to be, always respecting their boundaries with consent."

My mouth dropped open, and Orlando's, Brian's, and Brandon's faces transformed into pure panic.

"Awwww, that was lovely, mi cielo. You really have been listening to my advice, haven't you?" The light in my chest shined so bright it blinded the entire block.

"Well yeah, but this particular thing, not you, but Orlando taught us that. He tells us a lot about how to be a cis, heterosexual, responsible man," Brian said with that awkward, embarrassed-but-proud posture boys did when secretly pleased with what their parents had to say.

"Yeah, he's also teaching us how to talk to you and Dad and, y'know, our elders."

An elder.

I mouthed, "An elder?" And glared at Orlando, who had the decency to cringe and mouth back, "Sorry."

Whew, this had been a whole journey. I was glad Orlando was instilling the right values in the boys. It filled me with admiration and reluctant acknowledgment that he was a man.

Who was I kidding—I always reacted to him as a man, but I tricked myself over and over into seeing him younger. I didn't have time to train no young man in how to make love, nor did I have the patience for waiting for him to mature past his twenty-five years, which in woman years were really twenty. I needed to keep myself contained, so anytime I felt desire, I clung to these stereotypes, because what else did I have?

There were boys twice his age who did not understand the very easy concept of women's agency and their sexuality, but here he was, fully comprehending it in his midtwenties. But still I was certain his maturity levels were severely lacking in other areas to take a ride on my amusement park so he would always remain a cute fantasy only.

Yup, there it was, these were the facts that helped me from pouncing on him every time he proved me wrong.

"Boys, why don't you go put your shirts on inside the school and wash your faces, at least, before we head out?" For once Brian and Brandon listened without a *Jeopardy* round of whys, whats, and wheres. They both waltzed away, their lanky limbs longer than the rest of their bodies, giving them that youthful endearing look of their teenage years.

Once my "mom antenna" recorded that the twins were inside the school, my gaze focused on smooth dark brown skin glazed by perspiration. Nothing else was relevant but the torso and limbs that were in perfect grown-man proportion. No lanky arms and legs here. No, this was a grown-ass man.

My focus zeroed on Orlando, the only man that made my body do things I didn't need it to do.

Tranquilo, Bobby, tranquilo.

Not even our patron saint, Juan Luis Guerra of the bachata hits, could encapsulate the conundrum that erupted whenever Orlando and I were on our own. I made sure it didn't happen often, but the twins had been struggling with math, and Orlando had promised to help.

I had been skeptical at first, but soon the twins started focusing on homework and some of their difficulties working on their math. They started advocating for themselves in a way I had not been able to fully get across to them.

Speaking of the boys critically wasn't something I did in front of them. They might think they were grown, but their egos were as delicate as Fabergé eggs and I couldn't mess with that. So with great reluctance, I started setting aside time to speak with Orlando one-on-one during pickups.

My teens were worth the risk of getting overheated or letting my mind run wild with sexy scenarios of what I could teach Orlando.

"You wanted to ask me about their math, didn't you?" Orlando nodded in perfect understanding, the ridges of his cut arms and chest doing a mesmerizing dance that robbed me of my capacity to multitask.

I could only thirst; my age gap defenses slowly melted as his shoulders squared and his lush lips opened. Words flowed from his mouth, coated with the warmest honey that sweetened the smokiness of his voice. Maybe it was the fact that Demarquis III and I had just had a session, but all my synapses were firing the same urge. One single thought was all I could manage.

I want to run my hand down his marble chest and detect all his sensitive spots.

Dios mío, Trinidad, get it together!

"Ms. Velasquez?" Orlando's stance broadened somehow, the air thickening, the scent of clean, subtle male cologne and sweat rushing through me, lightning up my solar plexus. This was no child. He knew exactly what he was doing. I needed him to stop, stop immediately.

Nah. Keep going.

"Oh yes, yes, I...should I get a tutor? Is it bad—what do you think? Porque, listen I'll do what I need to do for those kids. Because education is first in my house. It really is, okay?

And I hope it is the same for you. People like you and me, you know, we need to uplift each other, and work together because if it's not us then who? You know?"

Oh my God.

What in the world salad did I just say? This was ridiculous; I did very well under pressure. Shit, anyone would say my job was one of the most stressful out there besides first responders, so why could I not get it together to sound like a normal person.

"Nah, I think Brandon needs to practice more and Brian is sabotaging a bit to spare Brandon's feelings. I can work with both of them—incorporate an hour before we play ball…" His lips kept moving. All my focus was on multitasking between ogling and keeping up with the conversation.

Everything Orlando said was on point. Too on point. This is what I needed, someone that spoke that Man Code that only men could. I sure couldn't. Gender existentialism wasn't something I ascribed to at all, but be it personality or age, Orlando understood my twins in a special way.

A way that stimulated my brain and other parts of me.

He understood them in a way that made him extra dangerous.

There was a respectable distance between us, but every centimeter of my skin could sense him. This type of awareness of everything that is soft and yielding in me and everything that is hard and rugged in him made me lightheaded. It was not a common occurrence.

It was an almost never occurrence.

Especially in my current state of impending couplehood.

Not quite there, always suspended in time.

Milton had a date tonight with one of his other almost girlfriends. Not IG girl—she had gotten the boot real quick after demanding more of his time and space. He replaced IG girl with a slightly younger model.

Which was not an issue.

When the thought skidded through my brain, I felt nothing. No anger, no jealousy, no joy.

Nothing.

I believed in different types of loving. I had read all the polyamorous books when Milton explained to me what he was. To be honest it sounded refreshing. Instead of people playing the field out there and lying about it, everyone was up front. The thing was that I was starting to understand that I was an occasional, maybe even situational, polyamorous person.

I was ready to jump back on the monogamy train.

Something to talk about in my next therapy session, right after confessing how my nether parts vibrated at the mere proximity of a man that was not my almost boyfriend. In fact he would never be my boyfriend because someone like Orlando would mean indulging in all the decadence and joy of living that I used to chase in my youth, regardless of being polyam or not.

Orlando reminded me of that feeling of jumping into the unknown without having to consider any consequences beyond tomorrow, without letting anything but pure desire and instinct guide your actions. Impulsive and full of happiness. All the things that could lead you to marrying a man that never loved you, and maybe even subconsciously used you to stay in the country or even worse until he could find his own feeling of pure joy.

Orlando kept talking and I nodded and said all the right things because I was back oto my full senses.

My ex-husband was the aggressive reminder I needed for not messing with the adrenaline that Orlando ignited in me.

I took a step back, widening the gap between us. He instinctively mimicked my motions, putting his own space in stark opposition to mine. Even in this he was the ultimate gentleman. Noticing my need and giving me more of it.

Space.

That's all I needed from Orlando.

Any other thought was a dream. Orlando was a sweet fantasy. That was all.

A steamy, cute fantasy that tormented me on a daily basis. So keeping my space was the best thing I could do.

Four

Orlando

The sizzle of the onions and garlic made my stomach grumble after my hours with my mentees. As soon as I arrived home, I went straight to the kitchen, pulled out Mom's paila, and started cooking dinner.

Without even having to peek into her bedroom, the scent of incense and loud mystical music blaring told me she was having one of her days. The grumble in my stomach morphed into unease. Would she take the time to come out and eat tonight? Having no other option, I focused on the rice and peas in the pot, steering the creamy coconut water until the bubbles prompted me to lower the fire. Chicken thighs went into the mixture of garlic, onions, and other seasonings. Maybe the scent would break her out of her episode.

Food is how she took care of us when she could, teaching me all the meals she learned from her mother, who grew up in Roatán, and her dad's favorite Bayan dishes. Food is how I attempted to take care of her now that things had changed. With anxiety settling in my stomach, I pressed Rewind on the day, focusing on the highlights instead.

When I decided to join the mentorship program my old school organized, my main consideration was how well it would look on my law school application. Low-key, I was also yearning to connect with someone the way I wished I could connect with my younger brothers.

My mentorship program with Brandon and Brian became one of the highlights of my week. The kids were bright, not the most studious, but each had their individual interests that showcased their critical thinking and hunger for knowledge, which was fine.

Brandon was fascinated with anything that had an engine and could spend hours talking about videos he'd watched on the matter. He sometimes mentioned one of the boys he had a crush on, but he was very aloof about his sexuality overall, so I never pressed him in that area. Brian was more on his *damn, girls are fine* moment, but my mans had figured out a creative way to focus that attention. Women sports. He was a damn near expert on all the WNBA key players' stats, and don't get him started about soccer.

Each of them showed the potential to be great at whatever they wanted to be if someone took the time to guide their enthusiasm to open doors to discover opportunities. That's all I'd ever wanted, so when Mr. Thompson reached out to me about the mentorship program, I knew this would be a good fit for me.

What I hadn't been expecting was Trinidad Velasquez. I don't know how dudes have types. I mean, I get it; we all have things we look for in the person we like, but for me, it had to be more than looks. Honestly, all types of women were my preference: small, tall, short, plump, you name it. If the vibe was right, I was open to exploring where the attraction could lead me.

When I met Trinidad the first time, I hadn't been ready. The boys had talked about their mother as this perpetually tired, staid workaholic that somehow managed to be kinda cool when she tried.

Instead, a thick bombshell strutted down the pavement, her hair in locs, coils burning mahogany brown under the sun. The flower dress she wore spoke of afternoons by a bar on the bay with cocktails.

She reached her hand out, and maybe I moaned a little bit because she smirked.

"Hello, Orlando, the boys told me you were twenty-five but I could have been fooled to believe you were a little older," she said, then set me at ease with her smile.

Damn. The twins hadn't prepared me for anything. They hadn't even hinted at how gorgeous their mother was.

No hint of her beauty, or how her mouth quirked up when she was trying to hold back laughter.

"Yeah, I get that a lot. I am way more mature than my age." Whatever my vocal cords did, it sounded mad goofy to my ears. Placing extra depth on my words had been an instinctual action. There was nothing but to go with it. I hadn't met a woman that made me this nervous and excited in like ever.

Damn, how could the twins not warn me? Give me a little heads-up at least?

Nah, they didn't say shit. No mention of her dry sense of humor and how she tried to hide it and act all proper around me. No thought to warn me of the impact on my solar plexus when we first shook hands outside of the basketball court.

"Oh, I bet you think that." Trinidad smirked again, her hand still in mine. I still remember the warmth radiating from the spot where she laid her palm on mine. It stayed with me for hours after seeing her. I lay down that day still surrounded by thoughts of Trinidad Velasquez. I cheesed all the way home, and till bed. Nose wide open from a few inconsequential words.

And before I could think twice, I jacked off to the thought of her lips around my dick, while I moaned "Ms. V, your mouth is magical," over and over again.

Trinidad had lived in my head ever since. She had me simping the minute I met her.

She had the type of body I used to draw back in school when trying to make my classes go faster. Soft, brown-skinned, big-hipped, big-assed anime heroines with midlength locs, big expressive eyes, and mischievous smiles. And there she was, Trinidad, one of my anime heroines come to life.

But the light in my heroine's eyes didn't live in Trinidad. My chest contracted when I first realized that. I was convinced Trinidad needed an adventure. Something to jog her out of the everyday bustle. Something like what I was searching for in Ofele Town.

In the first few meetings with her, I did too much, talking

and boasting about my job and my friends and well...sounding exactly like a twenty-five-year-old. Trinidad seemed unimpressed, and why wouldn't she?

After several meetings I finally got her age from the twins. At ten years my senior, and with two children and a divorce, she'd seen plenty of life and had shouldered many responsibilities. Maybe if I'd share that side with her...nah. It was fun having a crush when everything else weighed me down. When the responsibilities of my day-to-day felt like my best personal deadlift record over and over again. Getting heavier by the minute. I had no shot with Trinidad, and worse than that, I didn't think she liked me that much.

Trinidad Velasquez was a guilty pleasure and as unreachable as my dreams of pursuing a career in creative arts instead of law school. My paycheck was a biweekly reminder of that. And here I was supposed to be cheering myself up.

"Damn, arroz con guandules again? And chicken? Can't you cook something else?" Camilo complained as he and Marcelo trampled their way into the apartment.

"It's not arroz con guandules, it's red peas. And take off your trainers. Neither of you helps to clean the apartment, but when it's time to mess it up..." My two brothers had grown as tall as me in the past year. Marcelo was a couple of inches shorter than Camilo, and he couldn't wait to join Camilo at Stony Brook this fall.

"Same shit, listen, Imma take Celo to a party tonight," Camilo said, plopping down on the large sofa in our flower-splashed living room. Mom had interesting taste in decor.

"I thought the three of us were gonna play video games

tonight?" I did a good job keeping the disappointment out of my voice. Eighteen and twenty were interesting years in a man's life. Transition from school to college or work, moving into the world with a larger sense of belonging and responsibility. Or maybe that was my experience because these two acted like they were still teenagers. I didn't have time to be as immature. At their age I was parenting them. Camilo and Marcelo had benefited from having an older brother. Just plain old luck that they got to act like overgrown children and I never did.

"Yeah, but there is this girl and…" Celo started explaining as I stirred the chicken, the aroma of the seasonings permeating the little living room and kitchen.

"You know you cannot drink, right?" I asked them both, looking up from the paila, refusing to let them see my disappointment.

They both looked back with bored expressions. Whoever broke first would lose the battle of wills. So I kept my gaze steady until Celo blinked first. Camilo kissed his teeth and waived my concerns away. Parenting brothers was a pain in the ass.

Now that my Friday had gone truly to the whole trash, I needed to pivot. Maybe I could hit up my friends, or if Trinidad gave the boys permission, maybe I could play video games with them. Brandon and Brian had been unable to contain their excitement when I told them about my Friday night plans. See, my cheerful thoughts had worked and presented an opportunity.

"Why are you smiling like a you won the lotto?" Camilo asked.

"Why are you minding business that ain't yours?" I asked back.

"It's that lady, the mom of the boys he goes to play ball with." Celo explained that he'd met Trinidad a couple of times when he had joined me for a game of two against two with the twins.

"The one you said has a huge juicy a—"

"Camilo, what if that was your mother?" I asked, silently agreeing with the adjectives he used to describe Trinidad's ass. But I wasn't about to discuss Trinidad with them. She was a lady and older, and they had to show respect. My memories of Pa were scarce, but that advice I remember always. *Respect women.*

"Celo was the one who told me about it." Camilo pointed at Celo, who leaned against the kitchen counter to watch me chop tomatoes, cucumbers, and radishes—greens. Mom needed greens, and these two probably didn't eat a lick of vegetables unless I put them in front of them.

Celo shrugged and grinned. His expression said it all.

"Fine. Abandon me to your party—the party that you are going to and not drinking at 'cause I'm not leaving Mom alone to bail anyone out of jail. A'ight?"

Two sets of heads nodded solemnly.

Solemnly my ass.

"And remember the two of you promised to watch out for Ma while I travel to Ofele Town in two weeks, okay?"

"Oh damn, that's in two weeks? 'Cause there is this day party that I want to go to."

I wasn't a violent man nor prone to anger, but damn if I didn't want to throw a couple of punches right now. Preferably at Milo. He was second in command and balked at the responsibility. Everything about home weighing on my shoulders would have been easily managed if each of us played our part. We could, the three of us, divide responsibilities for taking care of Mom, but that would require me telling them some ugly truths about themselves.

Their selfishness... But that shit would only cause another rift between us, and we couldn't afford that.

"Y'all gonna watch her, or do I have to ask someone else?"

"Nah, we'll watch Ma..." Celo nodded, looking toward her room. We all stared at the closed door.

The hunger that propelled me to cook a meal for my family fled quicker than my poise disappeared around Trinidad.

Cheerful thoughts.

Ofele Town had never looked better.

Five

Trinidad

Rush hour in Brooklyn meant what should have been a ten-minute drive ended up being a half hour. At this point, I didn't even know why I'd moved the car instead of making the twins take the subway, but getting some quality time with them was always a good idea.

"…Orlando also told us about his years in college and how, even though he partied, he focused on getting good grades and graduated at the top of his class…"

Not today, though. Not when I yearned to relegate Orlando to the back of my brain, where I placed all the items I needed to compartmentalize. Not when they had chosen Orlando as one of their favorite topics of conversation and decided to give me a dissertation on all things Orlando.

There was no need for me to see that man-child without a shirt. That was knowledge I didn't require, and on top of that, I didn't need the reminder of how kind he could be and how he actually loved spending time with my sons. Unlike many a high-vibration man, or whatever they called them now, who felt an unmarried woman with children meant a woman that had failed at life. Especially at love. Immediately we are deemed broken.

"Yeah, he's asked to work on our math grades, so I'm gonna ask Ms. Solis," Brian continued.

"Man, more homework? We already do too much," Brandon interjected.

Orlando had my two sports-driven, nonacademic children talking about math and homework—*willingly* talking about it. He had this way of pinpointing what they needed to be improving, either at home or at school, that worked every damn time.

I remember the first Saturday I woke up to the smell of Pine-Sol and the sounds of deep murmurs debating which room to clean next. My mouth opened in quiet awe; I stayed still in my bed, enjoying the sound of the two young men I birthed being responsible and helpful.

The twins were maturing—whatever maturity looks like on a fifteen-year-old child—but some of those gestures came from beyond their evolving brains. Orlando was doing a great job guiding them during their sessions.

Beyond anything physical, that was the most attractive to me. Their father lacked in imparting any type of wisdom to them on how to prepare for life. Anytime they were with him, he would find ways to spend the least amount of time with them and fill their weekends with so many activities that quiet, quality conversations were few and far between.

Hearing that Orlando had referred to me as older was a good reminder. Talk about a splash of water over my over-active libido. I hadn't checked my period app, but without pulling my phone, I knew what moment of the month it was. Hopefully, I would be out of the thick of things and back to my stressed normal self until next month if I was lucky.

"And he is gonna go on a trip with his friends soon! I think one of those historical towns you're always telling us about," Brian said, gifting me with so many words. I planned to write this in my journal as a moment to remember when we got home.

"Yeah, he was telling us that when we're older, he'll take us to carnival. And maybe we can come out with him for Labor Day and whine with the ladies," Brandon interjected.

"Excuse me, you're gonna what?" I exclaimed. My babies, talking about whining with women? At least Brandon said *ladies* instead of something else. Thank God for small mercies.

"Well, yeah, you know how Dad doesn't take us to anything Caribbean even though it's his heritage. He ain't never including us when he travels to Barbados to see Grandpa and Grandma, so we've never seen Crop Over, but Orlando said…"

And so it went until we arrived at the house and settled in for the day.

My pantry was running low. The few boxes of pasta sat there waving at me, whispering that they'd be the quickest thing to make for dinner. I had already cooked today, but a brief glance at the pot on my way out told me the twins had eaten their weight in gold again. This would be the third trip to the grocer's in five days.

Their father's contributions barely covered the food for the month at this point.

Feeling overstimulated, exhausted, and ready for bed, I fixed up a quick dinner of chicken, pasta, and spinach with a creamy sauce I whipped up and hoped the twins would enjoy.

By the look of the empty plates an hour later, I could audition for *Top Chef*'s next season.

"I guess basketball was a lot today, huh?" I smiled as Brandon and Brian finally pushed back from the table, hovering over the plates as if they had been hanging out on a deserted island with no food for three months. Satisfied grins on two lean, smooth, brown, handsome faces nodded in unison, their locs bobbing with their nods. They rarely gave me such open praise anymore, but whenever they did, my heart filled with light and joy, a rush of pure warmth filling me at seeing them growing so well.

"Yeah, and our cheerleading practice."

"That's right!" I completely forgot about their practice. This current client I was working with for their upcoming event was truly driving me wild. I needed to sit down this weekend and straighten up my calendar and the boys' to keep track of it all. This weekend was their father's, which meant cleaning, organizing, and, hopefully, a few glasses of wine with my girls. Oh, and maybe another date with Milton.

Suddenly, the pasta hardened in my stomach, becoming a ton of granite.

I'd been postponing speaking with the boys about possibly going to the Poconos with Milton in two weeks. I'd never taken a weekend away from them like this. The few vacations I had in the past were with them. The only time I'd gone on a girls' trip was in August of 2019 while the boys were visiting my parents in San Pedro de Macoris. I had a time with a gentleman I met in Trinidad during a night out, one of the best nights of my life.

If only I could have sex like that again... Trinidad, focus!

Milton was great. He was...a communicative partner with very specific and particular ways he liked to perform in bed, which I respected. He liked cleanliness, no sweat, a leisurely pace, calm, and peace. I understood peace. I craved peace. But once in a while, I craved chaos, passion, and ecstasy. But I very much understood the price I'd pay for that type of burning chemistry.

I bet Orlando was the opposite of Milton. Wild, energetic, acrobatic—

"What's wrong, Ma?"

Oh my. My brain needed to take a chill pill. Pausing for a second, I took in the comforting air of our living room, a mixture of my cooking, my sandalwood candles, my own lemongrass scent, and male teenager-raging hormones.

Home.

"So...if I were to have a...trip with Milton soon, how would you both feel about that?"

Their downturned eyebrows were not a good sign. The subsequent silence wasn't either. My heart plummeted to the depths of my body, wondering if the boys truly didn't like

Milton. I'd attempted a few outings with the four of us, for them to connect on a deeper level. Still, any of those times, the twins stayed resolutely by my side, polite and kind to Milton but never saying much more than monosyllabic responses or audible nods, the most Caribbean thing they ever had done since I birthed them.

Their Bajan grandparents would have been proud of their grandsons' quiet but clear disapproval masked by quiet, *polite* but clear disapproval. It was an art many couldn't master. By the end of the third time we hung out together, I could sense Milton's desire to spend time with the boys decreasing by the second. Not that the levels were ever high to begin with.

"So what do you think?"

"I mean, not like you asking for our permission, right?" Brandon's deeper timber resonated in the dining room. That deeper voice was something I was still trying to get used to; one day, he woke up and had no falsetto, just a baritone exactly like his father's. Brian's voice had dropped, too, but he still had moments where his old little boy's voice would try to creep in at the funniest times, to his overwhelming embarrassment.

My instinct was to ask Brandon to remove the bass from his voice, but raising Black young men meant understanding that people around them would attempt to remove their power on a daily basis. It was a fine line between allowing Brandon and Brian to assert themselves confidently while understanding and abiding by the rules of my home.

"I understand you might not be thrilled about my potential relationship with Milton but..."

"So you planning to claim him now? I mean, y'all were dating, but we…we thought it wasn't super serious," Brian asked, a thread of panic underneath his self-assuredness. His face scrunched up, just as it did when he couldn't play with his favorite toy as a toddler, and my heart squeezed, wanting to reassure him. Another lesson I was imparting to them, wishing I didn't have to—we do not always get what we want, and we have to live with the uncertainty and unfairness of it all. I wished they weren't learning that lesson this way.

"We are discussing potentially becoming serious, yes. And let me remind the two of you that I am a grown-up, and I make my own decisions. I will always take your needs into consideration, but I need you both to remember, I am the adult here." The more resolute and decisive I sounded, the better for the boys.

"Yes, Ma, sorry. I'm sure we can hang with Dad or…maybe Orlando would be down to letting us stay."

My insides vibrated and warmed. Their dad had them this weekend; I doubted he'd volunteer another one so soon, but Orlando? He'd probably jump at the opportunity to spend more time with the boys; he'd offered to watch them on occasions when I was extra busy at work. Of all the three men currently in my life, the two that I needed to be attentive to my boys didn't cut it, but Orlando…

"How about you start your evening chores? We can discuss more in a couple of days. There is no rush. I only wanted you both to know what was coming."

"Can we do the chores a little later please? I needed to do some quick homework, and Brian wanted to shower. You know how he is," Brandon said with uncharacteristic calmness. His jaw was rigid, and I could see a vein throbbing on his neck.

Brian stared at his twin as if he'd put on a clown suit, got on the table, and started dancing. Brandon's eyebrow twitched, but he kept his eyes resolutely on mine.

A gathering tension rose in the kitchen; the boys rarely asserted themselves as the "men of the house." I understood gender constructs and society enough to try a balanced approach at home: this all-gender shit is bullshit, but you gotta understand it well in order to be able to smash it. So watching him apply some of the things I had tried to explain was disconcerting, at least. As the pack leader, I sat calm, not letting Brandon's temper activate mine.

"I what? Oh, oh yeah, that homework." Brian broke the impasse with a burst of movement, standing up and drawing my attention away from Brandon.

"We'll take care of the kitchen, Mama; we'll be right back," Brian assured me with his sweet smile.

The diplomat of the family.

A rush of air left my chest cavity as soon as the twins went to their rooms. Their empty plates and my half-eaten one lay there. Ignoring the pull to clear everything myself, I navigated my way to the living room where my laptop sat with several emails and deliverables waiting to be answered. The magic of working for myself meant I set my own schedule. The sucky part of working for myself was that I seldom set boundaries around when not to work.

Getting lost in emails, I barely reacted when my boys returned, both showered and clearly in a different state of mind. The china and stainless steel clanking against the sink soothed me while I typed away answer after answer for my upcoming event.

"So, Mom, Coach told us she signed us up for an additional competition."

"Really?" This vendor should have already sent me a full quote to present to my client. I had been chasing this particular transportation company for days. I hated when I worked with unprofessional partners because, in turn, they made me seem to be unprofessional.

"Yeah, so I wanted to see if you went with us. It's a weekend, so that's pretty dope," Brian said.

"But it's the same weekend as your thing, with that old man... Milton," Brandon said, disdain dripping from every word.

"Excuse me? Milton is not old. He's about ten years older than me, and for my age, that is not old..." The clank of dishes and the water faucet stopped, and we all stared at each other.

"Ma, for real? With all due respect." No sentence that started with all due respect ended well. "That dude is lame; he ain't for you. He doesn't have the same vibes as you. Yes, you work hard and shit, but you don't make your entire personality your job," Brandon explained.

I was gifted with many, many words by my boys. Just not the words I wanted to hear from them.

"He's not for you, Ma; he don't show appreciation for you the way he should. Men should shower their women with love, affection, and gifts and always make her feel like number one. At least that is what Orlando says, and I can see he is a stand-up dude, so it must be correct. Real men don't play games about what we want; we make what we want to happen. Milton ain't try to call you his girlfriend all this time; we can hear your convos with Auntie Miranda," Brian said.

Words dissolved from my lips. Every response I wanted to give faded to nothing as I gaped at my two boys who came for me and my life choices. When you give birth to Black children, you hope you gave them strength and audacity to live in a world that is so against us, but when that audacity is used against you…you start reflecting on your life choices. Running my nails over my keyboard, I hoped the ASMR could calm me enough not to end up in the evening news: my mug shot with the caption "Mother of two snaps."

"Orlando is a child; he doesn't know how things change as you continue to grow up." Why in the world would I decide to say that first? I'd never know. But the fact that the twins felt Orlando was a better example than Milton didn't sit right with me. Not if I was trying to make Milton a fixture in my life.

"Ma, Orlando is a grown-ass man. He is ten years older than us, not our contemporary; stop calling him a child. He supports his entire family and has been teaching us a lot of things." Brian turned around, drying the last plate and placing it on the correct shelf. The boys never put things in their right place, but they had started paying more attention—since Orlando.

My chest caved like an empty helium balloon; the boys very rarely asked for me to go on their cheerleading trips with them. They never bothered asking their dad because, well, homophobia. When their father and I realized Brandon might be gay when he was about ten years old, we did the best thing we could have done as parents. We took it in stride and never required him to come out of the closet. One day, I asked him if the boy he kept mentioning over and over was his crush, and Brandon froze; then I remember my little boy nodding, and when I smiled at him, he smiled right back.

And that was that.

Their father, taking in all the good things he'd learned in his life in New York and not the unfortunate homophobia from our Caribbean heritage, decided not to ostracize his ten-year-old.

Instead, he made sure his gay son would be the most manly gay man in the world. Cheerleading did not fit in that definition. So, their father didn't bother supporting any of the related activities.

I really wanted to go with Milton, but the boys seldom asked for my company. They were too grown for their mom to tag along. This invitation was a big opportunity to spend some quality time with them. Milton would understand. And who knew? Maybe instead of going to the Poconos, Milton could come with me. He'd said the trip was optional, so missing it wouldn't hurt him. This would be a perfect opportunity to show the boys that Milton cared, that he was about them and me…and maybe Milton could convince me too.

"Alright, boys, I will go with you."

Six

Orlando

Time accelerated without my permission these past two weeks. Work had been nonstop. The letter of acceptance for law school loomed on the top shelf of my bookcase with all my anime DVDs and fantasy books, luring me to check it again and ensure time hadn't run out on my response. My brothers acted like fools the whole two weeks, worrying me if they'd do a good job of taking care of Mom while I was gone. But Camilo had dutifully showed up this afternoon with a small bag, ready to stay for the weekend. Meanwhile my social life stalled as I focused on home, work, and the mentorship program. My brain had little capacity for else.

Staring at my packed suitcase, I sifted through my mental list. Forgetting something meant I'd potentially be on the first flight tomorrow to Ofele Town without my boxers or condoms. That shit couldn't happen, so I ran through the list one last time. The condoms might seem premature as I wasn't going down there searching for a fling, but if a fling searched for me, I wouldn't be opposed to a ride or two. And I don't want to be caught lacking if something were to pop off.

The sea breeze had been calling my name for days, infiltrating my neat room, bringing an airiness I seldom felt in my home. My friends would all meet me there a couple of days later, but I'd wanted to arrive first, settle in the house rental, and start my search for my baby's mother and my daughter.

My child. Shit! Whirling around, I found the pink paper bag lying on my desk, waiting to be noticed.

My palms grew moist as I refolded a little dress over my gray duvet. Would my daughter like it? The white-and-purple dress was big enough for a five-year-old. At least that's what the lady said at the boutique close to my office. I didn't want to show up empty-handed to our meeting, knowing I hadn't been part of her life for years.

Would it be enough to erase my absence? No piece of fabric could be enough; gifts were just empty gestures when replacing true affection. My mother had taught me that every time she went overboard with birthday and Christmas presents to compensate for the free parenting she got out of me.

Would my daughter even understand what was happening? I sure as hell barely understood myself, so I couldn't expect much from a barely grown toddler with their frontal lobe still in development. Shit, mine had only stopped developing a few years ago.

Closing the suitcase, I left all the insidious thoughts inside. Walking toward my large whiteboard with all my scribbles and plans, I picked up a marker, letting the quiet satisfaction seep into my taste buds so sweet I could taste it. There was nothing better to chase my anxiety away than checking things off my home to-do list.

Well…that was a damn lie… I could think of at least two other things that could be better. Sex and a certain mother of twins who inhabited my dreams, the wet and dry variety.

Fuck. Here I went, objectifying that woman with my dirty, filthy thoughts of bending her over her car hood, lifting one of those mom dresses she wore, the flowery ones with straps on the shoulders that flowed around her ankles. They made her ass look like Easter bun on Resurrection Sunday.

No…there was no time to jerk off, so I needed to focus on other things. Like the whiteboard in front of me.

Meds, check. I'd portioned all of them out and placed them in a daily medicine dispenser, which I handed to Celo.

Food, check. The freezer overflowed with easy-to-defrost and reheat meals for the three of them.

Security: Double check. I asked Seño B to keep an eye on the apartment. There was no one more nosy, stubborn, or careful than her. She'd hit me up in a second if things were going wrong.

I did a damn good job but I couldn't even be proud of it. I remember my mom being well…a mom, leaving me empty. *Why?* This is the question I ask myself daily. Why my dad, why my mom, why me? I am twenty-five. I should be enjoying myself and living life. *Why?*

Nah, I wasn't about to indulge in depressing thoughts. It was better to lean into the power of my mind. Feeling sorry for myself fit me like the huge-ass jeans my father used to wear back in the day when he thought he was fly. That's why I preferred that slim fit and positive thinking. It was how I moved forward.

With dinner already prepared for everyone, I could, in theory, relax for the evening, but my nervous energy wouldn't leave me be. The high-pitched groan of lasers and the vibrations of the sound system in our living room pushed me to leave my privacy and enter our apartment's common space. Mom sat on the recliner, watching her two youngest boys play video games, her hands clutching the fabric of her pj's at her knees. A different pang hit my insides, this one tasting like regret and sorrow as it crawled up my throat.

Age had not been kind to my mother. Deep lines marked the corners of her eyes, mouth, and between her eyebrows. Her skin, once a gorgeous deep mahogany, had turned dull the more she refused to go outside. Her hair shined prematurely gray, and her gaze was always focused on some faraway memory. I wish I didn't believe in soul mates. But how couldn't I when I had the consequence of two souls separated too early for their time right in front of me? The psychiatrist may be right about her medical diagnosis—bipolar disorder—but without her heart engaged in maintaining her well-being, grief was really the thing to blame for her current state.

Cabanga. That is what Seño B said my mom had when she found me sitting outside our apartment with my head bowed as my mother had one of her episodes. Sometimes, nothing helped. I was so good at calming her that it became second nature, but there were days that the memories assaulted her, and Dad's ghost whispered in her ear until she couldn't keep herself straight.

Seño B had pulled me up with impressive strength and brought me to her apartment for a cup of sorrel with a little rum; never mind, I wasn't twenty-one back then. She'd sagely said there was no external cure for cabanga.

No medicine that would cure such devastating and hollowing pain.

Cabanga was a yearning beyond comprehension, a hunger for something or someone so strong, your entire being transformed, and a cloud followed you. The only cure would be my mother wanting to be better and finally allowing herself to heal.

I hated thinking that way. But in times like this when I saw her wearing her pajamas from the day before, even though she'd assured me this morning she had showered, I wondered if cabanga was truly what she had.

None of my three family members acknowledged my presence. My phone pinged in my pocket as the common emptiness threatened to take over. My mood shifted as I read the text message.

Brandon: So you gonna travel next week and miss our weekly get-together

Brian: So we were thinking you should come thru for dinner tonight

Brandon: And we can play video games after! Mom is cool with it; come thru!

Mom is cool with it. Shit, I wish I believed that. That woman barely gave me the time of day, but to see Trinidad again would be exactly what I needed to leave for Ofele in good spirits. My shower walls had been painted several times these past two weeks, evidence of how bad I had it for Ms. Velasquez. Just the thought of her and I started bricking up.... again... Damn.

"Ma, comiste? Did you like what I cooked?" I asked, a thread of guilt coursing through me as I contemplated leaving my family behind to spend time with Brandon, Brian, and Ms. Velasquez.

"Ay...well, I didn't want that, so the boys went out and got me some McDonald's. But you can eat the food tomorrow. That way, you don't have to cook," she said it so matter-of-fact. I told her several times a day for the past two weeks that I was traveling. *Days.* But who cared what Orlando had going on? Certainly not my mother nor my brothers.

Fuck...focus on the positive.

Focus on what you can control. My father's voice always took over on days like this when I was at my lowest energy levels.

"I'm traveling tomorrow, Ma. It's all good. Imma go out to Brandon and Brian's. They invited me for dinner and video games. I leave really early tomorrow. My flight is at 6:00, so I won't see you in the morning. Okay?"

I stared at the three people closest to me in the world, and none of them looked up. Milo acknowledged my words with a brisk nod; damn… I guess I would take that, at least. Chasing away the void forming in me, I walked toward the front door, grabbed my keys, and exited the apartment. Leaving behind the noise of running feet and laser guns and the louder indifference my family clearly felt for me.

Focus on what you can control.

"Maaaaaa, Orlando is here!" Brandon hollered into the apartment, making my ears ring. I'd been to the Velasquez humble abode before. The turquoise walls reminded me of a calm afternoon at my paternal grandparents' home in St. Mary, Jamaica. Every little corner of the apartment had personality, from the mustard-yellow sofa to the glass jars and knickknacks on the walls; the functional way Trinidad had arranged their home made me jealous.

Our apartment, with its stark white walls, beige furniture, and nondescript art I bought in Home Goods had zero warmth compared to this place. I wish I could bottle a tenth of the vibes in here and take them home with me. Maybe then we could be a proper family.

"What's up, man, you good?" We clasped hands, and a rush of goodness trickled through me, attempting to erase the sadness clinging from my nonconversation with my family.

"Yeah, I'm alright. Ma made bandera…shit is fire. Can't wait to eat. Hope you brought your appetite."

"Yo! You came through; that's dope. I thought you were gonna flake on us, knowing you have that early flight." Brian popped out from a corner, his locs arranged haphazardly in a bun on his head.

"Que escándalo you both have. You'd think he's the second coming of Christ instead of Orlando. How are you?" Trinidad floated from the kitchen toward the front of the apartment to greet me. She also had her locs in a bun, black yoga pants, and a white tank top.

The back of my neck heated as I studied how fluidly she moved around her place, picking up one of the twins' backpacks and situating it by the entrance. She picked up a cup of water, walking a ring around her wood table toward a side table with a coaster, then fluffed up the pillows on the sofa. Every time she bent, the fabric of the yoga pants caressed and highlighted that huge, juicy ass that started all the trouble during my showers and had me cleaning the walls every morning. Words tumbled in my head and, without permission, started flowing out of my mouth. This happened every time. Shit.

"What's up, Ms. V? Looking good today. Thanks for the invite; you know how it goes. Sometimes a man don't know where he gonna eat, then someone makes that call, and you saved." *Da fuck? I cook.* Why did words that make zero sense come out of me the moment she was around?

"Oh, so you have a lot of young ladies inviting you to their apartment for dinner?" Trinidad turned around from fluffing the pillows, giving me a much-needed reprieve to my chest cavity, which valiantly fought to keep my heart in check. I had enough sense to wear the loosest basketball shorts because I already knew what would happen.

And what did she just ask?

"Uhhh...well, sometimes, yea." I hoped that I had answered correctly, but looking at Brandon's and Brian's scowls, I was off.

"Nah, Ma. We've told you Orlando is not like that; he doesn't have a bunch of girls, he don't play them like that."

Shit, there I went, talking to talk. This woman always made me forget my poise. It's as if I reverted to my twenty-year-old self around her.

"Mm-hmm, well, Orlando, I guess I have to believe them. I have no other choice, do I?"

"I mean, you could believe me when I tell you I'm a chill dude, but I know you're not buying that, are you?" My right eyebrow rose with a mind of its own, taunting Trinidad with a swag I seldom showcased. But that wasn't what I wanted to showcase, damn it.

"You guessed right; I'm thankful that you try to temper your escapade stories for the sake of my boys' innocence, though. I do see that. Come on over to the kitchen; the table is already set. Miranda is in there too."

Trinidad granted me a mild smile and turned around, the sway of her hips and ass hypnotizing me once more, ensuring I followed. I tried my best to keep my facial expression straight because I didn't want the twins to feel like I was violating their space or having improper thoughts of their mom, but gotdamn. It got harder and harder to keep the charade of happy-go-lucky dude going.

Besides, Trinidad needed to know nothing about my sob stories and my life hardships. She had plenty going on herself, and she kept a tight ship with her boys and was always poised. Women like her made men like me want to be better. Show up better. There were zero cracks in her armor, so who was I to come here and burden her with my stuff?

The kitchen and very small dining room sat in a different space, each with its own room. The dining room walls were a light green, and pictures of paradise surrounded the space. From previous visits, the scenes were not only art; they actually were some of Trinidad and the twins' favorite places in San Pedro de Macorís and Bridgetown. Even though she'd divorced, her love for Barbados ran deep, and it was showcased all over her home. Trinidad left me and continued to the kitchen, the sway of her walk making my chest tight.

"Ah! Orlando! Good to see you! Sit down, sit down. Everything is hot." Miranda, one of the teachers at Basquiat High and Trinidad's best friend, greeted me with a kind smile. I suspected she knew I had a crush on Trinidad, but she was always very kind when I saw her, so I reciprocated in kind.

Miranda, with her ample hips and thighs, navigated the tight corners around the table, holding two bottles of wine—one red and one white—until she plopped herself on her own seat and gave me a bigger grin, her light brown skin flushing red.

"So, carnival, huh? You gon wuk up dem gyal ova there?" Miranda had a glint in her eyes that I couldn't figure out.

"Uh, not sure about all the wuking up I'll be doin', but yea. Carnival calling my name." A quiet thrill traveled through me. I hadn't given myself time to truly think about it, but I was amped. I really was going to carnival in Ofele Town.

"Mmmm, good! I know you're gonna have a good time! We leave on the school bus early tomorrow as well, right, twins?" Miranda smirked and poured Riesling into Trinidad's empty glass, filling up to the brim. "She had a crappy day, she needs it. Red or white?"

"Nah, I gotta wake up very early tomorrow." I declined Miranda's wine offer while Brandon and Brian gave her an evil stare, which they quickly wiped away when their mother walked back into the dining room, bringing some freshly squeezed lemonade and placing it in the middle of the table. Each seat had a gold placemat, a glass full of ice, a heaping plate of white rice, pollo guisao, a couple of tostones, a small ceramic bowl with red beans, slices of avocado, and wine glasses for the adults. My stomach rumbled at the sight and the aroma of the holy trinity carrying the dish. Having home-cooked meals was one of my favorite things, especially when I hadn't cooked the meal.

"So yeah, the bus leaves tomorrow real early. So Mom's gonna take us, and then she'll fly in the afternoon, right, Mom?"

Trinidad sat at the head of the table with a quizzical smile. "Well yeah, you two made sure to buy my flight and take charge of my arrangements. I've never seen you both be so diligent about helping me out with my travels, but I appreciate it 'cause these two weeks have been a whole mess with that damn man changing the date of the event last minute."

"So…where is this carnival you're going to?" Miranda turned around and stared at me, smug amusement dancing all over her face. My instincts seldom failed me. I was certain Miranda liked me as a person, so my confusion grew. I fixed myself to answer her when Brandon's foot slammed against mine below the table.

"Eat, everyone! It's gonna get cold," Trinidad exclaimed, and I nodded, frowning at Brandon, who instead was focused on Miranda with the same screw face as his brother.

"Damn, Trinidad, all of this looks amazing; thanks for the invite again. I love home-cooked meals, and I can tell you put a lot of love into this one." I gave her what I hoped was a genial smile instead of the adoring one I felt seeping out of every pore. Trinidad's ochre hue reddened, and her gaze grew misty as we both stared at each other. For a second, I forgot we had company. My solitary soul reached out to hers, and my chest compressed at the sensation of hers touching mine.

Goddamn, I needed to stop reading those fantasy-illustrated books with romance. Trinidad had me believing we'd turn the page and skip away happy in the jungle of New York.

Two souls finally connecting.

Trinidad bit her lip, and I followed the perfectly white square of her tooth digging into her plumpness and gave a brief thanks for thinking of basketball shorts yet again. Needing a distraction, I cut the staring game first and turned to Miranda, who didn't have the smug expression anymore. Instead, she looked pensive. Up to something.

"I'm traveling to Jacksonville."

For some reason, I did not say Ofele Town. Trinidad already had a skewed view of my wild, nonexistent ways, and I didn't want to fuck it up by naming the town famous for hosting the hottest, newest Caribbean carnival in the States. Stories of last year's carnival spread all over Black social media, with videos of people wilding out in the coastal town. Maybe she'd think I'm going to like an American style carnival. Best leave things to the imagination.

"Well, that's dope. We're going to Florida too! Not Jacksonville, though," Trinidad said with interest as Brandon squirmed next to her.

"Ma! Stop saying dope, please! So, I was thinking, though, maybe you should let us go with Auntie Miranda; she is chaperoning too, so she can drive us to the bus."

"Don't be offering your auntie. The bus drive to Florida, girl… You are braver than me going in that bus for fifteen hours…" Trinidad shuddered.

"Well, someone has to do it, and I get extra pay, so if I need to watch a bunch of horny little fifteen-year-olds to get some overtime, then I will do that."

"Auntie!" Brian chastised her, but Brandon stopped making eye contact with everyone at the table and focused solely on his chicken. Damn, little homie probably had plans for the weekend. Not trying to blow his spot, I tried to keep the laughter from creeping up my throat, but it was a lost cause. Trinidad and Miranda soon joined me—all of us probably remembering some good times when we were teenagers with roaring hormones taking over every single logical thought.

Trinidad's chest rose and fell, the jiggle of her hidden breasts making me dizzy. The laughter subsided as my own horniness conquered any other rational way of thinking. I attempted again to wrench my gaze away from her, but I caught her biting her lips again. Shit. I was in trouble. This woman was pure trouble.

"A'ight. A'ight, it's not that funny. So, Ma, you're all set for tomorrow. The confirmation number is in your notes app, so you don't have to search a million emails in that inbox of yours."

"Giiiiirl, you need to do better." Miranda shook her head. "Thank God for Brian and Brandon arranging all of this for you 'cause you need it."

Trinidad stared at me for a second until she released me from her hold, and I was able to breathe easier.

"Girl, you ain't lying. I definitely need this trip." Trinidad shrugged and got back to her rice. And I went back to thinking she was completely out of my league.

"So, the boys doing better at home? Helping you out?" Not knowing my limits, I offered Trinidad to help with cleanup and washing the dishes. Miranda took one look at the pile on the sink, murmured something about the dishwasher and Riesling, and left us in the kitchen. The boys went to their room, letting me know they'd be ready to beat me when I was done with helping out.

The kitchen glowed with its yellow buttery walls and appliances. Such an old-school design, but it suited Trinidad; she was such an odd mix, and I couldn't quite crack her. For an observant person, that was enough to drive me wild with interest. She could be a little stuck-up, sometimes goofy, sexy, cool, strict—I could go on and on. Every single facet I discovered kept me hooked.

The need to make sure she was good, though? That had been growing little by little over the past few months. With all I had to take care of, you'd think I didn't want anything else on my plate, but if it was a serving of Trinidad, I'd gobble it all up. All to make sure she was good.

"They are, and I know it is not their good-for-nothing father...so thank you. You are an amazing mentor, and the boys really look up to you." We finished with the last dish, the scent of cinnamon and cloves boiling in the pot Trinidad set up to cleanse the house of the garlic and onion scent from before.

"Nah, you're an amazing mom. They really look up to you, you know? They get it even at their age. They get that you are their rock. Their father..." The boys' father was always a touchy subject. Brandon and Brian talked about him in an admiring but distant way. Trinidad had moments where she cracked and showed some of her frustration about her ex-husband, but for the most part, she kept a neutral way of handling anything related to their co-parenting.

"He's living his best life, and I am saddened for the boys. I'm saddened they never met the real man he was when he just moved to the States. I swear that man came to this country so hungry for love and for community. And I poured myself into him; I was his family, his connection to the culture here...all, and now it's like we are strangers. He got what he needed: two sons and that was it. He was too good for me after that. I was too... Dominican, too Black, too *barrio* for him. He wanted a bit of a more elevated life, you know? He moved to Manhattan, passed the Bar, and that's it. Now he has his beautiful blonde wife and...he barely teaches the boys about his Bayan background. Thank God for his parents."

Damn. I hadn't expected this. She never opened up. I didn't know what to say.

"Sorry, I don't know what came over me...probably that large-ass glass of Riesling Miranda served me."

"Nah, you're good. I...honestly, I am glad you feel comfortable opening up to me. I see you," I confessed, unable to keep the words from tumbling out.

"You see me, huh? What do you see? A tired thirty-five-year-old barely making it?"

"No, I see a beautiful, amazing woman, intelligent and capable, loving and so brave." Might as well spill my guts here to her. I don't know what it was about her, but damn, it felt good saying this.

"Wow, that was...lovely, made me feel things, or maybe it's the Riesling..." she whispered into her glass, her gaze lost for a second. Staying still felt like the best approach. Staring at her mouth, on the other hand, felt like a recipe for a night of tossing and turning. It was worth it.

When she licked her lips and took another gulp of wine, I followed the liquid down her throat and wondered what it would be like to press my lips right there where her neck met her shoulder. Fucking hell, I was standing in Ms. Velasquez's kitchen with a full chubby. Egregious behavior. Inevitable.

"Thanks, Orlando, that was... I didn't realize I needed to hear that, but I did. I'm going to turn in for the night, but you are welcome to stay with the twins; just make sure they lock up, alright?" Her eyes roamed down my body and, for a second, paused around my crotch area; at this point, I was fully hard, and there was no hiding it. I tried standing a better way, but the shift made things worse. Ms. Velasquez licked her lips again and I'm ashamed to admit a groan almost escaped me.

"Yeah, I should go to bed…it's getting…hot," Trinidad said and brushed past me, her perfume lingering behind. "Good night, Orlando."

"Good night, Ms. Velasquez. Sleep well."

I hope she did because there was no way I would.

Seven

Trinidad

The amount of patience and bandwidth I spent these past two weeks had me exhausted. My client had decided to change his event date, with two thousand people attending and a month and a half to go. It created such chaos and confusion that I worked nonstop, staying awake till past midnight, cajoling vendors and providers via email to switch their dates with minimal budgetary impact because my client also thought I walked over water and would get everything changed with no additional cost to him.

One particular vendor was giving me the run for my money. Anxiety coursed through me as we negotiated the date move for the tenth time. My flight boarding time loomed in the back of my mind as I finally managed to get the vendor to cooperate. Cursing my client's zodiac sign, his father, mother, and anyone who thought he was a good person, I kept it brief as I had no time left to get to the airport.

My plane to get to the closest airport to Ofele for the boys' cheerleading presentation was not gonna wait for an over-worked mom and event professional. Thank God my ride was already waiting downstairs. Hopping on, I was lucky to get the fastest, most imaginative driver in the city. He got me to JFK in less than thirty minutes and accelerated my heart rate so much that I recorded a thirty-minute workout.

Powering through with my rollaway, I flew by thousands of travelers, some jittery and excited about their trips, the buzz of their excitement melding with the soft instrumental music blaring through the hidden sound system in their air-port. Many business people sped by with stony faces, clearly hating every second they spent in the brightly lit building. And then there were people just like me, hassled and trying to catch their flight on time. A mix of luck and preparation saved me thirty minutes as I cruised through TSA pre-check.

An hour and a half after the meeting and five thousand steps later, I was sitting on my flight, ready for Florida and my cheerleading mom duties. The twins had been oddly quiet. Not one text checking in on me, as they usually did when I traveled. My cell phone lit in the dim cabin, displaying no text messages. My heart still hammered in my chest, my breath-ing so fractured, I vowed to up my cardio sessions starting next Monday.

Me: I'm on the plane departing now. See you soon!

Sweet oxygen coursed through my system as I shot a quick text to Miranda. Finding no reprieve to my anxiety, I opened my text thread with Milton. We spoke hours ago…and then he left me on read.

Milton: The welcome reception is in a couple of hours. I think Imma rest a little in case you write to me, I might be asleep.

A cracked tooth was not what I needed right before this competition, so I unclenched my jaw and let my chest fill with the recycled plane air.

Me: Thank you for wishing me a good flight.

Milton: You wouldn't have had to deal with airports if you came with me. I am going to nap now.

My temples throbbed at the casual dismissal.

Milton, what was I going to do about this man? The moment I told him I couldn't go on his work trip, things went from warm to frosty.

I got it, I was disappointed too. His refusal to come along instead of gallivanting to his optional work trip stung. Attempting to find a middle ground and giving him another opportunity to bond with the twins, I invited him to join me in Florida. But deep down, I knew he'd deny me.

Those high hopes I had when I met Milton had been morphing into dread. I didn't know why. Milton was exactly what I needed in my life. He was all green flags; all my boxes were ticked by him. So why, why did his name glowing on my screen make my stomach rumble and coldness cruise through my veins?

This feeling of vague disenchantment was not normal this early in a relationship.

I remember how excited I was when I met my ex-husband. How helplessly in love. The signs, I missed them all. Missed that he was looking for community, shelter, and love, that he was emotionally immature, and that he only knew how to use. All the things he needed I foolishly provided. And as I poured myself, *all* of myself, into him, he never poured in return. My glass ended up empty while he left me behind to figure out other ways to be fulfilled.

The well-being of my children was my main priority. The second priority was living my life in sexual chaos. I went out on one-night stands, partied during the weekends. Any activity that ended with me getting well sexed at the end of the day.

A single mother, desperate for attention and love, like the love I knew my parents had. I searched for it in the wrong ways. Protecting my heart became my priority, so I shared my body instead. My sexuality, the dusty old bat, discovered under cobwebs and neglect. A hidden flower, the one thing my ex could not use all up. And I let it flourish.

Until it threatened to overtake my focus.

Needing a change, I traded my old ways. I stopped going to parties; I stopped shielding my heart. I healed. And then I met Milton. My experience told me that even though I didn't feel those old butterflies for Milton that had frolicked in my belly during my first marriage, I didn't need them anymore.

Infatuation blinded you to the reality of the red flags. So,

I fell in love with the feeling of comfort and peace. But now those feelings had decided to abandon me. Instead of peace, dread had moved in.

Maybe not having the same tingle in my stomach as the first time I fell in love was a good thing. Maybe never feeling it again was the key. But I had felt it again. Just last night.

Last night…it had been so good to chill and talk to Orlando about the boys in a way that I couldn't get anybody else to, except for Miranda. The flutters in my stomach had intensified as I basked in the recognition Orlando provided. He saw me and saw my children. He understood, without words, what I was trying to accomplish in life. Why did it have to be a twenty-five-year-old who was starting to live? Why couldn't I find the same connection with anyone else? And why did he have to be so lean, sturdy, and chocolaty smooth…

Trinidad, portate bien.

That boy was so irresponsible. His mom was sick, and here he was, gallivanting to some type of party somewhere in Florida instead of being with his family. That is not what I needed. What I needed was stability. Banishing thoughts of butterflies in my stomach, I instead focused on Milton's steadfastness.

Me: Hey, Milton, I'm on the plane. Last chance to change your mind.

Milton: Hey, love. I'm sorry I got mad at you. I know this is important. For you and for me to meet your kids. But maybe we should talk. When you return. I am still going to go on the trip even though it's a couples one. I explained to them that you have a last-minute event to attend for the children, so they were okay with it. So let's have dinner when you come back and talk some more about the next steps for us to solidify this as something more than casual...maybe.

Well, that went well.

Me: Okay, Milton, I'll hit you up as soon as I'm back.

I put my phone down and closed my eyes, hoping sleep would take over. Every inch of my body screamed in protest and exhaustion. I should have taken an edible to relax; my brain had the tendency to take over, not allowing me to sleep during flights.

The flight attendants traveled up and down the aisle, assisting guests with their luggage. Damn, everyone on this flight seemed to have some oversized carry-on. It would take us twice as long to leave at this pace. Most passengers were my people, and most of them seemed my age or younger. The buzz of excitement was contagious; laughter and elevated voices transformed this regular plane into the ride to a summer cookout. One passenger held an intricate headpiece with feathers, the crystals on them reflecting all across the plane's ceiling, lending to the festive feel.

The beautiful colors reminded me of Labor Day here in New York, or my days when I used to go to carnival in Miami in October.

If only I were on my way to carnival... I was seriously overdue for a break. I used to prioritize some time for self-care before, but I needed to be everything for my children now. Everything that my ex-husband wasn't. They needed stability and normalcy, not a mom that flew to Miami for carnival with her ass cheeks out for everyone to see.

Thoughts of my client, of Milton, of the twins all invaded my mind, keeping me from the sleep I so desired. It was time for a quick meditation to empty my brain. Popping out my cell phone, I quickly found my guided meditation app and inserted my headphones to listen. Finally, slumber and I made peace, and as I drifted off to sleep, the last thing I heard was, "I can't wait to enjoy my first carnival in Ofele!" from the same passenger with the headpiece. Warning bells clanged, but tiredness overpowered any other thought as sleep finally took over.

Eight

Trinidad

There was nothing like landing in Florida and being greeted by the beautiful palm trees and sunshine. Now if Florida could keep the excessive humidity that seeped in as I walked down the Jetway into the airport. Already beads of perspiration traveled the middle of my back as I maneuvered the packed small-town airport.

This cheerleading competition must be a big deal. I still didn't understand how it wasn't in the original planning schedule of the season, but I was glad it was happening in a Black town with a beautiful history.

There were rumors that a lot of maroons from the Caribbean, the south, and other areas of the continent came and settled here. They took ownership of this little piece of paradise by the water and were mostly left unbothered by, well, everyone else. It was a feat to be able to have a town like this that had been almost untouched by time. A space where Black people had prospered and created a tight community that welcomed others like them every year for a vacation. It was a blessing of peace and tranquility, a land to be ourselves.

Ofele Town had been on my bucket list for years, and I had yearned to come and bring the boys to visit. There were so many historical locations here, as well. Many luminaries had either lived here or come to create in this area.

To be in Ofele felt serendipitous. While standing at a cross-roads in my life, without planning, I ended up here. Work had not been feeling as fulfilling as before. Maybe it was this douchebag changing the date, but I missed working on bigger events like this cheerleading town-wide event, where I was the head BAC calling the shots for big festivals.

A faraway thread of concern popped into my mind, like when you're trying to remember if you locked your front door or not. *What was the thing I wanted to look into right before falling asleep?* As hard as I tried, my brain refused to give the deets. It served me right for always keeping it filled with overanalysis, endless to-do lists, and worries. At this point, my brain was considering joining a union for mistreatment. Giving up, I left the faraway thread alone, hoping it would voluntarily return to me later.

All around me, people my age or younger wandered around, looking fine in sundresses and hooch daddy shorts. Now, I know my generation was the flyest to exist, but this didn't look quite like parents coming to see a cheerleading conference.

I had yet to see a teenager. That faraway thread vibrated in the back of my brain, still teasing me.

The sliding doors opened and closed, letting the humid heat creep into the cool airport as I finally approached the exit.

A banner hung on the top of the doorway leading to the rental car area.

Welcome, revelers, to Ofele Carnival.

Ofele Carnival? Was that supposed to be this weekend? It explained the people in the plane and all around me right now. My mommy sense tingled, my breath hitched, and just to be certain, I took stock of my surroundings. I still didn't see any kids—only adults, all beautiful Black people.

A quiet dread seeped into my pores as I took all this information in. The rental area brimmed with travelers; navigating through the space, I stood in line to wait to get my car.

Once I saw the twins I would get to the bottom of whatever hell was happening.

"Sorry, ma'am. Well, you know, today we got swamped with everything happening with the carnival. Everybody has come to get cars. I don't know how the town will manage all this traffic." A frazzled older woman stood at the counter with a look of inpatient pity.

This was the fourth counter I'd tried.

"Oh, I can imagine with all this activity happening in the town…is there another branch close to here?"

"Oh, no, no, no, no, we're too small for that. All of the rental companies are located here in our airport. I think there's only one in town and it's one of our branches. And by looking at it really quickly, they're equally as sold-out. Most people made reservations a month ago, at least. But you never know there might be some cancellations."

"Oh my God. Are you serious?" I really did not like depending on rides to be able to navigate this little town. Maybe walking would be the way to go. "Is it too far from here to the Ofele Resort and Spa?"

"Oh yes. That will probably be a twenty-minute drive. The airport is on the outskirts of the town. But there are a lot of rides, sure drivers. My brother is one. Would you like him to pick you up?"

"Oh well, if you don't mind, that's really nice of you."

"Of course. Of course. I would love to assist. I'm telling you. It is so exciting to host carnival every year. I get to see the most wonderful people. I love working these dates because I just sit here and like people's gaze."

"Oh yeah, I can only imagine. I'm guessing, you know, having the cheerleader tournament and carnival at the same time must be a lot."

"Cheerleading tournament? I haven't heard anything about a cheerleading competition happening but again, I don't have all the details of everything happening in the town. But if anybody knows what's happening in Ofele and its nearby towns, it is my brother."

My stomach twisted, and I pressed my hand over it to calm it down.

Something must be off.

Something must be wrong.

Maybe the cheerleading competition happened on the outskirts of Ofele. Maybe they called it the Ofele Cheerleading Competition, but it wasn't exactly there. The twins showed me a website when I asked them for more details about the event. It looked pretty straightforward.

I pulled out my phone and walked out of the airport with instructions on where to wait for the lady's brother. While I waited, I searched for the cheerleading competition.

Nothing came up in the Google search. Not even the website the boys showed that night when they made all my bookings for the hotel and flight.

Jesus Alabao. There was no way. No way. This was not happening. My breath caught in my throat as my chest accelerated its heartrate. I needed a course of action. Yes. I needed to get to the hotel; once I was situated, I'd think of a plan. These boys don't even know what they are thinking.

But no, no, no. This couldn't be, it couldn't be because Miranda was coming to Ofele, as well. Sweet air rushed through my lungs, accompanied by pure relaxation. It must be something like that. The competition had to be happening. It had to, there was no other explanation.

"Hey, are you Trinitty?"

"Ehh, No my name is Trinidad. Hello, John."

"Yeah. My sister asked me if I could give you a ride. You're going to the Ofele Resort and Spa, right?"

"Yes, that's exactly where I'm going. Thank you so much, John. You're amazing."

"It's my pleasure."

John had the AC blasting, and thank God for the man because he understood the assignment. The amount of humidity that hit me the moment that I walked out of those sliding doors was unbearable. Already, my locs were losing inches, curling to the top of my crown and holding on to all the moisture in the air. Putting them up in a ponytail to keep them off my neck, I settled in the back of John's car, my mind whirling with details and all the conversations I've had with Miranda and the boys in the past few days. Everything I remembered made sense, but they were the only three people I had talked to about the cheerleading competition and the whole world trip.

None of the other parents have mentioned anything in any of the pickups. The coach hadn't said anything the last day they saw me when I picked the boys up from practice. I had been so focused on getting everything situated for this event for work that I missed the signs, but I really was hoping I was wrong.

I wasn't wrong.

"Ma'am, we do not have a reservation for you. I've looked everywhere. I've looked at all the name combinations you've provided me, and none of them are in our system." The front desk agent couldn't be more exasperated if she tried.

"That doesn't make sense. My son made the reservation. I gave you a confirmation number."

"Yes, yes, you did. But as I explained, that doesn't sound like our confirmation numbers. That is not a valid confirmation number; ours starts with eight, and yours starts with a three. Seems like your sons might have been missing a number. Why don't you go ahead and call them?" the agent said.

I'd put her through a wild goose chase for fifteen minutes. She had a line behind me waiting to check in. Everybody was sighing and irritated because I was holding up their fun, but I currently didn't have a space or a place to stay.

"And you said you're sold out?"

"Ma'am...the entire town is sold out. It is carnival. Have you not heard of Ofele Carnival? I know that we're new. We're just starting to grow. But yeah, the popularity kind of went from zero to ten overnight, so the town is full. I don't know what to tell you. I really want to help, but there's really nothing that I can do." The agent finally thawed out, probably seeing the frustration seeping out of my sweaty pores.

"Please, please could check one more time. I'm gonna call my twins, and I'm gonna try to see if I can find that confirmation number, but in the meantime, can you just check one more time? They made it under Velasquez, please."

"Sorry. Okay, sure, ma'am. I will check one more time, but it would really help if you had the correct confirmation."

"Of course, I'm gonna pull over there, and why don't you take care of these fine folks?" I gestured to the line, my chest tight at the potential reality that I didn't have a place to stay. "I am so sorry. You know, my kids, they made the reservation," I explained.

A lady, two persons down, stared at me as if I had grown an extra leg.

"You let your kids make a reservation? How old are they?" I filled my lungs before answering, because if not my temper would escalate and they were not responsible for my predicament.

"They are fifteen years old, but they're very, very responsible." I couldn't keep the frustration from my tone.

"Oh, you brave girl, that decision wasn't smart. Now it looks like you won't be able to stay for carnival," the woman said. At this point I was frankly over with the conversation.

"I'm not here for carnival. That's the whole thing. I'm here for a cheerleading competition."

"Cheerleading competition?" the front desk agent asked while checking in another guest. "No way there is a competition, I would know."

"Yes, there is." I breathed for patience. "I think it's probably somewhere on the outskirts of Ofele. I think they call it an Ofele competition, you know how it is sometimes? You'll have something like a little rinky-dink town, like close to like a bigger town. And you know, they want to make themselves a name, but they want to be able to pull people in, so they call it something else." At this point I was explaining myself to the line and I had no need for that. Or maybe I was trying to convince myself.

"Ma'am. My two girls are both in the best cheerleading team in the county. Trust me. If there was anything cheerleading happening in this town, I would know even if it was in a hundred-mile radius."

I decided to move forward because this could not be happening right now. This could *not* be happening. So I just nodded as the other guests stared at me and pretended I had my shit together. I didn't.

"I hear you. I hear you. It must be something else. You

know how it goes?" Ugh, enough explaining. "But go ahead and carry on with your work."

A lounge area served as the perfect location to make this call. I had never hit the keypad of my phone as hard as I was doing now. I don't know how I didn't break a nail.

"Ah, what's up, Ma? You good," Brandon greeted me. His surroundings were too quiet. Would a bus full of teenagers be this chill? Or were the technology companies getting that good at isolating noise?

"Am I good? No, no, no, no, I'm absolutely not good. Estoy bien enfadada ahora mismo. I'm standing here in the Ofele Resort and Spa, which, by the way, is a beautiful hotel. And they're telling me that they do not have a delegation from Basquiat High. And of course, they don't, because look at this hotel. It's like five stars. Of course, Basquiat wouldn't be able to afford this. And then I say, oh, maybe the boys are trying to, you know, give me a little bit of treat. And I'm not staying in the same hotel as they are. And I asked for the confirmation number you put on my notes application, and they cannot find the room."

"Brian and Brandon, what did you do?" My voice rose in volume until I exploded on a crescendo at the end of my soliloquy.

"Mom, listen…what happened was," Brian interjected, probably standing right next to his brother.

"No, no, no, no. No, *what happened was.*' Do not even start. Tell me. Tell me, dimelo, don't give me the runaround. *Tell* me what's going on," I said through clenched teeth. People were starting to really stare now. The shiny marble floor reflected back my frazzled face.

"Well, we thought you needed a vacation…" Brandon said.

"What do you mean?!" Two men in suits appeared in the middle of the lobby. They must have teleported. A glimpse of a white earpiece gave me the information I needed to avoid being kicked out. This was hotel security. I walked away from the lounge area and settled beside a large column that covered me from the rest of the lobby.

"I really don't understand how this happened. How did this happen? What do you mean you want me to have a vacation? I don't have time for a vacation. That event is happening in a month. I don't have the time to be playing games in no, you know, paradise. Not right now."

Not during carnival. Because that type of vacation was not for the new me. The old me though? She'd be ready to party.

"Mom. We wanted you to have a fun weekend. You haven't stopped working in a long time. But both of us can tell that you need a break. So we planned to surprise you. And this was the only way to surprise you," Brian said sweetly. Such a deceptive little devil! My palm slapped the marble column next to me, the burst of anger demanding outlet.

"This was not the only way to surprise me! You know how you could have? You could have had a conversation with me and explained to me that you were concerned about me not having time to rest. And then I would have told you that I was planning some trips soon and Milton and I had been planning to go to the Poconos this weekend. And you know what? I don't need you both to be parenting me. I am the mother!"

The two men in suits stared at me, then each other. Then one touched his ear. Shit. I needed to lower my voice. I searched around for a quieter area but the lobby buzzed with so many travelers ready for their carnival weekend. You would think my voice would get lost in the hubbub, but my vocal cords were somehow competition for the quiet excitement filling the space.

"Ma, we you would have dragged and not done it any-time soon. And that weekend trip, wasn't Milton taking you to a work event?"

These children knew too much about my personal life. New boundaries needed to be set as soon as possible. Grab-bing my bag, I gestured peace to the security guards, my two fingers awkwardly bending away from my phone. Nodding along with my peace gesture I speed walked across the pol-ished marble searching for the nearest exit.

"Brandon Miguel and Brian Rodrigo, you both are in so much trouble, you know—never mind. We can discuss the consequences of your actions once I am back. I'm gonna try to get back home. I can't believe you did this!"

"Oh no, Ma, you won't be able to get back. You know, the city is packed with carnival goers and everything."

"Oh, now you are worried? I'll find my way, and the two of you are going to help me. Find me a way to get back home ASAP. Put your tía on the line." I was about to give Miranda a big piece of my mind.

"Hi, girl," Miranda said as if this was a normal call. The nearest exit felt miles away as my stomach knotted at what was to come next.

"Hey, girl?! What is going on? Why am I here?" Maybe if I approached this with the same calm I used when emergencies went off at events at work, I would get quicker answers. If I screamed at Miranda like I wanted to do, she'd tell me to fix my attitude and hang up on me.

Damned the healed hussy.

"I tried to plant some seeds to see if you were paying any attention to what these two boys were doing. They dragged me along in the plan. I said to them, look, your mom is too smart for that. She's gonna catch on. And then, lo and behold, they're telling me that you let them use your laptop for your arrangements. They made fake reservations for you and everything. So I said you know what, girl, if you're *that* busy, you really truly need some time off. So… I kind of let it roll. You know that they're safe with me."

"Miranda, this is ridiculous." My breath quickened at my sprint avoiding the security officers. The doors slid open and the fresh air quieted my thoughts.

"I need to be real with you. We tell each other like it is, and we support each other. The Poconos on a work trip is not a romantic getaway; you deserve better, girl. Just…why don't you enjoy your time there? And why don't you let loose for a minute?" Miranda asked.

"Why is everyone thinking I'm not enjoying my time??" I groaned.

"Because you are always a busy, girl. You don't rest, so you don't even realize you're tired. You keep on going and going and going. How many hours of sleep have you been getting lately?"

"Oh, five, that's enough." I waved my hand away.

"That is not enough, girl. Look. Why don't you just stay there for the weekend?" A place to sit would be a lovely reprieve from the drama I'd walked into without paying any attention. The boardwalk brimmed with excited revelers but a few steps ahead an empty wooden bench awaited me.

"I cannot stay this weekend. I need to be at the Poconos." My exasperation made way to despair. If my own friend helped my twins set me up, what did that say of my control of my own life? And what did that say about my loved ones' feelings for the man I wanted to get serious with?

"I tried to plant my seeds, but you let yourself be trapped, so deal with it now," Miranda said, and we ended the call before I cussed her out.

Before I could walk far, a discrete cough stopped me in my tracks.

"Hey, you need a ride?" Luckily, John was still sitting idly outside with a friendly smile.

"I had a feeling something like this was gonna happen." John grinned and opened the car door.

The cobblestone road merged into the smooth pavement as the mellow tunes in John's car helped me reset my thoughts. For a few minutes, I took in the stunning views outside the car. The palm trees waiving in the bright blue sky, the shimmering sea moistening the boardwalk's rocky and rugged edges. The flashing-by resorts and restaurants filled with smiling faces all different beautiful shades of Black.

Ofele might be gorgeous, but I had no intention of staying on this island.

"Okay, I don't even know where I'm going. I actually need to go back to the airport to see if I can get a flight back. Would you be able to help me to do that?"

"I doubt there will be any flights, darlin'. Everything is booked from here until the end of carnival coming and going. A lot of the locals end up leaving because they want to be able to have, you know, peace and quiet. Some people come for different amounts of days. We don't usually have a lot of flights to service this area. It's a very small town." John shrugged, extending his hand toward the window as we transitioned from the touristy area to the quieter outskirts of Ofele.

"So we usually only have a flight every three days." John kept going. Clearly, he didn't need much help from me to. "They've added a couple more today so that they could bring more people in and a couple more out, but the ones out are honestly very scarce until Monday when the carnival ends."

"No, no, no, no, no. I need to be able to get out of here. There must be an airport other than the Ofele?"

"I mean, there's the Jacksonville airport. It's about three hours." John chuckled and stayed on a local road. "If you are okay I won't get on the highway till you make a final decision. This here road is the older local road and will take us to the airport but the scenic route."

The search for a flight from Jacksonville to New York didn't provide a thing but more of a headache. I scrolled through all the booking engines I could think of, while John whistled and drove along the Florida coast, not a worry in the world. Well, good for John. I was about to start evacuating bricks as every possible way to get out of here quickly kept shutting down.

"Again, how are you going to get there? The buses are also all full. And there are no rentals," John asked, too relaxed for my liking.

"I cannot be stranded in this town. For four days. This cannot be, today was Thursday. I needed to be back. If I made it tomorrow, I could go to the Poconos, with Milton."

I should have listened to my brain instead of my instinct regarding this weekend, especially about Milton. A quiet dread pointed at the last possible worst scenario: staying in Ofele for the weekend. I texted the twins to see if they had any luck.

Brian: Hey, Mom, no, we're looking at Jacksonville. It's not looking good. We don't see anything. I mean, a lot of the flights just leave on either Sunday or Monday.

Brandon: Mom? Why don't you enjoy yourself?

Me: Where am I supposed to stay? How can I enjoy myself without a room?

Brandon: Well, there's somebody there that you know, maybe you can stay with them.

Me: Honey, I don't know a soul in this town.

Brian: Yes, you do. Orlando is there... Orlando.

Nine

Orlando

A functional but stylish place that matched my vibe. This two-story townhome did the trick. I arrived this morning and settled in nicely. The owner allowed me to check in early and now I sat in the living room wondering what came next.

I wasn't certain if I should attack and go on the search for my baby mother right away. I did not have a lot of information. Miss B had explained to me the little that she understood of Ofele Town and the location where her daughter could be.

Ofele Town was one of those burgeoning cities with that small-town feel. But really, the small-town portion was now on the outskirts of what people understood to be Ofele. The center of town had large resorts, hotels, and a big tourist attraction area combined with beautiful wineries on horse farms. All of them were owned by wealthy Black families. I knew that my baby mother couldn't afford to live in this area of the town, where it was clear that the high middle lived.

I needed to go to the outskirts where most of the people who worked in the service industry called home. I had a couple of spots that I could visit, but being a Black man asking around for a Black woman could cause suspicion. I knew enough to be cautious about how to go about the search. Mrs. Barranco had warned me that when my baby's mother had moved, she had been very careful not to share a lot of information with her family because she was hurt by the treatment that they had put her through. Maria did not feel like being found right now.

Thinking of Maria brought to mind yesterday's conversation with Trinidad. A strong woman who had also had to figure out how to parent on her own. I didn't want that for my baby's mother, and I certainly didn't want that for my child.

Even with all that awaited me, Trinidad invaded my brain the whole damn flight.

You would think that I would be anxious about meeting my baby girl, but instead, I kept on imagining all the ways that I could have helped *her* in her kitchen. How I could have given her kisses and reassured her that she was doing a great job. Shit, if anyone knew that she was doing a great job, it was me. I knew what bad parenting looked like, even if it wasn't my mom's intention. Reassuring her felt like such a priority to me.

And I'm not going to lie to myself, the clothes that she wore last night…she had me bricked up. By the time I got home, I pulled out the coconut, and my hand made quick work of the rod that rested between my legs most of the night.

At this point, it felt like a compulsion—just being around her, how my body reacted, how my mind reacted. This wasn't normal. That woman wanted nothing to do with me. It was clear as day, but, man, she had me thinking of her instead of focusing on what I needed to do.

Not wanting to waste more time, I picked up my backpack with my iPad sketches and decided to go out to one of the coffee shops that Mrs. B had mentioned that Maria referenced during their calls.

Before I could even find my backpack, a knock on the door startled the fuck out of me. No one had the address of the rental. Well, no one but the twins. It was probably the owner coming in to check on me.

I swung the door open with a friendly smile on my face. The smile dropped, my mouth gaping. No other muscle could move. A shiver went through it, and all my veins caught on fire. My heart leaped to my throat.

And there went my dick, back on brick, as hard as it was last night.

Just the thought of that woman conjured her on my doorstep. Whatever magic I worked, I needed to quit because I was not prepared to deal with her presence on top of searching for my child.

"What are you doing here?" Shit, that came out wrong. I could see it all over her face. She looked tired. She looked pissed—which didn't change her gorgeous face. God helped me; that shit was sexy to me.

"Well, what better way to explain than putting my children on the phone?" Trinidad said.

Her children. The twins. They had hit me up a little bit earlier, poking me about the digs where I was staying. They asked for a few pictures, and I dutifully sent them. I didn't understand what was happening.

"Brian. Brandon, you want to explain?" Trinidad insisted.

"Mom?" Brandon's voice came clear through the speakerphone.

"Man, no, no, no, no. Go ahead and explain what's going on. Because I'm certainly not going to do it."

"Yes, ma'am. What's up, Orlando? Listen, we messed up. We were trying to hook up my mom with a vacation. But we messed up. We didn't make a reservation at the hotel where she was supposed to stay. We thought that she would be able to get another spot that was closer to the beach, but the town is sold out," Brian explained.

Of course, the town was sold out. It was Ofele Carnival weekend. It was one of the most upcoming carnivals in the country. What were these kids thinking?

"Yeah, you're right. There's no room left to stay," I parroted back, a thousand thoughts racing through my head. My brain had already caught up to what was happening, but my mouth and body lagged a few seconds behind. They were still reacting to the close presence of an agitated Trinidad. I could see her chest falling and rising, the anger of the deception of her children making her beautiful in her wrath. The top of her cleavage had trickles of sweat, clearly from her exertion with her luggage and probably her ordeal getting from the airport to my doorstep.

"So, what you're saying is that you need to stay here?" At last, my mouth worked enough to form a sentence.

"What I actually need is a plane to New York right now, but apparently, that is not going to happen anytime soon. So, yes, I need a place to at least figure out how to get out of here. Even if I have to drive or get a rental to get out to another town. I'm going to figure it out." Trinidad's anger was a sight to behold; her cheeks burned red, and her eyes slanted until they barely seemed open.

We both knew getting out today was a pipe dream at best. Ofele didn't have the kind of around-the-clock transportation that New York did. Their buses were scheduled based on the needs of the town. Probably didn't even fluctuate whenever they had bigger events.

Trinidad might be stuck here for days. She was also clearly in denial.

"I'm so sorry to put you in this situation, but I don't know anyone else in this town. And these children shared with me that you're here, as well. Are you okay with me hanging out here for a couple of hours until I can figure out how to get out of here?" Trinidad shifted on her feet awaiting my answer.

"Sure, sure. Come in. Come in. Let me help you with your luggage," I said as she switched off the speakerphone

"Brandon, Brian. I'm gonna call you later. No…save it for later. Bye, guys."

The way Trinidad pressed her phone screen, I was surprised it hadn't cracked. I helped her with her rollaway. Why did she have three pieces of luggage for a four-day trip? My sense was honed enough not to ask the question in her current state. Instead, I dragged her little rollaway and hoisted her backpack and her weekender bag.

Trinidad plopped herself in the living room. I'd expected for the space to just be for me. But now, it would be for us. My chest warmed as I pictured the two of us chatting and enjoying the day.

"I don't know what they were thinking, Orlando. I get it. I've been tired. I've been busy. These past two weeks have been a mess. But they knew this weekend was important to me. That I was going to the Poconos with Milton. They're saying that this was for me to relax and to have a little vacation, but that doesn't track. I mean, I've taken a solo vacation here and there."

"When was the last time you took a trip for yourself?" I asked.

"I mean, that's neither here nor there. I took them to Barbados last year!" She snapped her fingers capturing the memory with a proud smile.

"Yeah, but that's not what they think you need now, is it? They know that travel with them is not full relaxation for you." I shrugged. The twins managed to pull the maddest prank I'd ever seen fifteen-year-olds pull, but I still felt oddly defensive of their motives. Placing her luggage in the corner, I joined her in the living room, sitting opposite to her perch on the sofa.

"No, those are my children. It's not work. You know what I mean?" Trinidad said, getting animated again. Not that I was mad at any of her animations; she was gesticulating and waving her hands, and I tried my very best to focus only on her face. Her gorgeous, dynamic face.

"Not work, like you're not enjoying yourself, but they can see you're the planner, you're the one who's responsible. You're the one who has to think of where the hotel is and where to get the rental. The one figuring out what you guys are gonna eat and what's the budget and keeping track of all of that stuff. They could tell because you have raised very mature men, very responsible men. I know that this particular situation doesn't feel like they're mature. But hey, just a reminder that they are still kids. They're fifteen years old."

I don't know what I was doing. I don't know why I was defending Brandon and Brian, but I had a feeling for what they really were trying to accomplish. I couldn't be more perplexed but simultaneously honored. Honored that they thought that I could be a good choice for their mother.

They've known my plans for a couple of months. The fact that they chose this particular city for her to go on vacation was telling. They could have made up any other plan, but it was here. They brought her to my doorstep. This was their way of giving their blessing in the most fucking-convoluted way I would have ever imagined.

Still, that didn't mean that their mother agreed. That didn't mean that their mother wanted to be here. And that's the part that they were missing. This needed to be consensual. This needed to make sense. Not wanting to blow their spot, I would keep my peace for now. Besides, I could be making wild-ass assumptions, and their motives were not as clear as I felt. So, instead of making it worse for them, I sat beside her.

"So, what do you need from me?"

An intense search was deployed in my rental living room. I sat with my iPad on lookout for flights. Trinidad had her laptop, and she hadn't been successful with buses or rentals.

Trinidad started constructing a mask to keep things out and still be in denial about it all. Staying here wouldn't hurt her, but she wanted to be back with her man. I wasn't going to compare myself with other men. It was a waste of time. But from everything I'd heard from the twins, Milton didn't seem to be the right fit for Ms. V's joy of life. That joy she thought she kept hidden under respectability and age.

I couldn't believe this. In New York, you have millions of people. Ofele had probably five hundred thousand people if anything, and that's counting the outskirts of the town. I could never live in a place so small that getting around or out of town was a damn hassle. Nah, give me New York any day with its thousands of flights.

"Oh my God. I can't believe this. I need to take a break. I'm hungry, and I'm pissed at the two of you, and you're going to be so grounded," Trinidad said to her laptop screen. She'd deployed the twins to help with the search, as well.

"Yes, Mom." The two boys knew they were going to be in trouble. You could see that they had made all those calculations, their faces dropping as they hung up the video. But there was also a resolute quietness in them that I could only admire.

"You want me to step out and get some food while you still search?" I asked her, eager to help.

"Honestly, I think I need to physically go to the airport and try to figure something out. And well, I don't know. You came early, and I know there are not a lot of activities for carnival yet. Maybe…could you drive me?"

I knew this was coming…but I really needed the time before my friends arrived to search for my baby girl. I could, in theory, use my rental car to drive her to Orlando or Tampa, where there were flights that would get her out, or maybe even Jacksonville, so that she could get on standby for one of the later flights for tomorrow. Could get her somewhere, but I would have to jeopardize my plans. Of course. When was that not the case?

"Listen, any other day, at any other time, I would have taken you wherever you needed to go. But I came early to Ofele for a reason. There is something that I have to do, and even now, I've lost some time. I am sorry."

"I know…this is not on you. I just…" Trinidad deflated, and my chest caved at the sight. Feisty Trinidad was a sight to behold. A defeated Trinidad was a sight to correct immediately.

Suddenly, a solution materialized, and it became as clear as day. My head was probably glowing with my great idea.

"Actually, if you do something first for me, Ms. V, I can give you a solid."

Ten

Orlando

It was like watching a tornado come to life. As if she was a hurricane reincarnate. Storm from the *X-Men* had nothing on Ms. V. She puffed her chest, locs flying out of their ponytail, her eyes narrowing in suspicion. I sought shelter behind one of the sofas; I recognized danger when I saw it.

Then, just as lightning, thunder, and rain coalesced in the living room, the air cleared with a pop of pressure as Trinidad rolled her suitcase right out of the rental at record speed. Damn, the woman could command the weather…or maybe it was her effect on me. I'm ashamed to say it took me too damn long to understand what was happening, but when I did, my stomach dropped to the bottom of my Jordans.

Rushing out of the rental with my head and heart pounding, I was lucky to find Trinidad in the corner of the quiet, picturesque street. Each house on the block looked far from the other.

"Ms. V," I hollered at her, and her shoulders stiffened at the sound of my voice. Shit. I really had messed this one up.

"Go away," Trinidad said in that Latina mom voice that made you wonder if you had ever done anything right in your life.

"Nah, can we chat? Listen. I just played back what I said, and it came out all kinds of wrong. That wasn't my intent." At this point, my stomach had become a rung-out sponge with nothing left but courage and audacity.

"I don't care. I realized this was a mistake. I thought I could maybe stay, but…no. I need to get to the airport," Ms. V said, running a palm over her sweaty forehead.

Damn, but she was fine as hell. I could imagine that the same sweat was caused by better reasons running down her face, her smooth chestnut neck, and her cleavage, which varied in degrees of separation depending on the outfit. Right now, the girls were sitting nicely together. Did they have that intriguing heaviness I'd seen in older women while browsing my porn? I got lost imagining what it could be and must have stayed quiet for a long time. Ms. V's loud "ahem" snapped me out of my trance.

"Listen… I can take you to the Ofele airport as part of my rounds today. We can also go to the bus stop and the rental car place. But I need your assistance. I need… I need help making people comfortable while looking for my five-year-old daughter."

Eleven

Trinidad

"Excuse me, what?" I stared at Orlando, looking so fresh and clean in his outfit, his New York swag unmistakable. Anger should have been the primary emotion operating inside me, and it was initially. Still, within seconds, I started imagining what I *could* do for him to get me back to New York, and then I grew angry with myself.

Zero self-perseverance, just lust and a clitoris that hadn't been appropriately touched save for self-touch in more than a year. That is what fueled my addled brain, images of Orlando settling himself between my legs to feast right on that sofa in his living room. Or me standing by the beautiful big window that faced the crystalline pool and palm trees in the backyard, getting pounded by a fully naked, ebony smooth, glistening trunk of a man. Orlando to be exact, in case there were any doubts.

There was no pride residing in me after these filthy thoughts. So without a word, I turned around and left that Airbnb of sin and temptation, not wanting even to consider what I would have said if I had stayed for a few more seconds.

I could have never expected this to be what he actually meant. A daughter? A five-year-old daughter? Bitter disappointment took over the anger and lust, leaving me empty and depleted.

What a day. What a week. And now the one man I thought had the type of fortitude and integrity to do the right thing by my sons was a philanderer who had a daughter. He didn't even know the location of said child.

"Yeah, I… I need help." Orlando shifted his stance, his shoulders drooping, his gaze pleading. Damn him and those pretty dark brown eyes. Why would God give him such pretty eyes? What a waste. Deserters of children should not have such lovely eyes. Reminded me of my good-for-nothing ex-husband.

You sure know how to pick them, girl.

Oh callate, como jodes.

Wonderful. I was now talking to myself. This day had reduced me to talking to my damn self.

"I'm not sure I can help 'cause I don't condone child abandonment." My voice crackled with the remaining anger from earlier, underlined by the hurt of knowing this man wasn't what he presented.

"Abandon? Ms. V, with all due respect, I'm fucking offended. What about me makes you think I would abandon a child?"

Oh, now he was the one mad? Excuse me, I didn't realize the tables had turned so quickly. Two seconds ago, he was looking all pitiful and in need of help. Now he stood tall and rigid, and my brain, the treacherous organ, tried to conjure more images of sexy, naked, glistening Orlando.

"Ohhh, you don't get to be mad! I'm not the one with a five-year-old. God knows where." I gestured wildly, my voice increasing in volume.

Behind us was a pretty blue house with white trimmings. The front window curtain fluttered, and a set of eyes appeared. Damn. I was making a scene.

"You have me in the middle of this quaint little street acting a damn fool. Those days are long past me!" I screamed. Well, I guess I wasn't *that* concerned about making a scene.

"What, what do you mean those days? Never mind, listen. Why don't we go back to the rental?"

Oh, he was now using the "this broad is mental" tone. All men had it, they started talking slightly slower, their inflections precise and modulated. Some even whispered. That shit didn't work with me.

"No, say what you have to say right here. That will determine my next steps."

"Aren't you the one with no place to stay and stranded with no flights out?"

"This man-child didn't just…" I paced on the concrete, the rollaway wheels struggling with the uneven little gravel.

"I can hear you, Ms. V."

Now that was his "don't play with me" tone, and there

went my brain, ready to fantasize again. That little rumble when he said Ms. V…mmmmm.

"Then hear away!" I whirled around and threw my hands up. At this point, I felt out of options. My own flesh and blood had put me in this situation. Damn me for thinking gentle parenting was the way to go; those two needed less communication and more fear. Great, now I sounded like their father.

"Let's go to the Airbnb," Orlando said, his tone changing once more to conciliatory.

"No." I didn't know what was wrong with me, but at this moment, this man was paying for all that had gone wrong today. It wasn't fair to him; this wasn't like me. Well, the new me, but I had zero ability to regulate my thoughts and emotions right now. He was encountering a version of me I thought I'd left behind: passionate, impulsive, risky Trinidad. Hot Girl Trinidad. Sizzling Trinidad, like Miranda still called me. That Trinidad had a lot of fun, but she also got into a lot of trouble.

"I really don't want to do this, but more neighbors are peeking out the windows now, and soon they'll call the police on us." Back to the rumbly warning. And what didn't he want to—" Up you go."

My body flew. That is the only way I can describe it. This lean baby man-child picked me up like a sack of rice and placed me comfortably on his shoulders.

Air deserted me.

I was dangling, face near his scrumptious ass, while my legs swayed in front of him. I should kick him in his most vulnerable place. I should press a kiss on his back. I should lie still and let him have his way with me.

Just as the last traitorous thought invaded my brain, the owner of the blue house came out, a cute little old Black lady with a concerned look.

"Are you alright, miss?" the lady asked.

Finally, it all clicked, and I calmed down enough to think things rationally.

"Oh yes, yes, this is my friend Orlando. We always play roughhouse. I'm sorry, but we are both on vacation brains and should be more mindful," I explained, voice strained from the awkward position I was in.

Whoosh! Air sailed through my locs, and my eyes watered as Orlando swiveled to face the old lady.

"That's right, so sorry, ma'am, we promise to act with more decorum moving forward. Thanks for your understanding." Orlando was back to talking normally, but the heat of his lean body seared mine; I felt every syllable, every rumble. *Everywhere.* "We'll leave you to it."

Orlando ended his charming entreaty and finished it with a friendly swat on my ass. The feel of his palm against my sundress would be engraved in my memories forever. What was meant to be a quick swat became a full-blown exploration of my behind; he even massaged it a bit before letting it go.

First, I would teach this man-child about enthusiastic consent.

Second, no moan would escape my mouth.

The walk to the house was quick; after all, I had only passed three houses before stopping. Orlando refused to drop me off until we crossed his threshold. His eyes were leery on me as I fixed my hair and dress once I was back on firm ground.

"You should have—"

"That wasn't right; I shouldn't have swatted your…your posterior area. I meant to put the lady at ease and wasn't thinking straight, but that is no excuse. You've never consented to my touch like that."

Oh. No lesson needed, I guess.

"Yes, well…next time, just ask."

What the hell? Next time, just ask? What, who? I was broken. That's what was happening. I was broken. My twins, and Milton, and my ex and this man-child, they had all broken me.

"Oh…it's like that, Ms. V?"

Oh, see, I hadn't seen this Orlando, and I wasn't ready for him. Confident, flirty Orlando was dangerous to my senses.

"Let's stay on topic, please," I grumbled. Annoyed, my nether parts wanted me to flirt back.

"This is the topic, Ms. V. Enlighten me. What will next time look like? I want to be prepared." Orlando sat on one of the love seats. His toned thighs appeared slowly as he spread, finding a comfortable sitting position. The circumference of said thighs felt incongruent with the rest of his lean body, but somehow, it all worked. I was ashamed to admit I got a little giddy when he finally found his comfort. That leg spread looked promising. "Ms. V?" A thread of surprised amusement and simmering heat accompanied his words. De-escalation was required. STAT. I was not about to convert into Hot Girl Sizzling Trinidad with this man. Oh no.

"You need me to find your daughter whom you lost." I plopped myself on the opposite couch, wanting to dissuade him from any other thoughts. His eyes seared me from top to bottom, then settled contently on my face. A girlish sigh escaped me, and we both froze.

"Are you…" Orlando leaned over, pressing his elbows on his legs. The predatory air surrounding me reminded me for a second that, no matter how much I wanted to think of Orlando as young, he was still a man. And I was reacting too much to this man while trying to get back to who I hoped to be MY man.

"I am fine. I am so sorry. This has been a very chaotic day. I just… I just want to go home. And I am the person who usually has the answers, and right now, I am running out of them."

"I get that…truly, I do—it's hard when you try to do everything right, and it still doesn't work out your way, isn't it?" He stayed in the same position, but now his gaze assessed me. Not sure what he saw, because I was a hot ass mess right now, but in his voice… I heard kinship. I recognized that long-ago pain of doing everything to be seen and loved and not getting what I needed in return.

"Yeah, it sucks. But you wake up the next day and you do it again. And as long as you are at peace and harmony with what you need for yourself, then the rest will fall in place." I nodded to him, hoping to alleviate some of his concerns. Even now, knowing he wasn't the man I thought, I still felt connected to him.

"I guess…listen. I did not abandon my kid. I…met this girl

a few summers ago. She was the daughter of my old neighbor. And we chilled for the whole summer, every summer. We got to know each other, mostly as friends, but you know…"

"Well, yeah, there is a five-year-old out there, so I do know."

"Yeah, well, we never had plans for long distance or anything like that; we were both clear with our expectations. We…probably did it a couple of times, and we used a condom all of them, so imagine my surprise…"

"Did the condom break?"

"Well, yeah, that one time, but I hadn't finished yet! I changed it, and we were good money," Orlando explained, looking scared and worried but oddly excited. That…that right there was the man I had seen with my boys.

"So, you really are out here just trying to reconnect with your girl and your kid?"

Orlando shook his head, stopping my train of thought.

"Nah, not reconnect with her. We were cool and all, but she kept me out in the dark. I have no beef with her, but I'm not looking to establish anything but a connection with my daughter. I cannot wait to be a father to her. That's it. I had to find out from her grandmother."

I nodded along, finally understanding the whole thing. He'd come early to search in private. His friends would probably not understand. He had a plan, and I was trying to derail it, and still, he was looking for ways to accommodate me.

"Listen, this what you are telling me is way more important than me getting back to New York to get to Milton."

"Oh…your man is waiting for you?" Orlando's disappointment could not be louder in this room full of sunshine and unspoken thoughts. And the reality was Milton didn't even know what had happened. He hadn't checked on me once; I didn't feel like disclosing the boys did this. It would sour him even more to them. My boys were my boys. They did wrong, but damn if I let anybody speak on them who barely knew them.

"I...let's say there are many reasons why I am looking to return early, but none of them are as important as you finding your child. Your deal is more than fair. I'll help you out today. And hopefully I'll find my solution along the way. Who knows, we might meet some people with more resources!" Somehow, the anger that had taken over earlier had dissipated in the salty sea air and the company of Orlando. Somehow, hearing his story, even though abbreviated, made me feel like we were partners in crime. Even if just for today, both searching for something/someone.

Both searching.

Twelve

Trinidad

The scenery around us took my breath away as Orlando navigated what they now called Little Ofele. A sense of otherworldliness infused every plant, every building, every rock in the town.

Usually, Florida during the summer is all blue skies and bright sunshine. Here in Ofele, the blue skies were present, same as the sunshine. Still, there was another color that beautifully blended it all. Some type of muted beige, that I would have difficulty describing to anyone. It was as if here, the sun shined but still protected our melanated skin. As if the air knew to take care of us, as if the water was extra clear and blue and shallow for us to feel comfortable in it. I might be desperate to leave for New York, but for this moment, I allowed myself to observe and enjoy Ofele and all it had to give.

"It's gorgeous, isn't it? I'm usually a go-go type of guy,

but the place got me. I drove around earlier, trying to get acquainted with the town, and got sprung."

"Young people still say sprung?" I stared at him in the driver's seat. He'd changed to slightly longer pants, not quite hooch shorts but almost, and a T-shirt, baseball cap, and shades. It suited him.

"We don't, but I gotta ensure you can follow." He kept his eyes on the road, but his lush lips were losing the battle, wanting to burst out in a smirk.

"Listen, if it weren't for my generation, y'all wouldn't have any swag."

"So old people still say swag, then?"

"I'm not that old," I grumbled.

"I know you're not. We are ten years apart, right? So, I'm not sure why you keep trying to put more age between us. I mean, I respect it…but still, I don't think you're old at all, just old*er*, and there ain't nothing wrong with more experience, maturity, and…knowledge."

Oh, why did those three things sound so…*so* when he said them? Like they had way more weight than I gave them credit for.

"Well, yes, I am more experienced than you, but you're right. The boys are not here this weekend, so maybe I can relax the Sra. Velasquez intensity a bit."

"You'd do that? For me? Wow, I'm honored." Orlando clasped his free hand to his chest.

"You're so full of shit."

"Nah, but I like this slightly more relaxed version of you, for real. Thanks for that." Orlando pulled up to a little variety shop on a road with several small-town businesses. We both descended the car and continued to trade jokes, the vibe between us relaxed.

"So, you think we can find your girl here?"

"She is not my girl, and her name is Maria. But no, I don't think we will find her here exactly. Her grandmother said she's been doing different work here and there, but she did not mention a retail shop."

"So why are we here?" I removed my sunglasses at the same time he removed his.

"Because this is where they sell bus tickets, the owner is also a travel agent on the side. If anyone can help, it would be her."

"Smart... I wouldn't have thought of a travel agent, even with what I do; I guess it's such a dying art. How did you know about them?" I stared.

"You know this device they call *smart phone*? And in there, it has a website called Goo—"

"Don't you even think of finishing that sentence." I shook my head, holding back laughter. Who knew? High school banter still did it for me. Maybe it was because we both knew that age was but a number between us, and maybe I needed to stop thinking in clichés before I got myself in trouble with this man.

A tinkling bell went off the moment Orlando pushed the door open, giving me the honor of walking in first. He was a gentleman, true and true. His momma had done right by him. I said so, and his face twisted but then cleared up with a big smile.

"It's all I know to be." He kept cheesing. We kept cheesing

at each other. Even as my cheeks started shaking, I held the grin. It felt so natural, so right to hang out with him. Without the boys around, it allowed me to see Orlando the man, not the mentor, not the twenty-five-year-old man—just Orlando.

"Good afternoon, how are you? I'm Delilah," a Black woman who appeared to be in her fifties greeted us. She broke the spell and we both acted like the teenagers currently in danger of being grounded for the whole summer.

"We're good thanks, Delilah! Appreciate you asking. I am Orlando, and this here is Trinidad; she is trying to get back to New York today or tomorrow, and we were hoping you could assist her?"

The woman's smooth features went from serene to "yikes" in less than five seconds.

Damn.

"That is going to be a hard one, ya' hear? This busy, busy season right now. I know the flights are all booked up from Ofele airport. And the bus rides to the closer towns are all booked up too. But I can search for you. It is going to take me a while, though. Do you want to wait? We have a little cafe next door; it's owned by my man."

Just as Delilah finished her sentence, a man walked into the shop. He was probably younger than me, tall and husky. He grumbled, "Good morning," made a straight line behind the desk, and hugged Delilah. I didn't see the resemblance, but based on the age difference, he must be her son or something.

"This Mikey, my man. He owns the shop next door. Why don't y'all sit over there and give me a half hour or so to make some calls?"

Oh, this was her man—her man. This lady could probably be in her fifties. Orlando bumped into me, and I was startled out of my reverie. I looked up at him to find him frowning at me.

"Oh, we get that reaction all the time. Don't worry, Orlando. The folks in the town are all used to us, but new folks take time to adjust. Usually, people assume Mikey is my son. Can you believe that? Well, technically, he could be with our twenty-year difference, but who cares? I never had children, so no one can tell me, 'He's as old as…,' and Mikey doesn't want any kids, so he doesn't mind being with a mature woman. I would think you two would understand."

Delilah smiled serenely and accepted a kiss on her cheek from Mikey. Then she proceeded to giggle. The woman was *giggling* in the middle of her business. At first I didn't understand why until I realized we couldn't see Mikey's hand, the one closest to Delilah, hidden by the desk.

Oh…well, good for Delilah. They exchanged a few hush words, and finally, the invisible privacy wall they created by being next to each other was lowered to include us again.

"So, the boss says y'all need a cup of coffee?"

"Oh, we need more than that? I'm searching for a family member, too, and I was hoping y'all could help?" I stared at both of them, and their faces grew pensive.

"Yeah, for sure. I mean, I was born and raised here, so if there is anything I can do, I will be glad to do so," Mikey said with his deep, husky voice and such a kind smile I could understand everything Delilah saw in him.

As if pulled by magic, my gaze switched to Orlando's, and

momentarily, the air grew still around us. His intense regard mesmerized me. Those damn pretty brown eyes seared me, and a myriad of emotions flickered through them as he studied me. I tried to understand what he tried to say with his looks, but my body responded quicker than my brain. A rush of heat traveled from the top of my head down to my feet and back again to settle in my core. It had been years since I felt flutters in my stomach, and pressing against my belly didn't stop the giddy feeling one bit.

"Oh, look, love, they got it too!" Delilah said to Mikey, effectively busting my bubble.

"Ah, got what?" I hated that my voice shook.

"That magic between you," Mikey explained in a bored tone, as if I should already know it.

"It's Ofele, you know, and with carnival almost starting… this is how the two of us got together; when Ofele Carnival was only locals and a few out-of-towners, he invited me to a fete."

"Whined her and juked her up the whole night. She went home with me that night." Mikey winked. Delilah tittered and hit his bicep.

"Nah, no no no. You're getting the wrong vibe here. I… this is my son's mentor and he so happened to be in town and is helping me, but no. No. No. I mean, no. LOL." The butterflies went berserk in my belly at the mere suggestion of Orlando becoming more than a harmless crush.

"Damn, Ms. V, you didn't need to say all those nos. I think the first nah was sufficient." Orlando rubbed the back of his neck, hiding his gaze with his fitted.

"Oh, it's okay, Orlando. If it's not her, it will be someone soon. I can feel it," Delilah said, and I started liking Delilah less and less. With all her commentary, it was making things awkward.

"Why don't we go to have that coffee and chat it up with Mikey while you search? Thank you so much for your help."

"Oh, yes, yes, let me get on that!" Delilah agreed, and we followed Mikey out of the shop and into the next-door establishment.

Just a few seconds outside in the heat and humidity and my back started perspiring. Thankfully the cool air in the coffee shop mixed with the delicious aroma helped calm my overactive nerves. The shop had murals of Ofele on each of its walls, with wooden lacquered tables and a counter that looked like it belonged in a Jamaican take-out restaurant but instead of curry goat, or oxtail, it boasted several savory and sweet pastries. I felt right at home.

"Are we good?" I asked Orlando, who'd gone stiff and quiet after that last exchange.

"Yeah, I'm straight. Listen, thanks for asking about Maria, it means a lot that you remembered." He guided me through the busy coffee shop until we found a small table with some privacy.

"How could I forget? Besides, we had a deal, right?" I tried to decipher why he looked so hopeful and guarded simultaneously, but then a swift flash of disappointment popped up, and I was even more confused. Orlando pulled a chair for me and waited for me to sit down. He didn't join until he made sure I was comfortable. The butterflies fluttered again, the damn pests.

"Yeah, we had a deal. It's just…fuck it, it's just people seldom remember things that are important to me. So that back there? It meant a lot," he said.

"Oh… I…well, that's not right. Not even your family?" I asked curiously.

"Nah, especially not them." He shook his head taking off his fitted and gently putting it on the table. "It was my dad's. Big Yankees fan." He nodded at the fitted, noticing my interest.

"I'm a Yankees fan, true and true, so I know your dad was good people. I…the twins have shared that he died when you were much younger. I'm so sorry for your loss. Damn, I hate when people say that because it sounds so empty, doesn't it?"

My stomach twisted in commiseration with Orlando as he struggled to say something I knew was meant to set me at ease. Without thinking, I pressed my hand on his, halting his words. "There is zero need to make me feel good; I was the one trying to give my condolences to you…okay? Just take it. You deserve for your father to be alive, and it's unfair that that is not the case. And I know we can't do anything about unfair shit, but, damn, it's okay sometimes to at least acknowledge that some things we go through are not okay. And that trying to be strong through it doesn't mean it does not hurt. It does not mean the pain and the sadness are less valid."

Orlando's eyes widened as he listened to me. They soon softened, and that hopeful stare returned.

I was scared of that hopeful stare.

"Thanks… I… I didn't realize I usually do that. Rush to make people feel okay that my dad died. I appreciate you calling it out." That smile of his. Mm-hmm. Eyes and smiles were my thing and this man delivered in both areas and then some.

This day of adventure, before I returned to reality, felt prescribed, but I didn't want to investigate why. For now, I wanted to be present. I'd have plenty of time on the flight back, analyzing each second and each word, and the feelings. Unless I conked out again, which was the most likely scenario because I was no spring chicken.

"Hey, it's okay to recognize people-pleasing tendencies." I shrugged, trying to dissipate the air of intimacy that continued to coalesce around us. Mikey approached our table just in time, my savior in flannel and jeans.

"I have Jackie, our barista, preparing your drinks. So, who are you looking for?" Mikey took the third seat and sat down, a weary sigh speaking of early mornings and hard work.

"Her name is Maria…" I paused, realizing I went into this with a lot of enthusiasm but zero planning. Very unlike me. I stared at Orlando, and he took over.

"Maria Roberts," Orlando said. "She came to Ofele about five years ago. Here's a picture of her; not sure if she looks familiar to you?" Orlando's tone couldn't hide the hope he felt. Mikey studied the photo for a long while.

"I thought she was your family member?" Mikey asked me, his gentle, giant demeanor slowly shifting.

"Oh well, yes, but…"

"It's okay, Trinidad. I appreciate it, but we can be transparent with Mikey. Listen, man…"

Orlando bared his entire story to Mikey. How Maria and he had been summer friends for several years. She'd been his solace and the only person with whom he shared how hard it was for him to be brother, father, and caretaker. Then, the last year she visited her grandma, they had a hot and heavy night. They had agreed to remain only friends after having sex, not finding any romantic chemistry between each other.

Maria ghosted Orlando after a while and didn't tell him anything about her pregnancy. He shared old messages from social media that showed they had a good relationship, then the many times he tried to reach her to no response from her. Orlando continued to explain how Maria's grandmother finally told him about his daughter, realizing it was unfair for him to be left in the dark. "...so when I found out... I just want to meet my daughter, man. I have two brothers and an ill mother back in NY, so... I'm not trying to make Maria's life difficult by any means."

Mikey absorbed all the information while I gaped at Orlando. I didn't know about most of this. The way the twins spoke about Orlando; it was this happy-go-lucky man who, yes, lived with his brothers and mother, but never in a way that truly explained the responsibilities he had. He didn't go into much detail, but it was all there in the pauses, in the way he maneuvered the conversation away from what clearly was a sore subject to him.

"Listen... I hear you, and as a man, I commiserate. But I gotta make sure I do right by Maria."

"So you do know her?" I perked up.

"I didn't say that, but I'm going to put some feelers out

there. If you give me your phone number, I'll hit you up with any info I have permission to share."

Smart man, I didn't blame Mikey for his caution, but selfishly, finding Maria quickly would have alleviated the guilt I felt from taking Orlando away from his task. We finished our coffees, and soon—after farewells to Mikey and his staff—we made our back to Delilah's.

"So, you found your family member?" Delilah asked the second we walked into the shop.

"No, but Mikey promised to help, which is all we can ask. Any luck?" Orlando asked.

In twenty minutes, he'd managed to change my perception of him again. I had no idea how he did it. A day with Orlando felt revelatory in ways I wasn't ready for. I wanted him to remain static in my mind, a fun, harmless crush. Someone to flirt with but always keep at bay.

Our lives were weirdly entangled for the day, and I couldn't remember the last time I felt carefree. But with him, somehow, I wasn't overthinking; I was not wondering about the next steps and what our picture-perfect family portraits would look like after our wedding.

No, I was getting to know Orlando and liking the things I found out because it was him. A warm shiver took over me as Orlando turned around, activating the air of intimacy that didn't ever fully dissipate.

"So what do you want to do?" His deep voice penetrated my idle thoughts.

Dios mío.

"So, so sorry, I completely blanked out; what did I miss?"

"No direct flights that get you home by tomorrow; all are Sunday onward. I looked at some connecting flights from the airports in the fifty-mile radius, but I am not done yet. I can call you tomorrow morning with any news?"

"Delilah, I appreciate that. Really, that would be...fantastic." This woman didn't need to do all this legwork for me, but here she was, trying to help out.

"No worries, hun, it's my pleasure! Besides, we felines need to stick together." Delilah winked, and a choked-back laugh escaped Orlando. I pretended the last words were never said, but my face? It was heated.

"Okay, here is my phone number; Mikey has it too. And here is Trinidad's. Thanks, Ms. D. You've been clutch today," Orlando said, deftly maneuvering the situation and giving me time to chill.

We walked out of the shop under the tinkling bell, side by side, with a sense of purpose. Orlando opened the door for me, his self-assuredness back in play. With his fitted, lean frame and those pretty eyes hidden behind his sunglasses, he felt present in a way I could not describe, and another shiver traveled all over my body.

Ay Dios mío, what was this?

"So, people still say *clutch*?"

"Certain felines do..." He flashed me a big smile.

"Boy, if you don't stop!"

"How could I when you get so pretty while flustered?"

My chest expanded, and my heart imitated the rhythm of the wings of the earlier butterflies.

My God! Qué es esto? Why are you not answering?

"Oh, here you go; I'm certain you say that to all the young ladies." I got into the car, pretending my face didn't feel ten degrees warmer than the rest of my body. I needed him to turn the car on ASAP before I melted on these leather seats. Who rented leather seats in the summer? Ugh.

"Now, I thought we agreed you wouldn't do the Ms. Velasquez thing while the kids are not around?"

"But you *are* a kid," I nagged back.

"No, I'm not. You heard what I said to Mikey. I stopped being a kid a while ago," Orlando said, a peace offering—an open door. I could take the offer and get caught up in this weird cocoon we were building together, but then what? My plans had not changed. I would find a way to leave.

"Do you mind me asking some of your story?" *Trinidad Caridad Velasquez Rodriguez, this is not minding your business…*

"I don't mind you asking me anything, Trinidad," Orlando said.

Dios mío.

I was in trouble.

Thirteen

Orlando

"You shouldn't say things like that to me," Trinidad said after a long stretch. We made our way into Little Ofele, and I drove slowly, enjoying the views.

The quiet beauty of the town impressed me once more. The pristine cobblestoned streets, lush greenery, and bright, colorful flowers. The small shops, houses, and buildings, all in the French Colonial style, reminded me a little of my one Mardi Gras in New Orleans. The bright colors of the infrastructure transported me to St. Mary and my few visits with my grandparents in Jamaica.

Time had stopped here in this place, protecting its townspeople and keeping the community tight and friendly. Here every face looked like mine and Trinidad's. Shit was real. Not even Flatbush could re-create this feeling of belonging, and that felt like some damn traitor's thoughts.

"If I made you uncomfortable, I'm sorry...my feelings are bubbling out with you for some reason."

"Oh?"

"I don't like sharing a lot about my family...it's...it's been hard, and at the same time, life is hard. I don't like complaining." I shrugged, turning into a strip mall where we could ask around for Maria. My excitement to find her in a day was slowly morphing into the realization that this would be harder than I thought. My pride didn't allow me to ask for help from Mrs. B, clearly a tactical error.

"I get it, I...sometimes I feel like that about my divorce. But then I have Miranda and my parents. Who do you talk to?"

"Psh. Nobody. Maria back in the day, but then she started feeling a way about my ma, and I didn't like that."

"What...what's your mom's illness?" Trinidad brushed her locs, away from her face, her expression so attentive the words starting coming out.

"Honestly...the diagnosis is bipolar disorder. But Ma...she has all the help she needs medically, and still, it's like...stabilization can be lengthy, especially if the person does not believe they're ill. Ma don't believe she's ill; she thinks she's depressed because my dad passed away. Her depressive episodes are long, her manic ones are short and chaotic, and in between when she is somewhat regulated, she stops taking her medications, so it's like starting all over again. I finally persuaded her to stick to her psychotherapy consistently a year and a half ago." I gripped the steering wheel, remembering the hard conversations before convincing Ma. A quick glance to Trinidad was all I could manage to keep my emotions in check.

"Besides my brothers and my grandparents in Jamaica, no one knew this. Ma's parents had passed away before my father, so we had no help from that side, and she was an only child. My grandparents in Jamaica felt Ma needed to 'tek spoil 'n' make style'—get out of bed and keep going when she had that first depressive episode after my dad died in a truck accident while at work. It took until I was in my teenage years to realize something else was happening with my mom." Deep breaths and a brief pause to keep my shit together. Trinidad hums of understanding were hitting under my armor. It was so easy opening up to her, and at the same time, hard as fuck.

"I had to beg her when I was sixteen. By that point, I had understood that the mood swings were not just Ma being a Caribbean mom, ya' know? I made sure to shield my brothers as much as I could…"

We found a parking spot that provided top-tier people-watching. Opening old wounds never served me well. Keeping positive was my brand of therapy. A warmth settled on top of my hand as Trinidad's smaller hand cradled mine.

Comfort. A welcome but unknown companion.

"So…let me get this straight…you were how old when your pops passed?" Trinidad's soft voice whispered in opposition to the blowing air-conditioning keeping us cool.

"I was nine; my brothers were three and five," I said, staring out the windshield, unable to make eye contact with her.

"So, a child raising children, from what it sounds like? I'm sure your mom did what she could, but…wow. You're a brave man, and you were also a brave child."

I thought she was going to say, "I'm sorry." That is what

people around me usually said, even not knowing all the gritty details. But she instead focused on the positive... Fuck! This woman kept making me fall into...hope.

"Yeah, well, I didn't have much of a choice, and now, as a man, I understand my mother is ill, and a lot of the behaviors are not intentional, which is why it's pointless to dwell on the negative."

"I see...well, do you get some family therapy, you and your brothers?"

"Nah, before me getting my job, medicaid barely to cover Ma's medications and her choices of meds sucked under her plan, she responded better to brand names instead of generics. I love my job, and they have okay health insurance, but to afford the out-of-pocket costs I need a better-paying job. So, law school."

Shit, I didn't mean to sound like a fucking victim. This conversation was becoming too much. Now it was my turn to grow quiet. A group of Black girls around my age, clearly tourists, walked by the car with their costumes. One of the carnival bands had their costume pickup in one of the shops.

Purple, gold, and green feathers and crystals shined as they ambled down the sidewalk, excitement so palpable that I focused on them instead of the conversation inside of my rental. Trinidad's hand stayed on mine, and she held it tighter.

Recognition. Another welcomed but unusual feeling.

"The twins say you're really good at what you do, and your animations are, and I quote, sick."

"I doubt they said exactly that word."

"Listen, young man, enough of this bullying. I'm thirty-five, not fifty."

"You sure, old hot stuff?" I flipped my hand and captured hers in mine. We stared at each other, the air-conditioning suddenly not doing enough to keep the wet heat out of the car, or maybe it was the two of us.

"Yes, I'm young, okay!" Trinidad objectively was a beautiful woman. Her lustrous ochre skin glowed even with the little sun streaming through the windows. Her smile, damn her smile, it wasn't perfect, but it was perfectly hers with her cute big canines fighting for space. Those eyes of hers that had their own language framed by long lashes that made my knees weak whenever they fluttered...and her body... Her dress draped her so beautifully, showcasing her strength, leanness, and flexibility.

It all told her life story. Fuck, I was sprung.

"Good, finally, we agree on that subject; glad we got to a good resolution." I interlaced my fingers with hers, turning around to give my whole attention to her. Not that she didn't have it before. But now I held her gaze.

"Boy, if you don't stop," she whispered. This time, it sounded like a promise, a caress. What would happen if I didn't stop?

"If you were to stay behind, I would ask you, what if I couldn't help myself, what would you be comfortable with..." I couldn't finish the sentence. I wanted to be direct with her, but at the same time, my nerves were getting the best of me. My throat closed up as I waited for her answer.

"I have to go back... I'm, this trip with Milton, it might

mean a stable future…for my family," Trinidad said as if the words tasted sour in her mouth, but she still needed to say them. The cold of the air conditioner made me shake, and when her hand left mine, I held back the ball of frustration sitting at the base of my throat.

"I hear you. Maybe we should call it a day. I think we should head out early tomorrow; it will give us time to get to Jacksonville."

"What's in Jacksonville?"

"An airport, you will have better chances to get out and go to Milton," I explained. The air was extra loud now; another group of people exited a shop with white costumes shining bright in the darkening evening.

"Are you sure? You have a lot going on tomorrow and only the morning and afternoon until your friends arrive. Are you going to share things with them?"

"No, I can do this on my own; no worries, Trinidad."

And I meant it. I always did things on my own. Today's camaraderie with Trinidad was a mirage, and I fell for it.

Not her fault that I fell for it; it was all mine.

Fourteen

Trinidad

Living in denial was not my style, but these past hours with Orlando had made me forget the realities of my life. Now back in his rental, in the room he graciously offered for me to sleep in, I sat on the four-post bed, staring at my luggage, wondering how my day had gone so wrong and so right at the same time.

My two sons had lost their damn minds setting me up like this. It was wrong, plain and simple. How had I missed the signs, though? What was I thinking by letting them use my laptop for all the transactions? The lure of them maturing before my eyes had dulled my instincts. How could I forget how it felt to be fifteen, thinking you knew it all when in fact, you had no fucking clue?

Therapy had helped me mold my parenting into a way that I felt comfortable with; I called it gentle/strict parenting,

Dominican style. But lately, as they grew into the men they would be, I couldn't figure out quite how to meet their needs for fulfillment, for confidence, for self-assuredness. My relationship with Milton was the answer to my prayers, someone who could help me raise my teenagers and give them those examples their father was not fit to provide.

My first thought was to ground them for the entire summer besides physical activity and mentoring. Nothing else would be allowed: no cheerleading trips, no hanging out with their friends. Nothing. It would be a memorable summer for sure, but would it do the trick? I wanted them to understand the ramifications of their actions, of making decisions for me without my say when they were categorically not the head of the household. They needed to calm their young behinds and stay in their lanes. Because of them, I was stuck in this very beautiful room, right next to temptation, and I wasn't planning to succumb.

The room decor was more of the easy-breezy Ofele vibes with creamy walls and a white and yellow bed set. A little whitewashed wood desk and chair sat in a corner. No TV, because who in their right mind came to Ofele to watch shows? My toes reveled in the softness of the plush carpet covering the entire bedroom, the movements enough to calm me to have a civil conversation with my offspring.

Me: I need you all to find any connecting flight that gets me out of Jacksonville and back to New York tomorrow.

Brandon: Ma, we are trying.

Me: Con respeto, Brandon.

Brandon: Sorry Ma. I know we messed up. We trying to fix it. We know we messed up and let you down. We just wanted you to rest, you know? You always doing so much for us. I'm sorry, Ma.

Me: Good, but this is not the end of this. When I'm back home from the Poconos, the three of us are going to sit down and have an in-depth discussion about boundaries and each of our roles. You're teenagers and my sons, and even though I make sure to honor your decision-making processes, this one was very wrong and did not take into account any of my boundaries.

Brian: You still going to Poconos?

Me: Yes. My relationship with Milton is my decision, and we will chat about it too.

Brian: Oh. Okay. Sorry Ma. I agree with Brandon; we messed up.

Brandon: Any flight? Even if it's several stops?

My toes froze on the carpet, images of several airports flashing in my brain. Did I really want to spend my weekend like that? Was the Poconos this important?

Me: Get what you can, I will decide.

Brian & Brandon: Okay.

Me: Love you even though y'all still in big trouble.

Brian: Love you too

Brandon: TQM

Oh, my boys. The anger brewing at remembering every-thing dissipated, the calming sensation of the carpet soothing my chaotic thoughts. Calling Miranda would probably help me detangle some of my anxiety, but I didn't feel like being on the phone. My stomach groaned, an emptiness settling inside.

Of course, I felt empty; I hadn't eaten in hours. After our conversation, Orlando and I headed back to the rental in com-panionable silence. The air of intimacy morphed into a quiet disappointment I wanted to erase for both our sakes. Still, that instinct was Hot Girl Trinidad thinking, not levelheaded Ms. Velasquez thinking.

My watch said it was past nine, and the creaks and groans of the house settling into the cooler evening had subsided. Stillness.

Maybe Orlando had gone to bed already. Orlando, in the room next door, sleeping in his bed…his very pillowy lips, slightly apart as he gently snored. I imagined he probably snored with all the stress and responsibilities in his life.

If he was mine… I'd cuddle him and let him be safe in my arms. And maybe I'd play with his dick just a little, but that would be for me, not for him. If he were mine, I'd slide the sheets off his silky dark torso, reveling in the beauty of a man well-made. Kisses, and licks, and sucking would ensue until the sheets tangled around us and—clearly, I needed some food to stop the addled thoughts.

After food, I'd have a little get-together with my favorite toy, Mr. Demarquis. Maybe then I'd assuage the burning temptation eating me from inside.

I tippy-toed downstairs to keep the wooden stairs from creaking. There was no more stillness here; instead, the kitchen light illuminated the rest of the darkened common areas. The sizzling sounds of an active stove piqued my curiosity. The scent of bell peppers and tomatoes activated some seriously embarrassing growling and lured me all the way inside.

"Hey, Ms. V... hungry?"

Orlando stood in front of the stove, sautéing with basketball shorts on and no T-shirt. Did my addled thoughts follow me downstairs? My heart and stomach had a wrestling match to decide which organ would make the most fuss, but they had no chance against my pussy which purred at the sight of a cooking Orlando.

"I... I could eat. So what you making?" I settled myself on the other side of the kitchen, my attempt to keep as much space between us. The kitchen was large, with big windows by the sink, a large island with the stove and prep area, all white marble and whitewashed wood detailing complementing the stainless steel appliances.

Four barstools sat across the island, a perfect location to ogle; I mean, *admire* Orlando's cooking skills. All that inspection to not make eye contact. But I couldn't help myself... Orlando, with no T-shirt, carved chest, small lickable nipples... *Dios mío.*

Thank God he didn't pick up on my hormonal rioting. Instead, he avoided eye contact, his free hand rubbing the back of his neck. *Oh?*

"So I texted the twins and asked them what you like as a guilty pleasure. They said to make you revoltillo de huevo y tomate," Orlando confessed.

"You're making revoltillo?" I squealed. Pure, intense delight rushed through every cell of my body. Very rarely did I get surprised—besides, of course, this trip—and more importantly, pampered. The tingling in my chest intensified when I took his words into account once more. Orlando went out of his way to make sure I was good.

Estoy en serios problemas.

"Do you like revoltillo?" I asked, shutting down the overthinking for now. Enjoying the moment tempted me more than anything else in this kitchen, in this otherworldly town. Maybe there was someone else who tempted me more, but that would be my secret to keep.

"I haven't had it Dominican style, but I love trying new things." Because of the stillness of the house, we both were speaking in hushed tones. The air of intimacy swirled and surrounded us, warming my skin and teasing my senses. Here was my opportunity to leave things on a better note than the car ride.

"So how you making me revoltillo and you haven't had it?"

"I can cook, cook. A search for recipes, and I took the best notes and did my own." Sure enough, the aroma of breakfast en casa de abuela en San Pedro de Macorís hit me so strongly that my throat closed up for a bit. The plate had the revoltillo with the bright red tomatoes and colorful peppers, steam still rising from the plate. Next, to eat, two green boiled plantains awaited to be demolished.

"When, how?"

"I'd done groceries before you arrived; these are all staples in my kitchen." He pointed at the plate and nodded for me to eat.

"How about you? I'm not eating without you." My stomach grumbled at my comment.

"Stubborn woman. Here. I'll eat with you." Orlando moved gracefully, turning around to get another plate. The ripples of his muscles showcased how well he cared for his body. The leanness didn't hide the strength from within.

When he turned around and shoved a forkful of hot scrambled eggs in his mouth, I might have moaned a little.

"Thank you," I said, keeping my hot girl thoughts to myself and settling in to enjoy the food. For a few minutes, we ate with only that stillness accompanying us.

"So, what are your guilty pleasures?" I asked him after my belly had allowed me to take a break.

"I love me some bun and cheese; I don't care if it's Easter or not, get in my belly." He chuckled, those thick lips of his glistening with the revoltillo juices. Bendito, when had eating become such an erotic endeavor? "And I love me some cassava pone, shit hits every time."

"Cassava pone? I don't know that I've ever had that."

"Never had Belizean cassava pudding? I think some countries call it yuca pone…it's cassava flower and coconut and condensed milk, and…it's like pumpkin pie texture. The best way I can describe it." Orlando blew a kiss in the air, his gaze softening in a dreamy far, long stare.

"Oh…that sounds delicious, so you got a sweet tooth, huh?" I teased, forking some eggs and slipping them in my mouth. I took my time savoring the seasoning and the eggs. He'd managed to make them creamy and had gotten really close to the flavors of my childhood, and on the first try.

In my less wholesome days I used to say if I met a man that could cook me my food, the food of my people, I'd never let him go. He'd get the royal treatment over here. All orifices would be fair game for a man like that. Of course, I met him once I was a wholesome woman—horrible timing.

"I do have a sweet tooth, and I am a good boy. I always eat it all…cake, dessert, and other varieties…" Orlando said in a voice so raspy, I felt it in that other variety. His choosing this particular time to chase a minuscule piece of eggs from the corner of his lip with his tongue seemed premeditated and downright cruel. I was trying to be a good woman, but he was making it so difficult.

"Oh, so you're an eater. Is that what you're saying?" No overthinking. All in.

"The best of them. I pride in my capacity to…please." Orlando winked. Our plates were both empty at this point. The comfortable air of intimacy had another quality—a charged, dangerous scent—the scent of risky decisions and untold ecstasy.

Looking to make a swift retreat, I hopped off the stool

and carried my plate to the sink. Orlando turned and did the exact same thing. Now close to me, I could smell his musky sandalwood scent—one of my favorites. Of course it was one of my favorites.

"I can clean up," I offered, hoping he would show the usual traits of the man in my life.

"Nah, I want to do the cleaning after I eat. Are you okay with that, Ms. V?"

The warmth of his skin kissed my arm as we stared at each other. His lips were parted just like in my fantasy, but more tempting than ever. My breath escaped choppy and irregular, probably why my brain took a break and let my hormones take the wheel.

"We haven't even... I...fuck it." Pure adrenaline guided me. That and unadulterated desire. My lips crashed into his, and the fantasies did me a disservice because his mouth on mine felt as heavenly as Ofele on a cloudy day. Pure comfort and magic. A sense of belonging. A homecoming.

He took over the kiss, his command and ease calming me and accelerating my pulse simultaneously. It should not work. How could I be calm when blood pumped three times as fast everywhere in my body? But was; I opened up to him, our tongues entangling and finding their rhythm. He pressed all that lean goodness against me, enclosing me with his arms against the kitchen counter, and I reveled in how well we fit together.

The kiss grew incendiary as I sucked his tongue in mine. Soon, we were grasping at each other's clothes, so desperate for more contact that we did nothing but frustrate each other with lust. Finally, my sweatpants ended up on the floor with my panties.

Leanness was not a deterrent for Orlando and my grown woman's weight. I sailed in the air for the second time today, but this time, my behind ended up cradled by the cold marble underneath.

"You don't know how long I've dreamed of that kiss, of your lips, of holding you," Orlando confessed between ragged breaths.

Confessing my own fantasies felt a step too far down the road to perdition. Instead, I nodded and ran my tongue over my lower lip.

"Argh, woman. You're beautiful, you know? Inside out, your light…that's what drew me in, but damn, the looks didn't hurt."

Was that a giggle that escaped me? I could not remember the last time I had giggled. This man was going to have me giggling all the way to an orgasm. And I wanted that so bad.

"Boy, if you don't…"

"You don't have to tell me twice, Ms. V. Let me show you my eating abilities."

Wetness is to be expected if things are going right. Wetness is desired and required for things to go right. But this was not just wetness. This was dirty, filthy, drenched goodness. This was masterful flicks and swipes, a rhythm perfected by my moans and screams. This was mind reading business, a soul-sucking enchantment. This was not fair. He began slow, savoring every spot between my legs, from my knees, traversing my thighs, ending right where I needed him the most. He took his time, building up the suspense and tension, making me ask for it, beg for it even. Little direction was required.

"There...oh, do that again," I pleaded, and Orlando dragged his tongue right on my clitoris. Pressure, the right pressure, no shyness, no hesitation, he went for it. He understood the mission and applied himself deliciously. Warm shivers raced up and down my legs until they started trembling around his head. I grasped anything I could find; the hard brim of his fitted did the trick, but my desperation for an orgasm was so elevated I ended up knocking his fitted off his head. Even better, his soft coils served as my emotional support companions, my fingers and nails nestling in them, never to leave. At least not until he made me come.

"You like that, Ms. V? Huh? Is this what you need? To get my mouth all glistening with your goodness?" His rasped words vibrated against my pussy lips, making me even wetter. This wasn't a man-child; this was a sorcerer. My entire body replied to his question, gushing and shivering. The butterflies were doing an intricate choreography, an ode to Orlando, they called it. And my heart? It decided to show me the potential signs of sex-induced cardiac episodes.

"Sí, Orlando, por favor!" I was begging, but I didn't even know what I was asking for; I just needed so much from this, from him. All my troubles were outside of this room waiting, but here in the kitchen with the filthy slurp Orlando created and my desperate breathing, here I was just Trinidad. Ms. V, if I wanted to be extra nasty. And I wanted to be so nasty with this man. The scent of my arousal mixed with his sandalwood and my body wash had me wondering how my room would smell after a full session with him. It would smell like citrus, sandalwood, temptation, and bad decisions.

Eau of Risky Frisky Man Child. I would buy three bottles.

The heat of the outside seeped into the kitchen, and beads of sweat gathered on my brow. My legs ached as if I recently finished a two-hour yoga session, and all sensations coalesced right where Orlando's tongue met my throbbing pussy. His tongue went into turbo mode and kept the luscious pressure. Perfectly precise, exactly how I needed it. My senses dulled, the kitchen becoming a blur, sounds amplifying until a burst of light and liquid went through me, hot, immediate, and encompassing. All the tension popped, and I became a loud, sobbing, wet mess. Never in my life had I orgasmed like this. Orlando pushed back in the nick of time, the wetness arching out of me hitting his chest.

"So good, Ms. V. You did so good." Orlando grinned, delighted to see my fountain while I watched the mess I made on him and the kitchen floor.

"I've never, I…what just—" A loud vibration startled us both. My phone lay next to me, Milton's name flashing on the screen. Maybe shutting my eyes would make the image disappear and my racing heart calm down. The decadent feeling seeped out, chased by panic and terror.

"I… I gotta go to sleep; I…this shouldn't have happened. I am so sorry." The heat that cradled me earlier left me now feeling suffocated. Orlando's hurt expression sat heavy on my chest, but I couldn't focus on that right now.

"Oh damn, well, I can't say I'm sorry that happened, but I'm sorry you feel that way. Let me help you down."

"Oh no, no, no, you're good. And I think I'm saying this wrong. This—" I waved him away, and down there between my legs waved at him too but a beckoning one instead. "That was phenomenal. 10/10. I would write any reviews to the ladies you're dating if you need to, but it was wrong because I'm trying to have something serious with Milton, and even though he and I ain't exclusive, I don't want to…yeah, I'm blabbering." I chuckled, attempting to erase the somber mood that had overtaken us.

"I get it," Orlando said in a clipped tone, and his posture completely changed. No longer did I feel he fit perfectly with me. His aura screamed Do Not Approach. Coldness settled between us as he stood watching me scramble down off the counter. I hesitated, eying the pants on the floor, wondering how to bend with any sense of decorum, but his chivalry must have been deeply ingrained because he bent over and handed me my sweatpants.

"Good night, Orlando," I said, pleading with my eyes for him to understand my position.

"Good night, Trinidad."

And for once, I wished he'd called me Ms. V instead.

Fifteen

Orlando

Darkness greeted me early in the morning. The comfortable bed could not cradle away the frustration that settled in my bones after the night I had with Trinidad. Her scent of lemons, passion, and woman still lingered even after I'd taken a shower and brushed my teeth. Or maybe it was just my imagination, conjuring her yet again so I would remain taunted and unfulfilled.

I didn't care about coming; well, I fucking cared about coming, but I didn't need to come last night to feel satisfied. Trinidad's ecstasy had been a sweet reward until that man she dated called and poured cold water into the pseudo intimacy we had created together. One call, and we both stepped back into reality. A reality where the two of us had no future, not even a present together.

Damn.

Avoidance helped me so much in many ways, but not in this matter. My brain and heart refused to connect. No matter the reality, falling in love with her was nonsensical; my heart had started the process months ago with no input from me. Catching feelings for an unattainable woman tracked, though. When had I ever gotten what I wanted?

If the bed wasn't going to help, maybe an early run would do the trick. My mood needed to shift by the time I hit the road with Trinidad; I couldn't let her see how affected I still was from last night. Trinidad did not need the burden of my hurt feelings from her rejection. She'd set her intentions clearly from the beginning of the day, regardless of how well we'd clicked and how charged the sexual tension was between us.

Getting my shorts and trainers on, I quietly left the house, hitting the pavement as if it owed me for last night. In any other place I've traveled, I've never felt fully comfortable running for exercise unless it was at a gym or a park. Here in Ofele, there was no fear of being mistaken for anything but a tall, dark-skinned Black man on a morning jog. Shit felt good.

The heat subsided enough to make the run an okay one. By the time I came back to the rental, the sunrise sun glowed, illuminating the streets of Ofele with that otherworldly gleam. Upstairs I heard steps, probably Trinidad getting ready to head out. I had about fifteen minutes to shower and be ready to take her based on that time we had agreed upon. She'd texted me last night asking to head to the airport early, without knowing if Delilah or the kids had even gotten her a flight. We'd texted back and forth. I didn't think it was a good idea for us to rush there without a precise plan, but she was adamant.

Trinidad: I figure, if I'm there early, I can charm my way onto a flight.

As promised, I stood by the door at seven, and Trinidad emerged from her room with her luggage.

"Let me help you with that." I moved with the speed required to avoid her saying no. By the time she opened her mouth, I was already halfway up the stairs.

"Oh, you don't have—"

"I do," I said, grabbing her carry-on and going straight back down. Movement prevented my organs from rioting against me in her presence. I didn't need to focus on the ache in my chest and the hardness between my pants after seeing her today and smelling her citrus and woman scent. Just the scent reminded me of last night, and I half wished I'd waited to wash my face a little longer.

"Alright," I heard behind me as we made it outside. "Did you sleep okay?" she asked, attempting to pretend everything was okay.

"I slept like shit, but I think you knew that already."

"I didn't. I mean, I was hoping that wasn't the case."

"I know, sorry, I didn't mean to sound so...salty. My apologies." Once I put her luggage in the trunk, I rushed to open the door of the car before her. I stared, frozen in time and place, focused on her alone.

Trinidad, under this sleepy sun, shades on in a black maxi dress with straps. Trinidad, with the awkward, apologetic smile and glowing ochre-brown skinI now knew tasted like a spiced bun and all the good things in life. Trinidad, with her back to me, determined to head back to New York for a man who did not deserve or fit her.

"It's okay, Orlando, last night…yeah, I wish things were different."

But they were not.

"So, did you sleep okay?" I asked her, eager to erase the awkwardness settling between us. It was a long drive; we didn't need to be uncomfortable for all these hours.

"I didn't, but it's hard for me to settle in a new bed at first." She fidgeted with her purse strap while talking. Right now, she was full of shit. But I wasn't going to call her out on that. She could have slept really well after I put her to bed after a few sessions, which only our bodies were required to attend.

"Good, good." Shit, this was going to be awkward, wasn't it? Just as I got on the highway toward Jacksonville, my phone rang in my pocket. I connected the call to Bluetooth, clutching the steering wheel tight, bracing for whatever was coming.

"Yo, Orlando, you good? Listen, I don't know, man. I'm trying, but Mom's tripping. You said she has to take those pills at night, but she didn't want to take them last night. Today she acting a little funny. Should I give them to her now, or wait? I don't remember what you said," Camilo said, not stopping to hear if I was good or not. Typical.

"I'm alright, man. Listen, I left you all the notes in your notes app. What happened?"

"Shit, my bad, I erased that; I figured I got this. She's my mom too, you know; I try to pay attention. But yeah, I don't have it."

Thank God for the clear road. Trinidad's stare nudged

me, but I stayed put, holding it all in. The urge to punch the steering wheel was intense, but it subsided as I counted my way from thirty to one.

"Man, you there? I need to know what to do?"

"You can't give her the meds now, not those. Make sure she takes the morning dose, and she'll be okay. She needs to go outside today, no fussing. The sun helps her to stay regulated. A walk won't hurt. And if she's being stubborn, make her mashed potatoes and fried chicken tonight and hide the meds in the potatoes…. It works like a charm. Alright, I gotta go; I'm taking Ms. V to the airport," I said. No point in getting mad at him, for what? Camilo would just brush my anger off, which wouldn't solve anything.

"Ohhh fine ass Ms.—"

Sometimes, hanging up a call was all you could do.

The quiet in the car grew intense until I started my road trip playlist. The nudging hadn't stopped, but keeping my eyes on the road was very, very important. Super important.

"I don't know what to say first…" Trinidad finally broke the silence. "I mean. First of all, how old is your brother?"

"Camilo is twenty, about to be twenty-one," I explained.

"Huh…"

Silence again. But now, the curiosity wouldn't let me focus on the road the way I was before.

"Huh?" I stole a glance at Trinidad, and she was sitting facing me completely, her expression contemplative.

"It is not my business at all, but at twenty, what were you doing for your siblings and mother?"

The road widened in front of me. The sun shined a little

brighter, and the music suddenly sounded clearer. Then it all dulled again, and I stole another look at Trinidad.

"When I was twenty, I finally convinced Mom to be more diligent about her medications. I was in college and making sure my brothers were good. Apparently, I was also creating life without even knowing it." I chuckled.

"Mm-hmm. I think you know what I mean but you don't want to face it yet, and I respect that. I only wanted to point it out."

These were all thoughts I had before. My brothers could be more responsible; I had to be—I had no choice, but why rob them of theirs? They were allowed to be teenagers and young adults now; it was the right thing to do. If I had to carry the burden for them to have regular lives, then…that was the hand I was dealt. Miles Morales didn't complain when the mantle of responsibility fell on him. Why would I complain now?

"Nah, it's okay; I can thug it out."

You know when Latine moms disagree on something but are trying to stay quiet? That loud disapproval hovering all over, the passive-aggressiveness choking everyone out? Yeah, Trinidad was damn good at that.

"If you say so…" Trinidad was about to say more, but her phone rang. She immediately started miming to it and answered as she kept mouthing a name. It took me a second, but I quickly picked up it was Delilah.

"Hello! How you doing?" Trinidad said, animated.

"Yes! I am here with him," she answered after a brief pause. "Can I put you on speaker? Great!"

"So first, the good news, Orlando, we found a bakery we

think your girl used to work at. We are not certain, but you can go and visit it today! It's on the old part of Ofele. It's called The House of Sweets. They should probably be able to help you some!"

Damn, that had been quick and effective. My heart tripped at the news; I was one step closer to meeting my daughter.

"…news is that there are no flights today that would cost you less than $3,000 and two stops to get to NY. I even looked for Newark. I guess summer travel is back. Also… I kept looking just in case; Saturday has very similar pricing. It drops on Sunday."

"Oh…my flight leaves on Monday. Sunday, it makes no difference at that point." Monday was a day off for Milton and the office, so they were going to be there until that day, but that would be too late.

"So sorry, hun. I really wanted to help! It's a very busy weekend. Overall, there are a lot of activities happening across the state that are increasing the pricing. But now you get to enjoy our wonderful carnival!" Delilah said, trying to infuse some positivity to the bad news. My news had been fantastic, but I couldn't help the desire to comfort Ms. V with her bad news, news that sparked renewed hope in me. Maybe, just maybe, we'd be able to…nah. I needed to stop dreaming.

"You're right, Delilah. I have to look at this on the bright side. Alright, then, thanks so much!"

"You're welcome, darling. If you both are up to it, Mikey and I are hosting a fete on a yacht tonight; you should come through! I'll send you the deets via text."

I mouthed, "Deets?" and widened my eyes at Trinidad, and she rolled her eyes back at me.

After a final round of goodbyes, she hung up.

"Before you ask, *deets* is definitely some old people shit."

"Boy, if you don't stop." Trinidad's laughter filled the car and occupied my chest with joy. My God, but the woman was gorgeous. Her neck lengthened as she threw her head back, letting the hilarity of the moment erase her disappointment. I got it; I did that often, and she was doing it now, too, embracing the reality no matter how sour it was—making lemonade right before my eyes.

Once her laughter subsided, she transformed once more. Her shoulders, previously relaxed, went into attention, and she turned to me eyes filled with determination. Fuck, I wanted to kiss her so bad.

"You know, I bet you that's why the boys haven't answered my text messages. They can't tell me straight up they haven't found something. I'll taunt them the whole trip with the fear of being grounded for the summer. And I will enjoy the Ofele carnival. Milton will understand. Now, the only thing missing is finding me a hotel."

"Hotel? Nah, you staying with me. Listen, there are probably no hotels available, and I promise not to repeat last night's occurrence." Back to focusing on the road. At this point we were about half an hour away from Ofele, so I quickly changed our destination in my navigation system and got us on the direction back to the rental.

"I can't continue imposing, besides… I kind of want what

happened last night to happen again, which is why it is not the best idea for me to stay with you," Trinidad said nonchalantly.

Nothing felt nonchalant after hearing her words. We were lucky I was a good driver and didn't crash us. But then I remembered she still wanted to be with that goofball Milton.

There was a time to be respectful of another's dude woman, but this man had never claimed Trinidad from what the twins had explained. Why was I letting him take so much space this weekend? If anything, this was my chance to prove to Trinidad she had a better chance at all her dreams with...fuck, I was getting ahead of myself. One step at a time.

"Would it help if I promise I'll behave? I don't want you to waste money when I have that big rental," I said.

"Why did you rent something so big, by the way?" she wondered, sidestepping my question. I would allow it for now. I sighed, not wanting to share my silly expectations, even though I knew any silly, important, or vulnerable thoughts were safe with Trinidad. Yesterday, I had shared with her many things I kept inside, and if anything, it seemed to make her like me more.

"I thought I could convince Maria to stay in the other room with our daughter, so we had some time to get to know each other. I really thought I was going to arrive at the Ofele airport and magically find them waiting for me with a welcome sign and big smiles."

"Oh...that, I get that. It's a little fantastical, not gonna lie, but I get it, wanting the best-case scenario, seeing the glass half-full, that is how you make it every day, isn't it?" she asked.

Man, if only she knew.

"Yeah, that is how I make it day by day. Positive thinking. I mean, the few times I focused on the negative, my mood just...it didn't feel any type of good." That was the best I could do to explain my fears and concerns about letting my mind wander into a place where I wouldn't be able to retrieve it again.

"I do, too, but I've learned not to get so overly positive that I disconnect myself from everything I'm feeling."

I let her words sit for a minute, seeing their wisdom but not ready to fully unpack their meaning in my life.

"Does it work for you?" I asked instead.

"Sometimes." She gifted me with a bright, self-deprecating smile, and I smiled back at her, unable to contain my curiosity.

"So, are you gonna stay with me?" I kept my eyes on the road, driving us back to Ofele. The sky could not be a brighter blue, clear with a thousand possibilities.

"I will; thanks for the offer, but do not let it derail you from your plans with your friends. I can link up with Delilah and Mikey and hang out with them for carnival—"

"Nah, that's not going to work. Listen, you just told me you are equally as tempted as I am. So, let's do this; let's go with the flow this weekend. The kids are not here. Milton is not here. This is a golden opportunity. At least, that's how I see it, and I hope you see that too. Give me a chance, Ms. V. I'll make sure you have a good time."

"But Milton..."

"But Milton? Nah, he could have been here. He chose not to be. He could have been your man. But he ain't. His loss, my chance."

My words came out exactly how I needed them. They did not betray the chaos of nerves making my blood pump twice as fast. Signs of moisture appeared on the steering wheel, and I tried to hide them when she turned her gaze toward her window.

"Listen, I'm not promising anything but going with the flow. That I can do. Or at least I hope I can do," she said into the window. And for once, I realized Trinidad probably was feeling similar nerves to mine. I reached out, wanting to reassure her and calm any nerves.

"I get it, and that's enough for me," I whispered, holding her hand. Hers was equally damp. My heart hammered in my chest. This felt like a huge leap, and I didn't know if there was anything below to catch me.

"So instead of going to the rental, why don't we go to that bakery Delilah mentioned?" she said as tension rose between us, palpable.

"Are you sure?"

"Of course, this is so important to you, and it seems you don't prioritize yourself much. If I'm to go with the flow this weekend, my ask is that you prioritize yourself just a little." Trinidad fixed her eyes on me, not letting me go.

"Okay, so this weekend, we are letting go and prioritizing ourselves," I said, then winked at her. Her dazzling smile was the perfect reward.

Now I had to figure out how the fuck to prioritize myself…

Easy.

Sixteen

Trinidad

The delicious smell of baked goods and yeast welcomed us to the cozy bakery, where we hoped to find Maria.

Everything Orlando had shared about Maria made me think he might have some unresolved feelings for her, and every time that thought popped up in my mind, the butterflies in my stomach got very, very angry. The feeling was so familiar and unpleasant that I didn't want to give it space. It reminded me of every time my ex-husband met a new friend or woman and talked about them, and my insecurities would flare to life. He never made me feel secure in his love, and jealousy became my companion.

Orlando hadn't done anything but make me feel wanted, but I had no claims on him, same as he didn't on me. Our deal was only for this weekend; once we returned to New York, reality would kick in, and rationality would prevail. But for now, I craved the temptation he personified. He and this town with its beautiful tropical greenery and sweltering heat that made you want to walk around half-naked, and beautiful Black faces all brimming with excitement for the weekend and carnival.

If I'd thought the airport was full yesterday, I underestimated the number of revelers coming to town; it felt that overnight we, the tourists, had quadrupled. Everywhere we'd turned, there were groups of friends walking on the sidewalks, laughing in their summer bests.

A sea of umbrellas and towels adorned the beach, with all types of summer bodies frolicking in the sand and water as we'd drivenby one of the favorite tourist beaches. Old Ofele vibrated with excitement. Local vendors had tents all up and down Main Street, which they'd closed for the weekend. After we'd found parking, we'd joined the throng of people ambling around buying souvenirs and the local fare.

"There it is, there's the bakery!" I'd spotted it first, and Orlando guided us, holding my hand until we'd made it inside the shop. Even after we walked in, he'd still held my hand. I started at our clasp fingers and gazed up to him, so handsome today, wearing hoochie light blue shorts and a white button-up shirt with short sleeves. The outfit was right up my alley and didn't help the angry butterflies attempting to break through.

"Hello! Let me guess, are you the people looking for our Maria?" A stout man approached us as soon as we approached the counter with a jovial smile. Again, the feeling of similarity to New Orleans struck me again; if this man would tell me he was a Black Creole, I would believe him.

"I'm Francis Landau. It's a pleasure to meet you both, Orlando and Trinidad, correct?" He extended his hand to Orlando, then, with my permission, graded mine and placed a gentle kiss on my palm.

"News travels fast."

"This is not a big town, no matter how much new Ofele has grown over the years. Mikey shared with me your ask, and I agree with him. Maria needs to be the one to decide if she wants to talk to you or not. So last night I called her and let her know you are in town. She doesn't work here anymore, but we care for her and Maya deeply."

Orlando's hand tightened around mine till it hurt. His eyes were wide, and I had to jiggle them until he dislodged the tight grip. I shook away the radiating pressure and grabbed his hand again, which was damp. Squeezing with all my might, I poured all my reassurance and support until I felt the tension ease from his hand.

"Her name is Maya? My friend didn't tell me; she wanted Maria to tell me."

"Why…is it significant to you?"

"Yeah, it's my grandmother's name in Jamaica; it's a family name of sorts. Maria knew that," Orlando explained.

His eyes were misty, and he tried to hide by looking all around the shop—the silly man. My throat tightened at the news, and it wasn't even my daughter. I so wished he allowed himself space to be vulnerable.

"Okay. So...should we return here? What are the next steps?" Orlando asked, composed once more.

"No, young man, the ball is in Maria's court now. She said she'd come to you when she's ready. Please respect that and enjoy your carnival weekend. She'll reach out if you're okay with me sharing your contact information with her."

I searched Orlando's face for any disappointment, but he took the situation with equanimity. He left his contact information and after buying me a spiced bun and three for himself, we walked out to the torrid heat waiting for us outside.

"So, what do you think?" I asked him, taking a bite of my spiced bun.

"I think that went as well as it could; I did spring this on her, but I could have handled it differently."

I stayed quiet, impressing myself with my restraint. He didn't need my opinion on any of this; it wasn't my business.

"Damn, that silence was telling!" He put on his sunglasses, and we ambled slowly to the car, both wanting to enjoy the sights and the festive vibe surrounding us.

"You know what they say? I'm eating my spice bun 'cause I got no water..."

"So, you minding your business?" He laughed and took two big bites of his spice bun, obliterating something that took me several bites to eat.

"RIP, spice bun, you never stood a chance." I chuckled.

"You know me and my eating abilities..." he said, and flashes of last night materialized between us, raising my heartbeat and making me sweat more than I already was perspiring.

"Oh, I do know..."

"I have other prowess as well, in case you want to give them a try this weekend." He popped another piece of spice bun, his third one, and hummed happily. That hum initiated an earthquake in my belly, making tectonic waves in my lower area. Everything he did was alluring, and that was a problem. I wanted to indulge but didn't want to be sprung by this man. I'd done enough veering off my path to my goal.

"I'm certain, do you…we shall see which ones you get to put into practice." I, too, could play this game. If Orlando meant to keep me off-kilter, I would return the favor. Game on.

"Anything you consent to, I'm yours…" he said as we approached his car. He gallantly opened the door for me, a habit I was quickly getting used to. I was getting used to all things Orlando, and that wasn't fair to him or me because once I left on Monday, things had to go back to normal. They had to.

"So your friends are all staying in a hotel?" I asked Orlando as we hung out in the Florida room of the rental. The place had a wonderful sunroom surrounded by gorgeous vegetation, including a bush with pink flowers, which I searched and found out are called Bahama senna. The abundant small pink flowers adorned the perimeter of the backyard, their nice aroma calming.

"They are. I didn't want them all up in my business."

"You mean meeting your daughter?" I asked, sipping lemonade, which Orlando had made when we got home after hearing me complain about the heat.

"Yes, and other things…they don't know I'm applying for

law school. Well, I already applied. I haven't opened the letter yet, but I think I got accepted. I have to reply to the university by the end of the trip, so I needed some space to make the right decision."

"Congratulations!" I sat straight, stopping the rocking chair I was on as he swayed back and forth in the hammock he'd chosen.

"Thank you..." Orlando replied, a tinge of sadness clouding his voice. His eyes closed, and he kept swaying in the hammock, same way he probably swayed to make the right decision, and suddenly I understood.

"You love that animation job...the boys have told me how much you enjoy it."

"I do, but I have to quit to be able to go to law school; Columbia doesn't allow us to work while in the program." His arms flexed as he placed them behind his back, the lean muscles peeking out from the short sleeves of his shirt. I wanted to run my palms where the hardness met softness, snuggle on top of him, and give him the comfort he needed.

Calmate, Trinidad. Honestly, it was like Ms. Hot Girl V was trying to take over this weekend, but I couldn't let her. At least not fully. It wasn't my time in life for that anymore. Just a little indulgence; maybe I could sneak into his room tonight, but nothing more. No acting like lust-sick fools around Ofele.

I couldn't afford all of that; my heart couldn't afford to remember what it felt like to be infatuated, and...why did this man bring these thoughts to mind? I was so content with what I was building with Milton, I was at peace knowing that wild, passionate love didn't do me any good. But Orlando's mere presence threatened that reality.

"But why law school?"

"The year for a first paid associate would cover all the debt we currently have. I would have Mom on top-of-the-line medical insurance so that she could get all the treatment she needs. She could use more regular therapy sessions and more care, but right now, we can't afford that. I am good with animation, really good, but I am also good with retaining information. And I would be good at law school," Orlando said, his closed eyes tightening every time he said *law school*.

This man really was looking at this all the wrong ways, but was it my place to intervene? It was not. Just earlier, I'd told him I was minding my business. Orlando kept walking his path as if it was predetermined and he had no say in what happened. But he was the one in control. He didn't seem to know it.

"Orlando, I think you could find other ways to help your mother if law school isn't what you want. With the passion you have for animation, you could probably move up the ranks pretty quickly in three years." There went keeping my nose out of his business. If my mother would be here she'd call me *metiche* and then join in the butting in.

"Yeah...maybe—"

A loud knock interrupted Orlando, and he sprang from the hammock way more gracefully than I could have done. I walked behind him as the nice, quiet rental filled with boisterous sounds as two men and one woman walked in, all chatting at the same time.

"Yoooo, you rich son, this house is nice!" A tall, lanky man, with the same complexion as Orlando but with curly hair, clapped Orlando on the back and whistled after the embrace. Just a look at him, and I knew he was the loud one of the group.

"Ugh, why you so tacky? Let the man live. Hi, boo, you good?" A petite woman who I could probably carry in my pocket threw her arms up at Orlando, who dutifully picked her up and twirled her around, her short curls bobbing with the movement. She was gorgeous, with flawless mahogany skin and an impish smile.

"I'm good, Gracie pooh, now that you're here," Orlando said.

"Papo, lay off my woman, she's not your Gracie pooh…" said the third man, who looked like danger and sex on two long legs. His New York accent was tinged with something else, and I knew he was a fellow Dominican without having to ask.

"Here you go, you promise not to be on that bullshit," Grace growled, and the three other men laughed.

"You should have never dated this fool," Orlando said and turned around to find me standing by the entrance of the living room. Suddenly, seeing all their expectant faces, I felt completely out of place. This was Orlando's environment, and I didn't quite fit in it.

"Who is this?" Grace approached me with a big smile.

"Hello, I am Trinidad, I am—"

"Oh shit, we know who you are, Ms. V," the first man

said, and Orlando elbowed his friend so quickly I would have missed it if my attention wasn't on him.

"You do, huh? I hope all good things. What is your name?" I asked the girl first, who bounced on the balls of her feet, ready to take flight. She could be Black Tinkerbell in the live action film if they ever did one.

"I am Grace, that's Trevor—" she pointed at the loudmouth "—and that is Desmond," Grace finished with an annoyed tone as she pointed at Dominican Papi Chulo.

"Hey y'all, I'm Trinidad, even though it seems that is common knowledge; I'm gonna go upstairs, work a bit, and give you time to catch up. See y'all tomorrow!" I turned around and bounded up the stairs, hoping Orlando wouldn't follow.

No such luck. His steps reverberated heavier than mine behind me. Lean my ass; the man was pure mass. I'd learned that fact this week. Why I thought otherwise, I would never know. I reached my door just as Orlando's warmth caressed my back. I wanted to lean back and let him hold me, and kiss my neck and…

"Trinidad…what's up? I thought we were all going to the yacht party tonight. And why don't you wanna hang out?" Orlando asked, his hushed tone full of hurt.

With nowhere to escape, I turned around to him, wanting the conversation to be over.

"That is what you came for, to have fun with your friends who are your same age."

"We are ten years apart, not fifty. I thought we were past this."

"If all of us were in school, you would be in third grade

while I would have been a high school senior, not even in the same building." I gestured downstairs to the bickering and laughter floating around the house.

Orlando's widening glance was all I needed to open my door, but he was right behind me.

"Please, you said we would both enjoy this time, together." His deep grumble started melting my reserve.

"That's not fair; that was before your band of merry thieves arrived."

"What?"

"Sorry, I am confusing stories—Robin Hood, Peter Pan… who cares? Listen, I want you to have fun, and catering to me, making sure I'm good, and catching every reference from your tight group is not going to be fun."

"Why don't you let me determine what is fun for me?" Orlando said with a deceptively calm voice. Suddenly, the very large and comfortable room felt small. The calming walls with their rich buttery colors didn't soothe me. My pulse raced as I walked back toward the wall until Orlando was a breath away from me. He'd moved so smoothly I hadn't had time to react to anything but his alluring cologne and sultry warmth. The heat outside might feel suffocating, but this heat, the one we created together, felt incendiary.

"Don't do that, Trinidad; we both have promised to let go…let things flow, right?" Orlando asked, his eyes settling a little lower than my eyes. My lips tingled, remembering how great he tasted last night. I wanted to try again, taste him once more, and see if this time he would taste spicy, like cinnamon and nutmeg from the spiced bun. He didn't keep me waiting long; our mouths melded together, knowing exactly what to do. His hands were everywhere: my locs, my neck, my collarbone. Every single path of his fingers left a trail of goose bumps behind.

I moaned into his mouth, happy to taste the cinnamon and fruity flavors of the bun we ate earlier along with the essence of man, arousal, and need. A need so deep I couldn't help pushing off the wall and rubbing my body against his, to chase away the pool of desire that had settled in my core since yesterday.

"Fuck, I've been wanting to do this since the last time I kissed you," he said between breaths, and I chuckled into his mouth. I sucked his tongue, and that earned me a loud, needy moan from him. I needed to elicit that same exact noise again. My pussy agreed wholeheartedly. His hands traveled down my neck to the cleavage of my dress, and he paused, his deep brown orbs hypnotizing me.

"Can I touch you here?" Orlando asked, and I nodded desperately, my locs dragging against the wall. Orlando didn't wait for another second; he yanked the cleavage down until one of my breasts bobbed out, the cool air and the sweet arousal he created coaxing my nipple to full attention.

For a second, I froze. He hadn't seen grown woman titties before. These ladies had some extra miles he wasn't familiar with. Some extra swag and sag, as Miranda would say. But based on how he reacted to the sight, all tension left my body. The first touch of his finger on my skin galvanized me, and I undulated against him, his hardness settling against my belly. He realized what I was searching for and lowered himself enough for the contact between our private parts to match perfectly. He caressed and plumped and played with my breast until so much wetness gathered between my legs I grew desperate.

"Shhh, I know what you need." He moved again until he pressed his thigh between where I needed him the most. The pressure he created was perfect, and like a needy cat, I rubbed myself against him, pulling him down for another kiss.

The pressure built inside, his hard thigh the perfect ally in my climb to ecstasy.

"Go ahead, Ms. V, get yours; I'm right here," Orlando whispered next to my ear, his lush mouth pressed against my earlobe, then settled in my neck, licking and sucking while I dry humped him.

No way past me would ever believe this was possible. Me, Trinidad Velasquez, a thirty-five-year-old mother and wholesome woman, dry humping with the most alluring, gorgeous twenty-five-year-old. It didn't hurt that Orlando was beautiful inside and out, and something in him kept calling to something in me.

The warmth flooded through my veins, and when Orlando bent a little and the wet drag of his tongue touched my nipple, I cried out. An explosion of sound and light went off in me, releasing all the tension and worries until I slumped against the wall, a ragged doll with a satisfied grin.

"Fuck, that was amazing, you came so beautifully for me," he whispered. Orlando bent and captured my mouth again for a languid kiss that left my brain scrambled, and my arousal peeked again. "So, that's that. You are coming. No more talking about staying behind. Grace is gonna get you a dress of hers that she brought, just in case."

Words were coming out of Orlando's mouth, but there was a lust for me that didn't allow anything but "Yes, Orlando" to come out of my mouth.

Did this man-child just sex a "yes" out of me?

By the time I had my wits again, Orlando had departed and a gentle knock on the door signaled Grace's arrival.

"Trinidad, can I come in? Orlando said you were expecting me."

Allowing Grace in, I shut the door again, worried that the sex demon would come back and addle me again and convince me to escape with him to a tropical island or something. That had been so good, dry humping wasn't supposed to feel this great. If it weren't for his friends' presence, I would have taken things much further and fuck the yacht party. Orlando had awakened something long dormant in me, and I was finally ready to let it out.

"I'm so glad to meet you finally! Orlando speaks so highly of you and your sons; he really cares about your family." Grace, with her impish smile, immediately made me feel at ease. The age difference so apparent downstairs washed away while we chatted about everything and anything.

"Oh, I'm so glad you are here; I swear I travel with the boys all the time. Well, not Orlando; he's deeply responsible, so being away from home never feels comfortable to him, but the other two knuckleheads get on my damn nerves. I love them, but they get on my nerves."

"How long you've all known each other?"

"We met in college. We were all part of the Caribbean-American Association and ended up on the board—well, not Trevor, but the three of us. Trevor was a member, but he just wanted to link up with all the other Caribbean ladies on campus and felt the best way to locate them was joining the association." Grace laughed as she plopped on my bed and made herself comfortable.

"And Orlando?" I hoped I didn't sound too eager, but I wanted to know more about him. The picture in my head of Orlando had morphed completely since yesterday. I always thought of him as this easygoing, nonchalant guy, but everything I was learning painted a different canvas—one that captivated me to my everlasting dread.

"Orlando was the most studious of us. He joined the association as a tribute to his father. You know his daddy was Jamaican, right? Well, he wanted a connection to his heritage. He spearheaded several cultural events that year we were on the board, and because of him, we raised the most amount of money the association had ever raised. Honestly, I don't know how he did it and still does it now. Those brothers of his… They were just calling him as I came up, asking for things he specifically had left written. He tried to laugh it off when I asked if he was okay, but…he has a lot on his shoulders. I worry about him sometimes. But Orlando doesn't do worry, he is the most stubbornly positive person I know." Grace shook her head, laughing.

The fact that his brothers had called yet again with questions they probably should know the answers to must be hard for Orlando. You would think they would step up the way he did at that age, but it seems everybody relied on him. Again, the similarities in our lives felt eerily serendipitous.

"He will never tell you if he needs something, and he will always bend over backward for his loved ones, sometimes to the detriment of his own needs. I hope you keep that in mind," Grace said, and the warning was received. She was a good friend, and if I was her, I'd do the same. Here I was, a mother with two children who probably had a lot of needs in Grace's eyes. What could Orlando possibly want to do with a readymade family when his hands were already full? And why in the world was I even worried about that? Orlando and I didn't have a future.

But it didn't stop me from imagining one with him.

Dios mío, I was in trouble.

Delilah and Mikey's yacht party assembled the who's who of Ofele and all the carnival leaders and organizers. The double-decker boat had ample space in the front for partygoers to mingle. Inside, there was a bar and a steel drum band playing some popular soca tunes accompanied by a track. Everyone was decked out; my people were not here to play. Thank God for Grace's white dress. The strapless bustier A-line had enough give to fit snugly on me versus the loose fit on her smaller body.

The heat of the day hadn't relented; my locks were up in a high ponytail ready for any breeze and possible kisses from the man standing next to me. Orlando wore loose white trousers and a short-sleeve shirt, the easygoing look absolutely appealing. With his hand on my elbow he guided me through the throng of guests until we found our hosts holding court near the built-in bar.

"You made it! How are you?" Delilah gave us both big hugs. Once I said hello to Mikey, a sharp tug from Delilah separated me from the men, allowing us some privacy.

"Oh, I see you have opened yourself up to the possibility of more." Delilah held back a cackle, but just barely. I glanced at her, not knowing if to lean into my laughter or my annoyance. The woman was persistent; I'd give her that.

"I don't know what you are talking about." If she were going to be a busybody, I would be obtuse. It worked with the twins all the time.

"Now you are gonna play games, you know exactly what I mean!"

"Loose lips and all. Girl, let me live, okay?" I winked and made my way to Orlando, who'd turned around with drinks in hand.

"I wasn't sure what you'd like, but I made a wild guess, and I hope I'm right?" Orlando said, handing me the cold drink. I looked back at Delilah, whispering in Mikey's ear and winking at me. If I let her, she'd start me up in a cougar's club, and I wasn't out here trying to be no one's wildcat—sometimes, I had to lie to myself to make it day by day. The problem was, the lie wasn't working tonight because my wildcat had been purring since I saw Orlando and realized he had conspired with Grace for us to match colors.

A sip of my drink gave me a burst of flavors, herbs, caramel, and enough alcohol to keep me in bed for the entire weekend.

"Mamajuana? How on earth?" I asked, impressed. He knew I loved the cocktail, but this was our equivalent of moonshine. I didn't even ask for it in bars unless I was in a Dominican spot.

"Yeah, the bartender is Dominican and Haitian." Orlando gestured toward the tall man behind the bar, who offered a bright smile and thumbs-up. Orlando gave him the nod and then guided us toward a quieter spot in the back of the yacht. We sat down on the comfy lounge bench, both savoring our drinks and the gentle breeze, now that the sun had finally relented.

"When was the last time you had fun, Ms. V?"

"So, you're back to calling me that?" I grinned, looking at him over the rim of my glass.

"Yeah, but it's an endearment now, tú sabe."

"Oh, a little bit of Spanglish. You don't speak it much, why?"

Orlando's expression clouded, and the urge to comfort him kicked in. A second later, he was back to his easygoing self, smiling again.

"I speak it with my neighbors, but when I try to speak and practice with Ma…she doesn't like it; she was teaching Spanish to my dad when the accident happened, and now she barely uses her first language. And she never taught us Garifuna, so…yeah." He shrugged, the picture of nonchalance. He didn't fool me one bit. I reached out and held his empty hand and looked at the foaming water behind us, the motor of the yacht lulling me to relaxation.

To be in silence with someone, true comfortable silence, was a gift. I'd only had that with Miranda. Everyone else in my life, I had to be on. Even my children, because they needed me and were highly attuned to my moods. With Milton, I had always to be pleasant; he hated conflict, and because of it, I was always careful around him. At least my Dominican brava side came out to play. But here on this sultry night in Ofele Town, a few days before the bacchanal, I could be myself. With the person I least expected.

"Last time I had balls-to-the-wall fun was a happy hour turned into an all-nighter when the twins were ten years old, and my ex had them for the weekend. But then, around 1:00 a.m., Miranda and I were wasted and dancing, and I got a call from my ex that I needed to meet him at my place because he could no longer take care of the boys. I had to rush home and sober up as best as I could with coffee to put them to bed. They were so upset. They had been looking forward to their weekend with their dad." Just remembering that weekend made my blood boil. I'd never known I was so creative with insults till that night. I had whisper them so the boys wouldn't hear, but I sure got them all out.

"That doesn't sound like 'balls-to-the-wall' fun," he said gently, his face showing full understanding and not a trace of pity.

"You weren't there before 1:00 a.m.; trust me, it was balls-to-the-wall, okay."

"Okay… I trust you, so that was five years ago…" Orlando turned my hand over until he cradled it, his fingers caressed the up and down from the tip of my thumb to my wrist. The scent of the ocean and our mamajuana reminded me this was my weekend; this was my time.

"I know, I'm very much overdue. I've been focusing on wholesome activities," I said, laughing. His hand moved up my arm, trailing soft pleasure on its path.

"So, what would it take to meet the not-so-wholesome Ms. V?" Orlando crooned. I wasn't aware men could do that. Jesus Alabao. His question crept into every needy atom in my body.

"Mmm, we could start with dancing; I love dancing," I whispered back, gazing into his eyes, unwilling to show how much he affected me. When he closed his and licked a drop of the infused rum off his lush bottom lip, I squirmed on the bench.

"So, let's dance." He stood up, adjusting his slacks before offering his hand to me. I stared at where he'd adjusted and wondered if he was all grown there too. My thoughts were descending further and further into straight filth.

"Okay, let's dance." And I followed Orlando on my way to have ball-to-the-walls fun.

Seventeen

Orlando

Nothing prepared me for dancing with Trinidad Velasquez. No previous fetes, no signature moves, nor the perfect whine I thought I'd mastered readied me for the sway of her hips and ass against me.

Ms. V transformed into full Hot Gyal right before my eyes when we stepped into the dance area inside the yacht. Machel Montano tunes had replaced the steel drum band, and the area was full of couples enjoying the vibes.

We started with a slow whine, and I left a space for Jesus, not wanting to assume. Trinidad took charge, her white dress hugging her hips and behind as she inched closer to me to the beat of the music. The soca dictated our every move, and soon we were whining the yacht down, her soft ass cradling my inevitable nascent hardness.

Montano urged us to take it slow, and I did, getting lost in the goodness of feeling Trinidad so carefree and soft against me. Every few seconds, she'd bend completely over, speeding up the mesmerizing circles against me and sneaking a look over her shoulder.

"Ms. V, why you playin' with me." I groaned as she started an eight pattern up and down, up and down, until she had me hard as Mjollnir. Ten...nine...eight...seven, that was the only thing left to do. If I counted, maybe I'd be able to reduce some of the sweet tension gathering in my spine and the urge to bend her all the way down and cause a scene in this party. Because Lawd, this woman was tempting.

The song became a faster tune, and Trinidad gave me a reprieve, turning around and throwing her arms over my shoulders. Her gorgeous face glowed with excitement and the sweat we'd created together. She'd never look happier to me than this time. We both sang along to the popular soca song, bodies in tune, mimicking what I desperately wanted to happen between us.

"You were right; I was long overdue for a good time," she shouted over the music.

"I'm always right," I said smugly, holding on for dear life and my composure. I wanted so badly to kiss her.

"So, kiss me then," she taunted. I paused, wondering if she'd infiltrated my thoughts. She bit her bottom lip, inviting me to taste, and who was I to resist such an alluring invitation? We lost ourselves to the beat of the music and the taste of our lips until we were grinding together; soon, we'd end up dry humping just like earlier.

"Fuck, Trinidad, this feels so fucking right. You feel it too, don't you? You see how it could be?" I said, panting against her lips.

"I… I yes but…stability, I need…something like Milton… I—"

I kissed her again because fuck Milton, fuck stability—even though I was certain I could give everything she wanted and more. She was such a good mother, willing to sacrifice her happiness for her children because this was happiness; this was her fulfilled and living life. But Trinidad had convinced herself along the way that a staid marriage would be the answer to all her dilemmas.

I had four days to prove her wrong.

The door slammed behind me, the sound reverberating through the rental. I couldn't get enough of Trinidad. We ended up in the living area, standing in the middle of the room, my fingers pressed into her waist. The yield of her body under my fingers, the intoxicating kisses tasting of spices and rum. Everything about Trinidad had drugged me until I convinced her to leave the party, desperate for some privacy.

"Take this off," Trinidad commanded, and I rushed to remove my shirt. The rental had warmed while we were out, just enough for comfort. Soft fingers trailed over my arms, ghosting down my chest, snagging on the waistband of my pants. Trinidad paused, her entire being focused on me, and that shit hit me on the chest. My entire body trembled at the power of her attention. Her deep brown eyes kept me still as she shoved my pants down, underwear, and everything.

"I wanted to see the whole of you," she whispered, and I

reveled in the slow perusal she conducted with her eyes. Every spot she looked at tingled in attention until I felt I would burst out of my skin.

"I need you; I've been so hungry for you," Trinidad confessed.

Fuck. I needed to make sure she was whole. This was it. I needed to show her how it could be with us because words were not going to be enough, not for someone like her. Someone so secure and sure in her path in life. I admired her resilience, and I wanted to honor her bravery today with my body.

I knelt down in front of her, the scent of her earthy and ripe, ready for my worship. My mouth watered as I lifted the white cotton fabric, finding her bare underneath.

Breath whooshed out of me as her melodious laughter filled the room and poured into me.

"Sorpresa!" she said.

My hands shook, activated by the vibrations of her body as her hilarity subsided.

Somehow, I managed to wrench my eyes away from the prettiest pussy I'd ever seen, plump and wet, all ready for me. I searched her face. Last time we'd moved so fast, I hadn't had time to really enjoy the view, but this time was different. Fuck, she was beautiful. Once I paid close attention to her expression, I realized we were both truly in this together.

Bravado. That is what I found.

Her grin split wide but trembled at the corners.

"Ms. V, are you nervous?"

"Mr. Wiggins, what do you think?" Trinidad's eyebrow arched so high it infected me with her laughter.

"Oh, so we busting out the last names right now?" I showed her I, too, could arch my eyebrow with the best of them.

"Sí, if you can do it, yo también puedo." She winked, and somehow, I fell even more for her.

"Alright, Ms. V, let's see what we have here."

"Stop it; you already saw it!" she tittered. I made Ms. V titter. I'm not going to lie, my chest puffed out in pride.

"I did, but not in this type of detail; I was rushing last time. I want to slow down, enjoy, and eat my full," I whispered against her velvety, plump lips.

"Dios mío," Trinidad mumbled, and I guffawed.

"Nah, that's not my name, but I'm flattered." I couldn't help myself.

"Boy, if you don't start!" Trinidad shuffled and ghosted my finger over her mound until I found her swollen clit. My thumb took over, and soon, I found the right rhythm, evidenced by the glistening wetness growing between her thighs; the breathy moans she couldn't help but let out. Shit, her fucking scent grew stronger and more alluring, and I got closer, needing to lick her clitoris just a little. Touching her with my thumb wasn't enough anymore. I wanted to give her a different experience than last night, but damn if I didn't want to drown in her essence.

The warm nub brushing my tongue felt like heaven, and just as she gasped, I took advantage of her body, yielding to me, and I slid two fingers inside of her.

"Bendito! I can't remember the last time I was fingered," she exclaimed.

"How do you like it?" I separated myself enough from her

to watch her again. She'd dragged her dress down her cleavage, and her large chocolate nipples were on full display. And her areola… I had to squeeze tight to keep myself from orgasming too soon at the sight of the largest, most inviting areolas. I kept thinking it, but Trinidad was truly a masterpiece. Her titties with the sizable chocolate circles, diamond-hard nipples, and that little sag would ruin me. And I would gladly go to destruction if she just allowed me to keep worshiping her for the rest of our lives.

Oh shit.

A rushed mixture of cold and warmth flooded through me, the palpitations of my dick and heart in tandem as the full realization of my feelings for Trinidad settled in my head. I understood infatuation, and I understood love. But this was some other shit, some vast, indescribable feeling of fullness and emptiness all at the same time. Of craving, acceptance, and peace rolled in together. I'd admired her from afar for long, and now…. now here I was kneeling at her feet, showing her my feelings with deed and action.

Nothing had prepared me for this. Thank God for my body, which had kept the task at hand, my middle and index fingers making my dick jealous at the tight, gooey creaminess surrounding them. Trinidad's pussy became audible, the squelching sounds of my fingers indicating she was ready for one more. So, I gave it to her.

"Jesus Alabao!" She praised or cursed God, and I applied myself fully to my task. My hand rushed up her body, pinching one of her nipples, aiding her in her self-caresses as I continued to taste and discover all the ways she loved to be revered.

"Orlando, dale, por favor...dale, ya!" Trinidad's desperate pleas were barely coherent as I continued to read her like my precious Miles Morales comics until, with a last cry to the heavens, she dissolved into pure liquid heat, pouring her ecstasy onto me.

And I tasted it all.

It tasted like home.

She tasted like paradise.

She tasted like every day after today.

And that is when I realized I was in love with Trinidad Caridad Velasquez Rodriguez.

Eighteen

Trinidad

SOS text messages were frequent back in the day after my divorce. Miranda and I had our drill down whenever I made a stupid move and linked up with someone not good for me or my heart. I'd text her, and she'd come to pick the kids up and take them to her mom, then return with all the supplies we needed for a day of rest sprinkled with some tough love.

Heathen felt like a very hard word, but for a couple of years after my divorce, I searched for myself in different ways, and some of them were more slutty than others. There was nothing wrong with that. I discovered what I truly liked in bed and what I needed in a partner, and I enjoyed the hell out of my Hot Girl days. But then I hung my jersey and searched for the type of family and stability I deserved. Since then, the heathen days and amazing sex declined in quality and consistency. Nothing to do with anything but myself. Because I'd stopped prioritizing my pleasure for the sake of everything else in my life.

Now I'd decided to dip my feet in the heathen pool, and I'd come back with more than I'd bargained.

Hence the SOS text.

The sun had barely come out of the sky, so I prepared myself for the curses accompanying this call. Miranda hated to wake up early. Propping up my laptop in front of me as I sat in bed, I answered the video call, a frazzled Miranda on the other end.

"Girl, SOS text? What the hell happened? Did you sleep with a stranger at that party last night? Why the everlasting fuck are you awake right now? Shouldn't you be sleeping the good sex away?" Miranda's bleary face greeted me on the screen.

"No! Girl, what do you mean a stranger? What do you think this is?"

"A trip for you to enjoy and get your freak on, and I'm glad you're applying yourself to the assignment, but, girl, it's six thirty on a Saturday; you lucky I love you."

"I can't sleep." I shook my head, remembering how a fantastically naked, strong Orlando carried me up the stairs and tucked me in bed, declining anything to alleviate his hardness but a steamy good night kiss that made my pussy purr in protest. She wanted more, and I did too. "He made me squirt," I whispered at the camera.

"Oh shit, hold on. Let me turn on the light." After some shuffling, amber light brightened the screen and a more composed Miranda returned to the frame. "We are talking about Orlando, right?"

"Miranda, yes, I am a reformed heathen, not a careless heathen," I huffed.

"Gyal, don't yuh start we me. So, he made you squirt… I knew that boy had it in him. Good for him." Miranda nodded, impressed, completely missing the point. I waved my hands in the frame, demanding her focus, my heart tripping as I remembered every decadent detail from last night. Usually, with SOS meetings, I'd regale Miranda with all the details of my encounter, but oddly, I didn't want to do that right now.

"So spill, girl, tell me!"

"I…it felt more. You know? We haven't even had intercourse yet…well, I guess fingering is intercourse, but never mind that. I just feel like… I feel like…it was more. It felt emotional. It felt like I was betraying Milton."

"Here you go with Milton, who cares about that square? Girl, has he even called you?"

Miranda's question soured my already fragile mood, causing my anxiety to increase.

"No, he's busy with his colleagues. But you know he wants something serious now so maybe I shouldn't be leading Orlando on, I think this is more serious to him than me."

"Really? Are you sure about that?" Miranda questioned, her no-nonsense attitude usually a balm. Today, it was making my stomach cramp.

"I don't know, I mean, I… I was in the moment, but it felt very intimate; I wanted… I want more."

"So get more. Milton is not the end-all-be-all. He is a good man, but he doesn't need to be *your* good man. Not every good man on the face of the earth means marriage material. Expand your criteria, girl."

"I have, I did, and what did I end up with? A broken heart and single parenthood. I fucking knew my ex wasn't the right fit, but I fell in love with him anyway. And Orlando is a good man, but he is *young*, Miranda; he still has a lot of life to live."

"Are you about to tell me…that that man who cares for his entire family is not ready for something serious?"

My stomach flipped again, and I broke eye contact with Miranda.

"Because everything you've told me of what he's shared in this trip tells me he is right up your alley in the commitment and responsibility area, and it seems that he also fulfills your heathen needs too; when was the last time you squirted, miss?"

"This is not what I called for," I complained.

"Sure was. 'Cause you knew I would give it to you straight and without any fluff. I'm not saying you need to end things with Milton. I'm also not saying Orlando is your Prince Charming. I'm saying you need to stop looking for one-size-fits-all solutions and decide what your priorities and true needs are. When you discover that, then you'll be able to figure all of this out. In the meantime, girl, keep squirting!"

She was wrong for that last statement, but right at the same time. I had called for a reality check.

"I have some processing to do," I confessed, and she nodded along.

"No shit…listen, I'm going back to bed."

"Hold up, before you do, can you wake up the twins,

please? In the most loud manner possible? I have some chores for them today. They best not get comfortable thinking they did this prank and everything is alright."

"Girl, I doubt they think that; they've both been on their best behavior and very solicitous while staying here. But I'll wake them up, as long as they don't wake me up after I go back to bed."

"Deal. Thanks, girly. I miss you; you should be here with me."

"Next year, we'll plan it accordingly. Love you, boo." She blew me a kiss, and the screen went dark.

Before anything else I shot a text to the boys letting them know I wanted them to clean Miranda's kitchen, living room, and the bathroom they were using top to bottom. Just as Miranda said, their response was quick and solicitous, which meant they understood that the consequences of their actions were still ongoing.

My chest ached; I hated being at odds with my sons, but they needed to learn. Somewhere along the way, they'd gotten too comfortable with the empowerment I fostered, and I sat for a while with it. My solution to it all—Milton, marriage, a strong male presence at home and outside the home—I turned it all around in my head until I built up an appetite and a slight headache.

Needing time for myself, I checked work emails and had a few video meetings. Even though it was Saturday, it was still a workday for me, and with the fictitious tournament canceled, I had to prioritize some tasks I'd put on the back burner. By the time I stopped, it was late afternoon, and my stomach and head united in protest until I replenished.

After a lengthy shower and my skincare routine, I made my way downstairs to see what Orlando and his friends were up to. The laughter and voices floated up the steps even before I turned the corner from my bedroom, and I froze, riveted by the conversation at hand.

"Nah, son, this man got bread. We ended up all sharing one hotel room; he got a whole house for himself," Trevor complained.

"Listen, I don't blame him; look at his guest. We would have been in the way my man. I can't fault the game. That's why that job you got at the animation spot is sweet as fuck," Desmond said with a chuckle.

"Y'all stay counting each other's coins. It's weird," Grace said, and I smiled at her timely comment. I wasn't convinced about Trevor and Desmond, but they were not my friends so I had no say. But it seemed they didn't understand Orlando well.

"I told y'all I wanted to do some sightseeing first, and you fools couldn't take additional days off from work 'cause you both stay missing work. So yeah. And I needed some space to think," Orlando explained. I sucked my teeth; he didn't owe them, not one lick of explanation.

"Man, you ain't thinking about nothing; you just were trying to curve us. I see how it is," Trevor complained.

"This is your problem. You think the world revolves around you. I did need some time to think. I'm pretty sure I got into law school." Orlando's rough tone told me he'd crossed over to that space where his frustration couldn't be contained by his people-pleasing tendencies. My chest ached again. Twice this morning for the men I cherished while they navigated difficult experiences.

My stomach growled, and my heartbeat tripled. The men I cherished? How had Orlando joined those ranks?

"You're gonna be a suit? Get the fuck out of here. Why you going that route? Man, you love your job!" Desmond interjected, and for once, I sensed genuine care in his answer.

"Orlando, for real? Why didn't you?... Let me guess, you were trying to work it out yourself?" Grace said, hurt, coating every word.

At this point, it was too much for my Dominican temper to sit on the sidelines. Stomping down the stairs, I made my presence known well before getting to the last step.

"So y'all feel you're so supportive that you can berate Orlando for his choices now?" I asked, forgetting myself for a minute. A red haze clouded the room, and the surprised faces of everyone but Orlando gaped at me.

Orlando, though? His frustration and helplessness oozed out of him, which, in turn, increased the volume of my anger.

"Do you have any big-time responsibilities, Trevor? Like do you take care of a child or a baby momma, or your family?" Crossing my arms over my chest, I awaited his answer with a saccharine smile.

"Uh, nah, I still live with my parents, but I contribute!" Clearly, this was a sore subject 'cause that "I contribute" spoke volumes.

"And you, Desmond, when was the last time you called Orlando to check in on him and his caretaking duties?" Desmond had the grace to look down, then faced me again, contrition and acknowledgment clear in his expression.

"Trinidad is right, my bad, my dude. I've gotten used to you keeping things in, but I could do a better job at checking in from time to time." Desmond nodded, and Trevor's head swiveled between Orlando and Desmond with clear disbelief.

"Nah, but we hang out all the time; shit, he could have said something!" Trevor gestured at Orlando, who shook his head.

"You ain't lying, but when is there space for that? Whenever I bring up anything that is not girls, shooting the shit, sports, or anything like that, what do you say?" Orlando asked.

"Ain't nobody got time to be a grown-up," Grace, Desmond, and Orlando all recited at the same time.

Trevor sucked his teeth, his frustration escalating. He paced back and forth to the living area.

"Alright, alright, y'all have a point. I gotta work on that. Growing up…that shit scares me. And you have been doing that shit for so long, Orlando…it's….intimidating," Trevor confessed.

"Finally." Grace threw her hands up. "Some communication between us all. It took Ms. Trinidad to come and set us up for success. We've been friends for years. The friendship is and can be deeper than what we allow it to be," Grace said with so much fervor, that my temper finally subsided.

Somehow, these young people were trying to figure out themselves and each other. I remember how that felt. And I had kids already. Now I wondered how much my ex and I weren't communicating—how much we were keeping inside. Trevor's confession had triggered some long-lost memories of my ex, joking that he couldn't keep up with me and my dreams. I'd always dismissed those comments, but now? Maybe I should have allowed him to speak more about that to me.

"Fuck, I know we're here for fun, but this feels good. Talking to y'all feels good. I have other shit I need to share with you, but we can do that after we return, we can focus on the fun now," Orlando said with a smile, reverting back to where he was more comfortable, but I could sense his excitement. I hope he saw that his friends were truly wanting to support him.

"Yeah, that's alright." Grace rolled her eyes and mouthed at me, "boys," as Trevor dabbed up Orlando, and they hugged as if all was forgiven. Trevor and Orlando had a brief exchange while embracing, their words low and just for each other, and the weight that had settled on my chest lightened considerably. When Desmond pulled Orlando for a hug, doing that back-pounding thing men loved to do, Orlando drew back misty-eyed, everything inside melted. Without any thought, I was soon beside him, my hand in his. Warmth, support, and safety. Want, pleasure, and yearning. Orlando didn't need to say a word, because I felt the same.

Orlando bent over, and the soft touch of his lips on my cheek warmed my insides and calmed all my troubles.

"Are you ready to go to the fair?" he asked loud enough for everyone to hear. With everything happening since this morning, I forgot our plans for today. But I was ready—more than ready—to embrace this day and every day to come in Ofele.

"I am." I smiled and hoped that he understood that I was ready for that and more.

"Thanks, Ms. V...that shit was sexy as fuck; you can defend me like that any day." The caress of his warm, minty breath on my ear caused a shiver all over me.

"Thank you for letting me live out loud and be me," I replied, getting lost in his gaze.

His friends shuffled out of the rental, telling us they'd wait for us outside, finally giving us privacy.

"Are you good?" he asked, checking on my well-being even with all of this happening.

"I am. I'm really, really good."

And for the first time in a long time. I meant it.

Nineteen

Orlando

The way I kept myself balanced and positive all these years was by building my walls up enough that no one could bother my peace. But building up those walls meant happiness had a harder time reaching me, so I lived in a perpetual state of contentment. Having the twins and their mother in my life had slowly started to change that. A superhero putting his guard down for people to find out his real identity. A lonely man, realizing he was, in fact, lonely.

Trinidad, with her fiery temper and beautiful heart, kept chipping at that this weekend. My fucking face hurt from grinning like a fool all the way to the fair, and when she placed her hand in mind after I paid for our entrance, that happiness took over everything and everywhere.

The fairgrounds were located on the outskirts of Ofele, at one of their public parks near the beach. A sea of white tents, rides, and food trucks transformed the lush green space into a feast for the senses. A thrum of excitement vibrated through the crowds as revelers chatted with each other, flitting in and out of tents selling an assortment of Caribbean souvenirs, flags, handicrafts, and other services. The sun blazed, even though it was early evening, but the ocean breeze acted as the perfect foil for the heat.

Hand in hand, Trinidad and I ambled through the stands, while Trevor, Desmond, and Grace went to the rides.

"Are you sure you don't want to go with them?"

"Do you like rides?"

"No. Why would I put myself through that type of stress— my job is a roller coaster already," Trinidad confessed with a smirk.

"Do you like what you do?" I asked her, unable to take my eyes off her. Trinidad glowed radiantly in a short pink romper with some type of frills that enhanced her hips and ass. She'd started glistening due to the heat, especially between her cleavage, and I wanted to bend over and taste all over her salty skin. But honestly, that was just me being horny.

What captivated me was her eyes. They were full of joy, a joy I'd only seen when the twins had made her proud about something. Watching her now, understanding how the happiness filling me up could be similar to her joy, had me wanting to confess everything I felt for her. But I wasn't about to spook her.

There was Milton, after all.

"Wow, mister, what was that?" Trinidad asked, looking down at herself. "What do I have on me?"

"Nothing but beauty," I replied. Damn, that line was tired as fuck. My face grew hot as Trinidad guffawed at my pickup line.

"You're too much, and I really like it." The twinkle in her eyes, the hand trailing over the exposed skin of her breasts, her bottom lip glistening as she wetted it...yeah, this woman had me down bad.

"You're trying to kill me, woman." I pulled her aside, and we kept walking and chatting about everything and nothing. Trinidad explained more about her work and why she loved it.

"See, I get to be part of people's most cherished memories. It's so rewarding. It's exhausting, too, though. Because people never listen, but that's where my feisty personality comes into play," Trinidad said as we entered a stand with easels decorating every corner of the space.

A young girl, maybe eighteen, with long locks, light brown skin, and beautiful eyes, sat on a stool. An easel in front of her, lost in her craft. Her style was photorealistic, and her paintings were in oil or acrylic.

"Hello!" Trinidad called her attention.

"Greetings! Yuh good?" The girl sounded like my grandmother.

"Are you from Jamaica?" I asked. I was fascinated by her art; many of the depictions were of anime and superheroes, all with a twist. She'd retold stories in her paintings with a Caribbean sense. One painting was of a boy getting into a Spider-Man costume, but the colors of his suit were green, yellow, and black. Another easel had a woman controlling the weather with locs flying all around her as she floated over an island.

"Yes! You too…you look like dem Sewells in St. Mary."

"Yeah, my grandparents come from there."

"I see dat man. That's home six months a year. The other six months, I come to the States to sell my art." She nodded at the piece in front of her, a little boy holding a plantain by the beach while watching two superheroes fight in the distance.

"What's that?"

"The battle between the modern and the old," she simply said and kept painting.

"Have you ever considered doing animation work? I mean, the art for animations?" I asked her, my excitement mounting. Trinidad wandered off to one of the corners of the tent, but I didn't miss the grin on her face.

"Animation? How yuh mean?" the woman asked, finally placing her full attention on me.

"Anime, cartoons, that. I mean you clearly know your superheroes and comics." I gestured around.

"Mmm." She singsonged, lost in thought. "Nevah thought about it, but I'd be willing to explore." She nodded finally.

"That's fantastic!" This felt better than when I found that copy of Ultimate Fallout 4 in a store in the Bronx a few years ago.

"A'ight man, calm down." The girl chuckled. In the corner, I heard another smothered laugh.

"Sorry, I…just you are great, you have an amazing eye, and there is a lot you could do in that arena. Here, take my information. Why don't you call me next week, and we can set a more formal meeting?" I pulled out my phone, found my business card app, and flashed her the QR code. She frowned at the phone, then searched for her own device and faced it to mine until she captured the information.

"A'ight man. My name is Lulu. See there? That's my IG, you can look for me there. I'll call you, though. This sounds like something I might do," she said, back to her easel, ready to dismiss me.

"Sorry, Lulu, how much for this one?" Trinidad asked. It was a small canvas—a little hut, and a woman standing outside with two children holding her hands, all dressed in the Bajan colors. The woman had a flowing cape behind her.

"Dat one is $350, but for yuh, I give you $250," Lulu said.

"Oh, I wish I could get it. I didn't budget for any big spending this weekend, but you said we could find you online, right? Maybe next month I can hit you up, will you still be in the States?"

"Nah, man, this my last event before I head back to Jamaica. The heat too much for me. I live here in Ofele when I come and travel as needed. But I can always ship from JA if you like."

Trinidad and Lulu exchanged contact information, and we walked out of the stand hand in hand. Somehow, I needed to to buy that art for her without her realizing it. I wanted to feel her joy, for her to remember this day forever.

"So, you really love that job, huh?" Trinidad asked as we exited the ice cream truck line, both with Grape-Nuts waffle cones in our hands. The cold creamy concoction melted in my mouth, alleviating some of the heat of the night.

"It's my dream come true." I looked down at her with a big grin, and her eyes softened at the sight.

"So why law school, Orlando? You can do this instead. You are so good at it! Even during vacation, your eyes don't rest. Lulu is amazing, and this will be a great opportunity for her!"

"I hear you, but...see, this is a great-paying job if it was only me. I can grow in the company, but what I could make in three years after law school would take me at least five or six years in my career. Then, there are the health benefits a law firm could provide me. And this was my parents' dream for me, at least that's what Ma has told me in her good moments. My father always said I was always argumentative when young and I'd make a great lawyer."

"Argumentative? Wow, I guess I don't see it." Trinidad took a slow lick of her ice cream that had me going from soft to chubby. I was lost for her.

"Yeah, I have it in me; I just choose peace now."

"Oh, maybe you choose peace too often? I mean, I see how hard you do for your siblings and your mother, which, by the way, how are they?"

The topic got me from chubby to soft real quick.

This morning, I'd woken up to frantic calls from my brothers asking me what to do because my mother was again fighting them about the medication. There was not much I could do about it from afar, and the calls continued through the day, my brothers' attitudes and tones escalating. Both of them clearly felt put upon for having to deal with our mother in one of her hard days, but this was a regular day for me.

The fact that they couldn't take one for the team and deal

without calling and texting me had pissed me off, and after Trinidad showed up for me, I decided to put them both on Do Not Disturb. I'd deal with the repercussions later, but for now, I wanted to be present. As present as I asked her to be. I explained all of this to her and she gifted me with a brilliant smile.

"I know that's right!" She bumped against me in congratulations, her soft body making me harden again. Fuck. She was right. We didn't need a roller coaster. This was a thrill ride, and I didn't want to get down.

"I don't want to be the bearer of bad news, but that sounds like you, an old lady."

"Boy!" She kissed her lips, some of the ice cream smeared over, and I couldn't help it; I bent down and tasted her. The cold ice cream warmed between our lips, and our tongues entangled, wet, and desperate. I hadn't kissed her the whole day, and that shit hadn't felt right. Finally, my hand could grab her waist and slide down her lush hip to her plump ass, which I squeezed, making her giggle against my mouth. That sound made me even harder. Trinidad noticed my rock-hard dick and pressed against it, making it ten times a problem or a blessing, depending on perspective.

"Ms. V, you playing games when I can't do much about it," I growled.

"Who said we couldn't do anything about it?" she taunted.

"You don't play fair," I said, then chased her mouth, the taste of sweet Trinidad intoxicating.

"Oh, I never do; I play to win." She held my hand, and we navigated the crowd, getting closer to the edge of the fair.

"Where are we going?" I asked her, not really caring because wherever I was going with her, it would be good.

"You'll see," she said.

We turned the corner to find a trailer attached to a fun house. They'd painted it with colors of the different Caribbean flags. Most of the revelers were around the other rides and tents, the fun house not being top of mind to most of the crowd.

We paid our entrance and walked in together, loud soca played inside as we navigated the different sections and tunnels. The mirrored tunnel was my favorite, each mirror distorting our images. Trinidad made funny faces, her boisterous laughter floating above the music and carrying me away to a high I hadn't felt in a long time.

This was happiness.

This was it.

One of the last sections was a labyrinth with neon lighting and rotating walls.

"You want to play?" Trinidad asked mischievously, her body heat so close, I took advantage of her proximity, holding on to her soft hips and pressing her against me. She ground against me, her low moan letting me know I wasn't alone in this. Trinidad was affected too.

"With you, I want everything," I confessed, hoping that the music and the playfulness would mask how true the statement was.

Trinidad slid her body against mine, awakening my skin with every touch. Again, her hand held mine, and she found us a dead end, darker than the rest of the tunnel due to the minimal neon lighting.

"This is a false turn…are you comfortable with public sex?" Trinidad asked. Before I could open my mouth, her head bowed, and she gracefully dropped to her knees.

Air, I fucking needed air and a bag to breathe in. Shit, this woman was going to obliterate me.

Unable to talk, the sound of my zipper opening over the soca answered instead. Sweet relief coursed through my veins as I released the pressure of my hardness. The humid summer evening air caressed my weighty balls. Big brown eyes with pretty eyelashes blinked up at me as I pulled my dick out, the heaviness telling me this one would go quickly. Shit, I wasn't ashamed.

Nothing had prepared me for the sweltering suction of Trinidad's mouth. The tremors started in my feet, running over my legs until I felt faint. The pink tongue of hers shined brightly under the neon lights as she dexterously licked and sucked until my entire dick was engulfed, and she took all of me until the head of my dick received the warmest of hugs.

Then she swallowed.

And that is all I could take.

Not even five minutes. Probably not even three.

Who am I kidding? It was less than two, and everything tightened: my back, my legs, my chest. I saw stars. I stopped breathing for a minute. I…fuck.

Having Trinidad Velasquez's wet, hot mouth on my dick meant everything. I'd leveled up to the highest degree. This wasn't her accepting my "eager" infatuation and horniness;

this was her giving me pleasure. Wanting me to come for her. Wanting my pleasure dripping down the corners of her mouth as a proof of the force of my affection and regard.

Whatever she needed I would give to her, and I would figure out a way to show her that we belonged together.

I just needed these days in Ofele to make it happen.

Twenty

Trinidad

How easy it is to forget a side of you when you put it in a neat little box to never be explored anymore.

Ms. V exploded out of the box ready to play and with that a legion of fiery emotions, all vehemently taking over. There was nothing but for me to experience the journey, be present, and embrace every moment. Now all that was left was to get my sympathetic nervous system to get it together because the urge to retreat after my night with Orlando at the fair had become stronger than El Cuco dragging you off to bed during a bad nightmare.

The craving to sneak out of my room and into his that night kept me tossing and turning, waking up in tangled wet sheets. The wetness was mostly my sweat. Mostly.

After a shower and changing the sheets, I gathered my

courage and made my way downstairs, where Orlando stood, making breakfast.

With no shirt on.

At this point, the man might as well carry me to his bed and put us both out of our misery. All of me wanted to be so close to him, mind and spirit. Feeling like this hadn't been the plan. The plan had been to get my freak on and go. Fuck, if I'd said that out loud, Orlando would have never let me forget it.

"What are you laughing about?" He turned around, placing a plate of scrambled eggs with veggies and sausage on the kitchen island. A cup of steamy cafe con leche accompanied the meal. The twins had gotten much better at helping out around the house since their mentoring with Orlando, but I hadn't had anyone make me breakfast in a long time. Maybe since I left my parents' home. My chuckles subsided, and a pebble lodged itself in my throat. That could be the only explanation for the tightness in my chest and the lack of air through my lungs. It couldn't be anything else.

"If I tell you, you'll call me old," I managed to say.

"But you're old; we already established that," he said, sitting on the other side of the counter, his stare caressing every part of me he could see.

"Boy, you can't be looking at me like that," I complained. Savory goodness coated my tongue at the first bite of the breakfast scramble, and I used my appetite as a shield.

"What do you want to do today?" Orlando called my bluff, ignoring my cheeks full of eggs. Now what was I supposed to do? Fast chewing my way through the mouthful, I took a sip of the coffee to clear my still-tight throat.

"I have to go to Delilah to get something to wear for that event tonight. I hadn't brought any fete attire," I explained.

"Alright, do you want me to go with you?"

Before the words finished, my head was already moving.

"No, I think you should hang out with your friends today; it was what you came for...well, besides finding your daughter. Any calls?" I asked, moaning when I got a particularly delicious bite. The man really could cook. I wanted to throw my panties at him, but that would send the incorrect message.

"No. Not yet. Are you sure you're good with me hanging with them? I prefer to stay with you," Orlando said in his husky voice, doing things to me.

"I know, and I do too. But all of this, although wonderful, is overwhelming." I gestured between us. "I thought it would be this fun weekend escape, but I think, at least for me, it feels more than that. And I have to sit with that for a while. On my own. But we have tonight, and we will have a good time at the fete."

"Thanks. I know that must have been difficult to share. Not gonna lie, it is feeling big to me too." Orlando's hand went to his chest, and as he rubbed in the middle, my chest released some of its tightness.

"Okay, then, we have a plan. We go do our own thing, and tonight the night is ours." My face warmed as we both grinned like loons.

"I cannot wait."

"So, how many businesses do you own?" I asked Delilah. Walls of dark wood and plum velvet with colorful outfits surrounded us. The small boutique, called Delilah's Fashion, had a variety of dresses for different occasions, the perfect location to find a dress for tonight's fete. The giddy teenager rush coursing through me had overtaken any other sensible thought. Orlando, before leaving with his friends, had pushed me into a corner in the living area and proceeded to kiss away any nerves taking over. Still overwhelmed with everything moving so fast, I was glad to be here, even if it had to be with Delilah.

"Oh, we own a couple more; we have a mini-mart, and a bike rental, another bakery. You know." Delilah waved her hand as if it was all inconsequential.

"Was Mikey ready to build all of that with you...or have you had to pull extra weight?" I asked, intrigued by their relationship. Now more than ever, with Milton not having reached out once, and Orlando so...so everything, I was starting to wonder if my relationship-building assessment was incorrect.

"Girl, he was the drive behind all of this. I've been trying to lean into my soft girl era since my divorce. But he makes sure all the financials are tight, and we have managers for all the places, so we get to enjoy each other. It provides us with the comfortable living I've wanted. And, girl, we travel—a lot."

"But the age difference, don't you worry?" Because I worried. There are things I learned in this last decade that were essential to my healing.

Responsibility, commitment, and compromise were keys to my success as an adult. Leaving some of my childish ways behind had been hard but necessary. Leaving the partying behind felt like the hardest thing to do. I lost a part of me, but it was what my twins needed.

They needed someone always ready to adult, not a mommy who had fun sometimes and was extra tired on a Sunday morning, so that breakfast was only porridge that I had planned ahead to make sure they had food if I slept in. They deserved to wake up to the smell of sizzling bacon and freshly made golden bakes, their favorite Bajan breakfast.

They deserved all of that and I had needed to realize my time to shine was done. This new era was my mom's era, my giver era, my nurturer's era.

So, I did worry about the age difference. Orlando deserved to live his selfish era right now, and it didn't seem that it was what he was doing right now, and me adding to the mountain of responsibilities felt selfish.

"About what? Look at this? What do you think?" She pulled out a mustard-yellow dress with a simple draped cleavage and a high thigh slit.

"It's my favorite color," I marveled and imagined how the fabric would cling to every curve and how Orlando would hang onto my every move. I needed to have it.

"Then try it on. You look like a medium, maybe, but those hips look like a large. Let's see how this medium works!" The dressing room had a comfortable sofa, which Delilah commandeered as she shooed me into one of the stalls.

"I don't worry about the age difference because Mikey is an adult. He made decisions the same as I did," Delilah said, her usual jolly tone absent.

"Not that, I mean…we know what it was to be their age.

I remember being a mother and wondering how to do it all, and I had so many moments I wished I could do things a regular twenty-five-year-old could do." My therapist would be very proud of me, voicing my anxiety. Giving it a name and reason wasn't something easy to do for me. But as I started to imagine any type of future with Orlando, I began to see how mismatched our futures loomed on our horizons.

"Again, that is a decision made; you cannot make the decision for anyone by trying to guide the process and withholding your feelings. At least it didn't work for me when I did it. Damn Mikey." Delilah chuckled, lost in her memories. "He came to my house every morning and would sit on the porch until I came out, and we would sit down and talk. He'd ask me. 'Okay, fine, what's the excuse now?' And I would tell him what was bothering me, and we would talk it out. It took a while and more action than words, but eventually, I realized I wanted to choose happiness. And I did."

The dress draped me perfectly the soft material allowing the air to circulate. That must be why goose bumps erupted on my arms and legs. It couldn't be Delilah's words.

Delilah's gasp when I modeled the dress was all the validation I required to buy it on the spot.

"No, it's yours. It truly is. I mean, I couldn't sell that to you. It was made to be worn by you." There was goofy Delilah again, all googly-eyed. "Orlando will fall head over heels in love with you tonight if he hasn't already."

My temperature rose, my chest tightening again at her words. For once, I didn't feel like rolling my eyes at her insistence about the two of us. For once, I grinned, and holding hands, we squealed like little girls talking about their first infatuation. And for once, I allowed myself to imagine a full future with Orlando, even while my stomach dropped at all the repercussions that would come from the fantasy.

"Are you sure you want to go out?" Orlando asked, stifling a groan. Good, I'd put my locs in a high bun, moisturized each crack and crevice in my body until every inch of my skin glowed, and applied light makeup that had the unenviable task of standing up to the sweltering humidity of Ofele. Strappy sandals and my clutch completed the look. All I required was liquid courage to make it through the night.

"You good, Ms. V?" Orlando waited for me on the ground floor wearing tan slacks and a deep blue shirt opened at the top. If I followed my instinct and dropped a kiss where his pulse vibrated, we'd never leave the rental. Instead, I approached him, my anxiety washing away after the touch of his skin against mine. The support I'd been searching for my entire life resided between his arms, in the spot right above his chest, in his eyes as they gazed at me with so much emotion I choked up.

"I'm excellent," I confessed, the admission triggering a burst of activity in my stomach. The damn butterflies, which I'd been doing my level best to ignore, flapped their damn wings around until they left me breathless.

"If you're doing excellent, then I'm doing excellent."

Orlando navigated Ofele as if he'd lived in the town since birth. The venue for this fete was an open-air club. A hut by the beach, the wooden structure painted in purple, green, white, and yellow with exotic flowers and fauna depicted on the column of the open design. The structure had a surrounding second level where tables and chairs made up the VIP area. A large bar traversed the side facing the sea, the waves the perfect background to the busy bartenders taking care of the thirsty fete goers.

The breeze had finally won the fight against the constant heat of the weekend, the scent of salt and ocean reminding all the revelers this was a night of bacchanal. The beat of my heart synched up with the bass of the sound system as the DJ played the latest carnival hits. We paid our entrance and we made our way up to the VIP. Thanks to Mikey, we had a prime spot close to the DJ and close to the upstairs bar.

"Yo!! Y'all made it finally!" Trevor rushed toward us before we could make it to the table. Scrawny arms surrounded me, and his strong cologne suffocated me as he surprised me with a tight hug. "Thanks for making us see."

He detached himself from me, and I turned around, wondering what I had missed.

"We had a heart-to-heart during lunch today; I told them everything. Just, you know, everything. The things that were easy for me to share with you but not with them. The way my brothers are acting like damn fools and can't even take care of my mother for a long weekend without fussing. The fact that I don't know if law school is the right answer, but I don't feel like I have a choice."

Orlando's words floated confidently above the commotion of our group. And his eyes searched mine for something, something I was desperately afraid to give him.

"Oh."

"Yup. Oh. Thank you." He bent, and his soft lips kissed my forehead.

Jesus, Bendito Alabao! How was I supposed to wait until later to jump on this man? How was I supposed to keep my emotions in check the whole night? I had all the answers but didn't want to say them aloud. Not yet, not when the night was young, and our group was lively and joy filled every cell of my body.

After all the hellos, Orlando settled me on his lap, the music vibrating between the two of us, elevating my aware-ness of him. Every breath he took, every time I slid on his lap, and he settled me again, the hardness building below. I let it all flow. The fete grew in crowd and noise as the night progressed, and the drinks flowed on our table. Tonight, I wanted to be with him, skin to skin, nothing but our sweat between us. I didn't want doubts or tomorrow to intercede.

"I want you inside me tonight." I bent over and whispered in his ear. His soft earlobe tempted me, and Ms. V took over, my tongue giving him a lick. The groan I received in return was all I needed.

"Is that you, Trinidad??" A loud voice startled me out of my interlude with a very hard Orlando who settled me firmly over his dick so that his erection would not be visible. The woman in front of me looked very familiar with a long blond wig, and a dress that exposed more than it covered, her abun-dant curves in perfect display.

"Girl, is me, Milton's coworker! I thought you'd be in

the Poconos with them crew that is always trying to kiss the bosses' asses! Y'all separated?"

Under me, everything went still. Inside of me, everything exploded in pure chaos.

This was one of Milton's coworkers, Roxanna. I'd met her during their holiday party last year, and we'd hit it off, keeping each other company while Milton mingled with the leadership and left me on my own.

"Oh hey, girl, hey." I stiffened on top of Orlando, mirroring his stillness. His friends gaped at us; their stares so intense I had to shut down the heat coming off them.

"So, this is your new man?" she asked excitedly. Milton had told me after leaving me on my own for two hours not to chat too much with Roxanna because she was a gossip. It was only a matter of time before this got to Milton in New York. The lack of sudden air and the absence of the flapping in my stomach kept me rooted in place, uncertain of how to proceed.

"Girl, don't you worry, Milton is a whole bore. This looks more like you! I mean, sure, he always talks about you in the office and stuff, but you probably saw through it, it's all about status with that one…" Roxanna chattered without requiring any involvement from me. Thank God, because every word she said settled in the pit of my stomach until I wanted to rush out and get some air. And I was already outside.

Get a grip, Trinidad!

"Sorry, girl, my boyfriend is looking for me, but I hope to see you tomorrow! What band are y'all with?"

"Oh, we are with Power by Four." Grace came to my rescue, clearly reading my discomfort.

"Oh! Great! I'm in the green section! See you tomorrow!" Roxanna floated away just as she'd come, leaving chaos and destruction behind her.

"Are you okay—" Orlando hadn't finished his sentence, and my legs sprang into action, getting up from the only place I wanted to be but knew I couldn't indulge in.

"I…listen, I'm getting tired." I grinned, hoping he would allow me this little lie, this one lie, so I could escape and deal with all the turmoil inside.

"Trinidad, let me take you home." He stood up, not allowing me the space I needed.

"No, you should stay with your friends. I can catch a ride back to the rental. I will meet you there."

Orlando's concern seeped into my veins, not letting me close him off completely. For once, my protective walls failed me, the same as they did with my ex-husband. Somehow, my feelings were entangled with his, and I couldn't figure out where my unease started or finished.

"No, that is not safe; I'll take you."

"Orlando, please… I… I'll wait up for you. We will talk. Let me just…let me just go for now," I pleaded, my pride bruised at how much this man could get me to concede.

"I…fuck. Okay. But please call me with you arrive. And I'll give you an hour. An hour, Trinidad. Okay?" I nodded, knowing he wanted it. I had to figure myself out before the hour, dreading it would not be enough time.

Twenty-One

Orlando

An hour to wait to talk to Trinidad felt too long. The vibe of the night disintegrated with her departure, all my worries flooding in behind. I hadn't told Trinidad about my feelings because her readiness to speak on these topics seemed tepid at best. For me to open up and be vulnerable the way I'd practiced this weekend, I needed to feel secure. That security that surrounded us yesterday in the fun house deserted me, and everything loomed uncertain.

The music blasted in my ears, my heart and head hurting, as I sat next to my friends. Should I go to her now and ask for a talk? No, she'd been adamant about needing time; encroaching on her way of getting her head straight was an asshole move.

"You are overthinking things right now." Grace's warm whisper shook me out of my dark thoughts.

"What do you mean?"

"I can see how you are there convincing yourself this is not for you." She shrugged. "Come, I'll walk you to your car." She stood up, palm extended. Trevor and Desmond stared at me, and then both nodded.

"You good, man, go have that talk," Desmond said.

The fuck was happening? This wouldn't have happened a week ago. Trevor would have made fun of me wanting to leave, and Desmond would have sat there looking unbothered. Just a conversation today and Trinidad's words yesterday pushed our friendship to a different space. There was still more for me to open up about, but damn, it felt good to be vulnerable with my friends.

Grace's small stature was no impediment for her to commandeer space through the crowd until we made it to the parking lot. I swear the woman had the presence of a six-four offensive tackle.

"So…what are you gonna do?" Grace asked me once we both got into my rental car.

"She's not ready." I shook my head. Saying the words aloud hurt my chest.

"How do you know if you don't ask her?" Grace opened the windows, the melody of the crashing waves eerily similar to the goings-on in my gut.

How do I know if I don't ask her? Asking her exposed me. A talk meant opening to her, carving out my insides for her to inspect and decide if they were valuable enough for her or not. It was better if I kept it all inside, and then when the disappointment came, I could walk away with my dignity intact.

A tiny burst of pain exploded on my bicep, the force pushing me against the car door.

"Stop it. Think different. You've been doing that this week. Think different!" Grace's sharp reminder penetrated the fog of disappointment, clearing the way for other thoughts. Was I really going to let Trinidad and me scare ourselves away from something that could be great? Not just great; great was not enough of a word to describe what we could be. We could be as epic as Luke Cage and Jessica Jones if we got out of our own way.

"Fuck, you're right. How are you so wise?" I stared at her, hoping she saw the gratitude brimming out of me.

"'Cause someone has to be, in this group of obtuse people. It took Trinidad for you to open up and trust us a little more, for Trevor to realize his immaturity wasn't letting our friendship evolve, for Desmond to…well, you know Desmond. I'm thankful for her, and I'm rooting for you both."

"Even if she's ten years my senior and has two kids?"

"Is that a concern for you? Because I didn't think so." The soca music floated from the Big Hut toward the car, complementing the silence between us.

The silence was all Grace needed to know I agreed with her. Brandon and Brian, as an addition to my romantic life, might not have been what I had envisioned for myself, but I took their existence as the blessing they were. Trinidad was an amazing woman, and the boys only added to the gift that she was. But that wasn't enough; Trinidad had her own thoughts about the age difference. She was my hope and at the same time the biggest opp for my hopes.

"No, it's not, but I think it is for her. She wants stability and a set future, and I still don't know if I'm doing law school or not." A cold pang vibrated through me.

"Sometimes we have to make sacrifices; if law school is what it takes for you to have a solid future, then…it's worth looking at. I want you to do what you love, but hey, we're not kids no more; this is some real-life shit. Real-life shit requires some real-life decision-making."

"Okay, Gracedamus, with the knowledge."

The nervous laughter escaped me, and Grace joined me. All the energy inside transformed into guffaws until my belly hurt, and I could barely breathe.

"So, you good, you got this?" Grace asked me once the soca music filtered back into the car accompanied by the gentle sounds of the ocean.

"I got it now. I need to stand up." I nodded, and she punched me again.

"Man, what the fuck? Have you been training or something?!"

"I have! For moments just like this." Grace smiled. Man, I was grateful for my friends. Even in difficult moments like this, I didn't realize I had someone to lean on. With Trinidad's gentle nudges, her showing me the possibilities of what living vulnerably looked like, I understood better than before how much I had isolated myself from those who loved me. From tonight on, I vowed to do better.

Trinidad in pj's curled up on the sofa was the first thing that I noticed. The Grape-Nuts ice cream in her hand was the second. The tracks under her eyes were the third, and they propelled me to my knees in front of her.

"What happened?"

The smile that illuminated her face was so unexpected I leaned over to taste her sweet lips. Just our lips together eased the turmoil inside, sweetness and Trinidad. If that's all I tasted for the rest of my life, I'd be a lucky man. Trinidad whimpered, easing out of the kiss with a dazed gaze, and my chest poofed up at the sight.

"I called my ex-hus—I called Barry. This weekend, all of it has made me wonder if my perception of my twenties and my marriage, the failure I felt in my chest, the wanting to change things, and my goal-driven mentality were the right things feel, to aspire. I don't have the answers, but Barry confessed something to me. He never felt he could measure up to me and my dreams. All this time, I thought it was the opposite, that I was too everything, too loud, too Dominican, too strict, too demanding, and all along, he felt inadequate. Our communication skills sucked too, so no wonder we both have been under the wrong impression all this time."

This was so unexpected I fell back, sitting on the floor in front of her, as she stretched from her curled position.

"I was feeling overwhelmed today because I'm starting to feel the same expectations I had for Barry, for you, and for me. And I've never felt that for Milton. Milton, though, he feels safe."

"I can feel safe, too," I rushed to say, then pausing to relax. This required finesse, patience.

"Yeah, I know that—that's the scariest part. You feel safer

than both of them combined, but you also make me feel a lot of other things." She chuckled. "Bendito, I swear my coochie has never been this active, and I haven't felt you inside yet. You're trouble, Orlando Wiggins. A challenge to my heart."

"And you are worth the risk to mine. I just…it's scary as fuck. Trinidad, I know you're looking for a partner that can build with you and the twins. I'm young, but I want that exact same thing. You know when I go to your house, I feel at home? You have that sense of belonging and peace that I aspire to create in my own place. I want that with you. I want that with the twins. Both you and they have inspired me these past months to be a different man, one more in tune with my needs and emotions. I've put my thoughts in a box for so long to survive caretaking my entire family that I lost touch with myself. But in these past months, that joy of life has crept back in, loud as fuck, and it's not going anywhere. I worried that law school would be giving up on my dreams, but with you, it's taking a risk to get closer to you, so that we can build together. Give me a chance, past this weekend. Give us a chance."

"Bendito, how can I say no when you ask so beautifully?"

Trinidad leaned forward. The tank top she was wearing offering me a glimpse of her gorgeous breasts until all I saw was the plump cleavage. The touch of her lips on mine refocused my attention, and now, besides the sweetness and Trinidad, I tasted security and safeness. The kiss felt familiar and new, exhilarating and relaxing, arousing and never-ending.

When we finally came for air, my shirt was off, and her tank top lay discarded on the floor. Her satiny brown skin felt warm to the touch, and I got lost in exploring her. Everything we'd done so far had been quick; both of us lost in the passion of the moment. But now I could take my time. Savor the downiness of her with my lips and hands. Her heavy breasts lured me first, and the touch of her hardened nipple on my tongue was all I needed to be bursting out of my pants.

"Oh, Orlando!" Trinidad moaned, pushing her head closer, cradling me, urging me to take my fill. I lapped, licked, and nipped, elongating her nipple until her groans dictated her limit. Every vibration of her moans electrified me and incentivized me to continue driving her wild. Because she was doing the same to me.

With quick efficiency, I removed her bottoms and the rest of my clothes, the temperature in the room perfect against my skin. Or maybe it was cold, but the feverish excitement to see Trinidad Velasquez naked had broken my internal temperature gauge.

Desmond had once told me about this legend of a bombshell of a woman who lured men at night with her sensuality and looks, an insatiable being. A Ciguapa.

Trinidad, her neck tendons taut as she arched under my kisses, was how I imagined the Ciguapa. I'd never see another picture of the legend without thinking of Trinidad.

Her wetness called to me, and I ghosted two fingers between her thighs until I found her soaking wet for me.

"Que rico se siente, Ms. V." I groaned as she clenched around my fingers, sucking me in deeper into her. Trinidad was lost in her pleasure, and fuck me I was lucky to witness it.

"Síí, Orlando, sí." There was no coherence left in her as

I drove her closer and closer to her climax, a concert of fingers and tongue, all deployed to make her mad with passion. Maybe then she could understand just how wild I was for her. I still had my worries; maybe the heat of the moment would persuade her to agree with my proposal, but for now, I packed all those doubts away and focused on my Ciguapa.

"Que linda, Ciguapita," I teased as Trinidad spread her legs wider for me, tilting her pelvis until all I saw was her wet plumpness, her openness to take the risk with me.

"Bendito, stop teasing me!" she whined, and I put her out of her misery, tasting every inch of her until she gushed for me, soaking my hand and the floor. At this point, the owner would charge me for the liquid damage to the floors, and I would pay the fee gladly.

"Are you ready?" I checked in. Not wanting to assume that because she said she wanted me earlier we were still on the same wavelength.

"Where is the condom?" Her heavy breathing and her dancing fingers on her plump little clit were the perfect consent.

Ms. V might be ten years older than me, but damn, was she flexible. With impressive dexterity, she spread her legs wide using the sofa's pillows as a cushion for her back. All the blood rushed to the heaviness between my legs, and I shut my eyes, overwhelmed by the earthy scent inviting me to feast.

I accepted the invitation, inch by inch submerging myself into her offering. She engulfed me and squeezed me tight once our bodies touched, and I started the mental count to a hundred. If I got to that number before the orgasm swept me away, I'd change my name to Captain America.

One...

"Ohh, Orlando, you feel so good." Wet, tight goodness held me in a grip.

"Fuck me." I could do this; I had to hold it in.

I lost my mental count, giving all my attention to her, the force of my thrusts solidifying every promise I made her. I would be her safety. I would be her security. I would be her solace and her partner.

"MMM, oh OH," Trinidad whimpered as I leaned closer to her, the top of my length pressing against that good-good place that would get her gushing for me again.

"Dale, damelo, Trinidad, por favor," I pleaded, the little blood I had left in circulation heating up inside me, driving me faster in her, getting me closer to her. I wouldn't make it to a hundred. I needed her to come. Desperately, I searched her nub and pressed it just as I learned to do so when she was close.

That was all it took; light exploded behind my eyes. We culminated together, the force of our ecstasy shaking the sofa until I collapsed on top of Trinidad. Her body became my shelter, and as I slowed down my breath, I exhaled. Finally, I felt at home.

Moonlight bathed Trinidad's brown skin, the bedroom transforming into a fairy's hideaway. So much light emanated from her, I could only sit next to her, in awe. Her long lashes kissed her cheeks and the goofy-ass smile she had told me I'd shown the fuck up and given her a good time. All was right with the world.

Until my phone buzzed.

Unknown number: Hey, Orly. I heard u in town. If u gonna be in carnival tomorrow, be on the lookout. Ima find u so we can chat.

"Are you good?" Trinidad asked. She languidly stretched in the bed, the sheets that covered her belly and breasts shifted until she was completely bare. Fuck, I was a lucky-ass man to lie next to her. A lucky-ass man with a lot of shit in the bag to encumber her. Trinidad had said she was good with it all, but was she?

I was about to be a dad.

Fuck. I wasn't about to be a dad, I had been one for a while now, without knowing.

"Oh oh, whatever is going through your head, we better talk it through, Papi," Trinidad whispered, pulling me out of my spiral. My dick also perked up at her words, especially *Papi*. Damn my attention span was crap, but I was gonna focus on what was the most immediate thing.

"Papi?"

"Well, if you gonna be my man…but I can call you something else." Her shoulders rose and fell, and her pouty lips spread open, warm breath whooshing out in a yawn.

"Nah, nah I like *Papi*." My chest poofed up, imagining her sobbing and moaning "Papi" while I put her through the mattress. Just like that, I was rock-hard again.

"Oh, mi amigo wants to play again? Damn, this is going to be fun." Trinidad stretched again, her nipples perking up in the night air.

"He does wanna play. He wanna play every time we are next to you, and many times when you're far away. I got it bad," I confessed. Fuck it. Keeping things inside protects me a lot, but with Trinidad, I wanted her to know it all. Damn, she had me down bad.

"Bueno pues I could be persuaded to play…" she purred, and I could swear her pussy purred too.

"I… I want that very, very much, but first…" I sat up straighter, my dick bobbing in disappointment at my decision to postpone bliss.

"Oh-oh." Trinidad reached down and pulled the sheets over her, hiding all that beautiful skin, and shifting her body so her attention was fully on me.

"Maria…my daughter's mother, just texted me. She…she said she wants to meet during carnival to chat." I stretched my feet out, the warm sheets soothing my nervousness.

"Oh…that's good news, isn't it?" Trinidad said letting the question be the invitation I needed.

"It is, but at the same time I know its gonna change my life. Same as my dad dying changed my life. Same as my mother's diagnosis changed my life…"

"All adding more responsibilities to your plate…" Trinidad whispered, perfectly understanding me without the need of many words.

"Yes, but responsibilities that fill me with joy, that have made me the man that I am. I am grateful, for it all, but it don't mean it's not more responsibility." Fuck, saying this to her felt good. To lay down the heavy burden for a second and just share words with someone that understood them.

There was nothing she could do to change my reality. But her understanding and support gave me strength. She saw it in a way my brothers didn't, nor even my mother. They took my caretaking for granted. Things ran well in our household and it was a given. They didn't know any other life, and I had created that level of comfort for them all. I hadn't let my brothers help and contribute in ways that were age appropriate because… I hadn't wanted them to feel the same burden I did.

"I think I did my brothers a disservice," I said, jumping topics without care. Thinking out loud with the woman of my dreams.

"Nah, at your age, trying not to add to their bag made sense to you; now that you know better, you can help them grow in that respect. It's never too late, and you know they're good kids, spoiled from what you've told me, but good kids. What else can they be? They are your brothers." Trinidad pulled at the sheets, the soft fabric flowing right on top of my legs. The slight cold that had seeped in had gotten lost in the comfort of her presence, but she had noticed and had made sure I was comfortable. And she'd picked up on my pivot with ease. Because all of these things were interconnected for me. For her.

"Yeah, I'm going to have to if I want to be as present as I want in my daughter's life…and law school." I slid down from my seated position until I lay mirroring Trinidad, both on our sides, faces close by. Her soft skin over her hips beckoned me, and with the ease of long-time lovers, I gathered her close. Our legs entangling in the most comfortable way.

"Do you feel ready?" she whispered.

"I do, I feel like I was born for it. I'm nervous as fuck of course, I don't want to fuck up in any way, but I want to be present for her. Be an active part of her life." The scent of us together was intoxicating. I knew it would be. We lay in comfortable silence, our bodies melting into each other.

"Parenthood…is the most rewarding but hardest thing you will ever do in your life. Many times you will have to make decisions for the good of your children regardless of what you need at the time. It's selfless work. You have been putting in that type of work since your father passed away. So I think you'll be alright, Orlando, I really believe so. And you have friends and me to help you through the hard days. Without my family and Miranda, I don't know what I would have done." Her words started lagging, her brain going into slumber faster than she was ready to admit.

"Thanks, Trinidad, I…needed to hear that. I need to speak with my family, when I am back…and figure some shit out ASAP, but you're right I'm not alone." The weight of those words surrounded me in peace I hadn't felt in my adult years.

I was not alone.

I didn't have to do this alone.

And as Trinidad fell asleep in my arms, I thanked whatever deity was in charge of this timeline for letting me be part of her life.

Twenty-Two

Trinidad

The scents of sleepy male and Orlando's cologne were the first things I registered when I escaped sleep's clutches in the morning. The day's heat already battled to infiltrate the rental, the sunrise way past us. No Jouvert for us; after the first round downstairs, Orlando carried me upstairs, where he proceeded to show me his youthful exuberance and reminded me of mine. We fell asleep, tangled in his sheets, after words that only served to let us grow closer, and woke up for a fourth round as the sun first made its appearance.

He rolled away from me, mumbling something about texting his friends about not going, then gathered me close, the big spoon completed with an impressive semi-erect penis that currently lay deceptively calm against my behind. That dick wasn't fooling anyone; it had the girth, the stamina, and the capacity to go, go, and go. My sore legs and other areas were a testament to its prowess.

"Good morning, sleepyhead," Orlando whispered in my ear.

"Excuse me? I am not the sleepyhead; it's you; I could have woken up and gotten ready for Jouvert if only you hadn't—" My chest jumped in joy as Orlando handled me like a feather headpiece, placing me right how he wanted me. His heavy weight settled between my legs, and his strong arms extended next to me, keeping our chests a few inches apart.

"Don't make me remind you how you screamed my name while coming; you wouldn't have been able to do that if we had gone to Jouvert."

"Sir, we did that the whole night. What do you mean I wouldn't have done it?" The bubble of happiness nestling in my belly couldn't be contained.

"Oh shit, that's right, I did make you come, five times if I remember exactly. That doesn't count this morning," he bragged. The man-child was too damn cocky for his own good. That must be the Jamaican in him. But he wasn't a man-child, and I wasn't old; it was just Trinidad and Orlando, both of us exhausted after a long night of passion and ready for carnival day.

We both were caregivers, and thrived in it, and sometimes we both neglected our other needs. But the possibilities of what we could be together…my chest warmed at the thought of actually being with someone that understood all my values, and had similar ones. Someone that would understand that we would both sometimes have to put others first, but we together would always be the beginning and the end. My joy bubbled up in my chest ready to burst all over.

"No one likes a show-off."

"That's not what you said last night." He stared at me and shook his head in disappointment. "How you gonna be a good example for the twins if you be lying like this?"

My entire body shook with laughter, and Orlando's eyes almost went crossed, zeroing in on my chest.

"Your titties are so. Fucking. Beautiful." Each punctuation was a peck on each of my nipples. I moaned, moisture already gathering where I needed him the most. Pressing against him, I shared the urgency growing within me.

"Aht, aht. You said I was showing off, so no penis for you, ma'am." He shook his head.

"Did you just Seinfeld me?" At this point my laugh was so out of control I was gasping for breath and dislodged Orlando off me, rolling to lie on my tummy.

"I sure did, gotta keep up with you, old lady." Orlando winked, slapping my ass cheeks, the sting minimal; he'd purposely done it to make it jiggle. And it did.

"I'll show you an old lady," I growled, throwing my arm over him. We rolled in bed, tussling, warm sheets catching around our limbs until I couldn't decipher where he started and where I ended. When he slid in, after placing the condom on, I sighed, the delicious soreness so good I would be walking funny in the airport tomorrow.

The airport.

Tomorrow.

Not letting the intrusive thoughts take over. Instead, I let him take me on a sweaty, sensual ride, our hips moving in tandem until we both shuddered, mouths merged in a forever kiss.

"Now, get off me, woman! I have things to do!" Orlando playfully shoved me to the side after pulling out of me and went to the restroom, his smooth little ebony ass bouncing side to side. I should tell him that and see how riled up he'd get by my observation. I couldn't say anything, though, because when he came back, he took his time cleaning me up and wiping all the residue of our playing away with such gentleness my tough Dominican ass almost buckled and cried. But I didn't because I was tough and because we were an hour away from needing to head out to the carnival grounds.

"Are you nervous?" I asked him not wanting to remind him too much, but I was so filled with anticipation.

"Honestly nah, I am good, I can't wait to talk to Maria… I think she and I will figure something out that will work for both of us." Orlando's confidence washed over me with quiet assurance. To see him so determined to co-parent, and co-parent well, meant so much to me. A little annoying voice reminded me that he had too much on his plate to add me to it, trying to ruin my good mood. But I was done giving those types of thoughts any air. I wanted to be in the moment, with Orlando.

My needs had gone neglected for so long, that I'd lost track of what I required to make me happy, to make me healthy. Being Brandon and Brian's mom did not mean I needed to sacrifice Hot Girl Trinidad to the altar of motherhood. The beauty of being a woman was that I was all encompassing, all potential, all me.

"Alright, you gotta get your costume on!" I reminded him, unwilling to meet his gaze. The fullness of emotions there still spooked me, but the joy bursting out of my chest didn't allow the fear to fester. Today was a beautiful day.

Today was Carnival Day.

There would be time to think about tomorrow, tomorrow.

"What do you mean I get a costume too?" I wasn't proud of the girlish squeal coming out of me, but Orlando and Grace had surprised me with a midline costume from the same section of the Power by Four band they had joined. The headpiece feathers were a majestic aqua and green, a beautiful contrast to Orlando's light and dark blue headpiece. The body was a mixture of purples and aqua and blue, finishing the touches with a tight sparkly blue girdle.

"Of course you do. Your man had us on a mission yesterday! The band at first said they had no extra costumes, so we kept coming back until they finally confirmed they'd had a last-minute cancelation. The poor woman got sick on the plane and ended up bedridden for most of her trip, so she sold the costume to your man there."

Be still my tracionero heart. I didn't need this palpitation this early in the day. The way Orlando had shown me that being cared for was imperative for him had opened my eyes to how much I would have given up if I'd settled for someone like Milton. There was nothing wrong with him, nothing at all, but we were not compatible. Our ideals, although aligned, didn't seem to mesh well in the bright sunlight. It had taken this trip for me to realize my stubbornness had blinded me to the truth.

Damn, Brian and Brandon, I would take this epiphany to my grave…or I would be the imperfectly healed mother who would tell them that even though they were still grounded for the summer, I was grateful for their intervention, however wild it had been. Because the reality was that I needed to live it to see it.

"Go, girly, we gotta head out. If not, traffic is going to get worse; already, it took me twenty minutes to get here with the costume." Grace shooed me to the room, but before I went up, I launched myself into Orlando's arms, his warm embrace telling me everything I needed to know.

"Gracias, Orlando," I whispered for only his ears.

"De nada, mi Ms. Trinidad," he replied and the puddle between my legs increased exponentially. A relationship with Orlando meant I'd have to increase my underwear budget because of the number of times I'd have to change per day…

A relationship. The utter peace that flowed through me at the thought kept me in a state of high as I got dressed. We left the house and navigated the streets of Ofele until we arrived at the grounds.

Hand in hand, Orlando and I, with Grace and the boys in the rear, ambled around in a sea of colorful feathers and bright sparkling appliqués. The amount of melanin concentrated in one area was a grand thing to see. The soca music blasted from different band trucks. Each band had ample space for their revelers to get information. Tents of different colors stood next to each band truck, with food and drink all part of the inclusive packages from the bands.

The front-line costumes of our band were spectacular. There was one gorgeous Amazon with flawless mahogany skin, an expansive feather backpack behind her. The fit extended to the length of her arms on the sides, and almost half her height above her. Peacock feathers trailed behind her waist, fanning out, lending to the resplendent feel of herdesign. Her body piece was minimal: a top that barely covered her blessings and a string bikini that sparkled brightly in the hot sun.

"The only way we make it is by drinking plenty of water." Grace handed bottles of water around to all of us while Trevor gave us our band-branded cups, all filled with rum.

Oh-oh. Rum was my companion during my Hot Gyal days, and anytime I took too much my judgment got somewhat impaired.

"What's up, you don't wanna drink?" Orlando asked as we swayed to the Allison Hinds song blasting from our truck's speakers.

"No, it's not that I just...well, I only drink a lot when I'm with Miranda and..."

"You are with me, though?" The vulnerability in his words...gosh, it was so sweet I wanted to kiss him all over. Instead, I accepted Trevor's cup and draped my hand over Orlando, our bodies sinking into a sweet whine as Allison Hinds pumped us for "da road."

"You can trust me; I got you, Trinidad," Orlando promised, and for once in my life, I accepted the words, allowing them to shelter me.

"We gonna have fun today, aren't we?" I asked him as our hips synced into the rhythm of our islands.

"We are." His lush lips pressed against mine, tasting of rum and soca.

I would never forget this day.

Twenty-Three

Trinidad

The drinks flowed with laughter and dancing as we waited our turn to go on the road.

For carnival, each band had several sections, and those sections had distinct costumes for men and women; the women's costumes were full of feathers and sparkles, and the men complemented the women's wardrobes. Each section had different versions of the costume, some more extravagant than others, depending on the expertise of the revelers to manage such large headpieces and back pieces behind them while dancing to the fast soca songs that were the hallmark of each carnival. Every year, the biggest and brightest soca stars would put out hits that would be played on the road at each carnival in the islands and wherever there were large Caribbean communities. Ofele had started a little carnival years ago, mostly for locals, but once the secret was out, the carnival exploded into what we were experiencing today, a true bacchanal.

The grounds had a path around the stands about three miles long that ended in front of a stage. There the bands would show the best of their costumes, their king and queen, and would compete for the best band of the year. Power by Four was the undefeated champion, and I could see why. The level of care they had for their revelers, the way the drinks and food kept flowing, and the intricacy of their costumes spoke to their commitment to our culture and traditions with a touch of modernity.

By the time we hit the road, starting the journey to the stage, the rum fumes were clouding my head with fuzzy good feelings. The heat of the day no longer bothered me. I was with my man and he had myback, literally. Orlando and I whined down the road, my ass married to his hips as we danced and juked up down the road. Whenever there was a lull, and we stopped to wait for the next band to go up, we found our cadence, the cheers and encouragement of our fellow section members fueling my joy—intoxication by happiness. And rum, too, but happiness came first.

When my favorite song from Barbados played, Grace and I jumped around with our flags in hand, waiving them in the air while the boys surrounded us, their glistening torsos and hips moving to the beat of the music.

This was soca, this was life, this was passion.

Power by Four Posse knew exactly how to party, and by the time it was our turn on the stage, we showed every single reveler there why the band was the winner.

When the queen called us to the stage, the section erupted in screams and laughter, running toward the stage, making the ground shake. The vibrations of speakers carried me forward, Orlando just behind. We found a spot by the front of the stage, and my hips took over, Orlando's hands nestled on my waist, running up and down as he guided me to bend exactly how he wanted, his hardness now evident after hours of close dancing.

He was allowed. There was no space required between us like Grace and Desmond were maintaining. This was my man, and if I wanted to whine on his dick on stage, then I would whine on his dick on stage. With clothes on, of course.

Sweet heat made our bodies slick with perspiration, the sweating the only reason the rum hadn't put me on my ass already. The gentle sway of my head told me I needed more water before Orlando had to carry me back to the rental on his shoulder.

"Go ahead, Ms. V, get yours," Orlando encouraged me, and those were the exact words I needed. My locs fell in front of my face as I bent so far down, I could see between both our legs. Orlando never let me go, holding me tight against me, keeping me safe while I had the time of my life.

We descended the stage, full of an indescribable joy, the type that filled you up and solidified photographic memories in your brain for your viewing pleasure later. I would always remember the feel of Orlando's slick skin against mine, of the drooping feathers on my shoulders brushing back and forth as I danced, of the sweet savor of rum and coke, of the tangy taste of Orlando's kisses, and the scent of sea and sand and Ofele.

And I would always remember the drunk flapping in my stomach, the butterflies always present, reminding me that this moment was special.

We made it back to our truck as the carnival organizers got the stage ready for the second part of carnival. Local and international soca artists hit the stage and kept all the revelers dancing and vibing as the sunset and heat gave way to a warm breeze.

"I need to sit down!" My thighs were on fire, whining meant squatting, and Mama hadn't gone to the gym this whole week. This substituted five leg days in a row.

"We bought some foldable chairs," Desmond explained, pulling them out of the trunk of their rental and placing things a little away from the loud noise of the music. All the trucks had synced up with the music from the stage, creating a wonderful surround system.

Relief coursed through me once I sat down. Grace sat next to me, closing her eyes and relaxing in the camping chair.

"I won't be able to walk tomorrow," she complained.

"Who are you telling?" I laughed, knowing I would pay for it and gladly.

The ocean breeze cooled down my heated skin and helped clear my fuzzy brain. Ms. V, Hot Gyal, was back and stronger than ever, the vibes of the day solidifying that I could have more than what I thought I could. I deserved happiness and fun times, security, and steadfastness.

I had to pinch myself as Orlando and his friends stood next to Grace and me. Orlando's aura lightened through my stay here in Ofele with him; even with all that waited for both of us back home, his happiness was evident.

Somehow, I had missed that before this, he'd always walked weighed down, the load he carried a solitary task. The vulnerability he'd shown these past days held me in awe and made mine easier to bear. I hated opening up, but we'd learned how to do it together. There was still much more to learn about each other, and be tested.

But for now, the future felt good…with the exception of his law school and Milton. Those two topics needed full revisiting, but I didn't want to spoil the vibes. There would be time back home for the tough conversations.

For now, I stared at my man, his chiseled melanated lean torso glowing under the dying sun, his smirk enhanced by those crafty lips I couldn't wait to kiss again. His deep brown eyes so beautiful to me, so full of pride and joy.

My man.

Orlando caught me staring, and the wink he gave me made all the fuzzy feelings sharpen in full detail. The wink morphed into a frown as he put his hand in his pocket and pulled out my cell phone. Orlando's face slackened, and the shoulders that only a second ago sat proud and relaxed tensed up, the weight of it all returning with no explanation. What the hell could my phone say? Was it the twins?

"Qué paso?" My body acted before my brain could catch up. Heart in my throat, I stood up, extending my hand, flapping my fingers until the weight of my phone landed on my hand.

Milton: Hey, gorgeous. Can you see if you can change your flight tomorrow for an earlier one? I can pay for the difference. I want you to drive down to the Poconos for the farewell dinner. The partners want to meet you.

Relief washed over me, followed by retreat, leaving concern and a nervous energy behind. I should have called Milton and let him know about the end of our situationship, but a face-to-face conversation was the least I owed him. Now the procrastination meant I needed to open the subject, and suddenly, the rum made its presence known, the entire sky rotating against me, the floor shifting and vibrating under me. Stability. I needed an anchor, and my hand shot out in search of the first solid anything I could find. My hand landed on a firm, rigid surface and once my eyesight cleared, Orlando stood next to me, keeping me upright.

"You good?" he asked in a clipped tone.

"Yuuuup." Oops, that took much longer to say than usual.

"Okay, here, sit down." My feet obeyed his command instead of the ones I sent via my brain. My stomach cartwheeled, and I was grateful for the idea of sitting down. Sitting down was good. Chairs were excellent.

"Who invented chairs? Lord knows, but great, great call."

"I don't know who invented chairs, Trinidad." Orlando's beautiful face was right in front of me. I leaned over to give him a kiss, but air greeted me instead. Wasn't his face just there, just now? "Aren't you going to answer the text?"

"Text? What text?" I asked, my brain, trying to reach an understanding and failing spectacularly.

"Orlando, she's lit. You gotta give her a second," a lilting voice said, and I shook my head in agreement until my head told me to stop because it hurt too much.

"She was fine, not too long ago..." Was that shade? Did I detect shade in my man's tone? What was going on?

"I think it hit her right now, probably standing up and everything, let's give her a minute," the voice urged Orlando. The voice of reason, listen to it, Orlando.

"Fine, that's fine. I, fuck, I thought she and I were in alignment."

"Now, wait a minute, don't talk about me like I'm not here." The *r*'s and *w*'s gave me a hard time, and the vowels wanted to show off and elongate in my mouth. I should have stopped one drink ago.

"Fine then, let's talk. Are you going to answer that text message? Why is that dude texting you?" Orlando's clipped tones were not appreciated when my head wanted to run away from my body and leave the pain behind until things calmed down.

"Nah, I can't have a conversation right now; I don't even know what you mean. And you best get your tone straightened out!" Oops. This was the side of Hot Gyal I didn't fully embrace with joy and happiness—the sassy, angry side. But Orlando had me confused, and I was not about to let him think he could talk to me any type of way. I had enough sense to understand he was upset, and I needed clarity.

"The text from Milton, Trinidad, and you're right, I do have a tone; I am sorry." Orlando dropped the decibels but said it loud enough for me to hear him over the music. Milton...oh.

"I don't know what to answer yet; I need to think," I said, hoping he understood. I couldn't just text Milton and say, "Hi, nah, I'm good, I have a man now." That would be immature. This required a phone call, and I was not equipped to handle that at the moment.

"Wow, fine. Okay. Imma go take a walk with the guys. I... you do you, Trinidad," Orlando said, his retreating form becoming a blur of color in a sea of more color. My chest ached, and I didn't know how to make it better. But my head? That pounding was unbearable.

"Oh, Trinidad, listen, he's...this is...you're both drinking, it will be okay tomorrow." Okay tomorrow...but nah.

"No, he should know better; he's supposed to have my back. How can he walk away? When I'm not even doing okay?" The more I thought about what just happened the more I saw red. The haze grew at a faster rate than the cartwheels in my stomach until my body once more was in movement.

"Wait, wait, Trinidad, where are you going?" Grace's tiny steps were loud as hell behind me as I navigated the crowd in search of a place where I could order a ride.

"You can't leave on your own; I... I'll come with you."

Clearly, Grace didn't want to leave. I saw her and Desmond dancing a lot; she danced with all her friends, but Desmond stayed by her side most of the time; his going with Orlando was clearly a solidarity thing, and I understood, but I did not plan to ruin her night too. Whirling around, the rum slushed all around my stomach and head, and I needed a second to wait for everything to settle down.

"No. I'm a grown woman. This is not the first time I have taken a taxi drunk. This is how we'll do it. I will call you as soon as I am in the car, and I will leave the call open till I get to the rental. Okay? There is no need for both our nights to get messed up, alright?" The slurs were decreasing enough to convince Grace of the plan. She nodded sadly, holding me so tight in a hug more fit to a gentle giant instead of the tiny pixie she was.

"Listen, he is in love with you. The dumbass just doesn't know how to say it." All my veins lit up at the sound of her words, but clarity had a way of always inserting its way.

"Love is beautiful, and I do believe you believe that, but he needs to sort some things out first before he can love me like I deserve." Every single part of the sentence came out clear and concise.

No slurs. No doubts.

Twenty-Four

Orlando

Trinidad had me twisted. After everything I'd shared with her this weekend, after making me believe we had a future past Ofele, she hadn't texted that man to tell her she was done with him. I didn't care about him, wasn't jealous or anything like that. What I had to offer didn't compare with him. It was the fact she was still on the fence about us.

"Yo, slow down; where are we going?" Trevor asked, jogging behind me. I didn't have a destination in mind; revelers cleared a path as I powered through the crowd, trying to find some space that was quieter than this. The booming of the speakers reverberated in my head, exacerbating my mood. Now I'd lost any capacity to be even-keeled; of course, Trinidad would knock me out of my lane; I should have expected this. The fact I thought I had a chance was laughable.

"Nah, I was just looking for a quiet spot," I said, the calm in my tone reassuring me I hadn't fully lost my touch.

"Shit, Orlando, stop. Are you really gonna do this? Trinidad is drunk, man; give her a chance to explain once she is sober."

"She has been sober all these days; she was sober this morning; why not reach out to that man and tell her about us?"

"Dude, she's a grown woman. What type of childish move would it be for her to text or call that dude? Didn't you say they had been seeing each other for a minute? Remember what happened with me and Grace?" Desmond asked. I winced at the reminder of his spectacular failure with Grace; he'd really mismanaged what he still considered the best relationship he'd ever had.

At least he had a chance. I got a weekend.

"Son, you gotta pause and think this through the alcohol is dictating a lot of your emotions right now; you gotta chill," Trevor urged me.

Their words penetrated my thick skull, and I took stock. They weren't lying, I was not completely faded, but we'd been under the sweltering sun and had drunk enough rum to fell a horse. My feet were steady, but my head had long ago started thumping to the rhythm of the music, reminding me that tomorrow I'd deal with a hell of a hangover.

"Fine, you're right; my point still stands."

"Your point sucks, respectfully. That woman, if not in love, is very infatuated with you. She's stepped out of her shell to spend this weekend with you."

Every word they said made sense, but damn, the hole in

my chest wouldn't allow for reasoning. Trinidad, from everything I had known about her, was one of the most considerate, caring people I had ever known. She'd put aside her wants and needs to provide for her children and to achieve what she believed was a picture-perfect family. And I'd come in and in a few days had asked her to let that dream go, to be with me. Fuck. I... I was afraid. What if I wasn't everything she needed?

"I need space," I told my friends, their faces both contorted, Desmond into nothing and Trevor into disappointment. "I'm not retreating; I just literally need a minute to sort my brain out. Y'all speaking facts, and when I go back to Trinidad, I'm gonna take her to the rental and make sure we both get some water and ibuprofen and tomorrow we can talk."

Trevor grinned at my explanation, thumping on my back in a rough embrace. Desmond nodded, a very slight smirk telling me he approved.

They both made their way back to our area, and I finally found a spot with some large rocks where I could sit and explore my thoughts. I'd jump in headfirst to the dream of Trinidad and me, but all of that meant big changes. Having a girlfriend with two kids meant I needed to be stable beyond what I had now, but here I was thinking still of dropping law school. Time was another thing; I could barely keep up with Ma and my brothers and the mentorship program. Trinidad deserved time and attention. The weight of the world settled on my shoulders as I tried to figure out the puzzle pieces, how everything would fit together.

A soft touch shook me out of my reverie. My chest tightened, hopeful it was Trinidad, but it had only taken a few days for me to learn her touch. When I raised up, I got face-to-face with Maria. Even with all this shit happening, my grin couldn't be helped.

"Maria Roberts."

"Orlando Higgins." Maria's deep voice carried memories of summers talking about everything from comics to politics to our parents and our dreams. She hadn't changed much, still lean and tall, almost as tall as I was, with a creamy light-skinned complexion and pretty freckles all over her face, shoulders, and chest. She had a front-line costume, all white, but no large backpack. At this time of the night, if you still had your full costume, it was a miracle. Her eyes were still as kind as ever, and her smile was as gorgeous as the first day I met her.

What had changed was how she made me feel.

For the longest time, I had a crush on her. One of those teenage crushes that feel intense and never-ending—nothing like what I felt for Trinidad, robust and mature, fulfilling and encompassing. Now I only felt gratitude to see her well, and the nostalgia hit me square in the chest.

"You look good, Orlando." She sat next to me on the rocks, and we remembered our rhythms and silences.

"Thank you for finding me," I said once we found our comfort.

"I hesitated, I'm not gonna lie. When I found out about Maya—"

Maya…my grandmother's name. Fuck. I fisted my hands over my knees, overwhelmed by the tangible knowledge of someone out there being a part of me. I already was a part of Maya no matter if we'dmet or not.

"That's a beautiful name," I said. "Go on. Sorry I interrupted you."

"You good; I know it must be a lot for you, but yeah. When I found out I was pregnant, I took into consideration everything: my family and yours, my circumstances and yours. I was young, so I'm not proud of my decision, but with everything you already shouldered with your moms and your brothers, I didn't see any space for a child. And honestly…you kept things so close to the chest all the time I was afraid you'd just go with the flow to make me happy. Take the burden and not speak up that you needed help. I couldn't do that to you, so… I figured I would make my own way."

A deep pressure started in the center of me, holding me down, weighing down my limbs at her explanation. I wanted to tell her she was wrong, but that wasn't true. I would have done the right thing. I would have kept it all inside. and I would have never burdened her or anyone else with my worries and concerns.

"I wish you would have told me, though; I had a right to know."

"You did, and I have regretted that decision for a long time; I am sure my metiche grandmother was the one to tell you. I haven't called her yet, but when they told me you were looking for me, I put two and two together. But she had been pushing me to tell you, and I kept refusing; I was…ashamed and afraid, I guess, of your reaction."

"I get it," I said, my head too full, my chest too heavy to do anything but push the feelings aside until I had more time to process them by myself.

"So…you want to see her?"

"Hell, yeah, I want to see her! Can I meet her tomorrow? Do you have pictures of her now?"

"Yeah, I knew you'd ask." She pulled her cell phone from an undisclosed location I didn't want to study too much and unlocked it immediately. The face of a pretty little girl without a front tooth, with Maria's complexion and my whole face, stared at me with so much joy that my breath caught in my throat.

"Maya," I croaked, breathing shallow as she flipped through baby pictures. A progression of the growth of my child till now. By the time she finished tears ran down my face, and Maria was sobbing.

"I'm so sorry I kept her from you; I really am."

"I get it, I…hey, we were young and…yeah. It's okay. Well, it's not, but I know we'll work through it. I want to be in her life, so we need to. I want to co-parent with you, Maria." I threw my arm around her shoulder as she sobbed against me. The relief to have found her and Maya wouldn't be complete until I shared it with Trinidad.

Whatever she needed to face with Milton, I'd be there to handle with her. And whatever I needed to face with Maya, she'd be there for me. I knew it. All it took was for me to open up to her and be vulnerable, to apologize, and to hope she'd understand my lapse of judgment. Because I loved her, and I didn't want anyone but her.

★ ★ ★

"What do you mean she left?" I hadn't meant for my voice to rise, but between the loud-ass music and the shifty faces in front of me, I was losing all sense of patience. And my well ran real deep.

"She was upset after you...you know, with the text message." Grace waved her hand around as if that would explain why she had allowed a visibly intoxicated Trinidad to leave by herself.

"I wasn't planning to leave her here; why would she leave?" Fuck. I pushed the headpiece off my forehead, rubbing the mark it left behind. The headache that had moved in had big plans to make itself comfortable.

"So...well, she felt you kinda let her down, assumed the worst, and well, left her behind, so she left you behind." Grace shrugged.

"Fine, I'll see y'all tomorrow. I'm gonna go to her now." It was pointless to ask more questions. I understood now that I fucked up. I had reverted to my old patterns of isolation instead of communicating my feelings, and I'd hurt her in the process. She needed so badly to feel secure and safe, and I'd destroyed that with one stupid moment.

The drive to the rental felt worse than crossing the Brooklyn Bridge at 6:00 p.m. on a Friday. By the time I stepped into the rental, a sense of urgency pushed me up the stairs. Hoping to find her room empty, I was disappointed to find the sexiest lump curled up under thick blankets. A few locs dared over the pillow.

"Trinidad, sorry to barge in. I was hoping you were in our room." Our room. Damn, that felt good to say.

"No, I'm leaving early tomorrow, so I thought it best to sleep here. Don't want to wake you up. Actually, I didn't want to sleep in the same bed with you at all. It would send the wrong message." I was grateful she didn't pretend to be asleep. But why would she? Everything she experienced, Trinidad took face on, no fears. I wish I had the same bravery.

"I fucked up."

"Ohh, yes, you did. And in one fell swoop, you showed me that you still are operating as a child. And I get it; you haven't had time to grow, not with how you've had to protect yourself from hurt. But I saw the man within these days, and I hoped that that was who I was starting a relationship with. Instead, the boy came out with a tantrum at the first challenge. Not only that, you retreated. Again, to that, 'I'm fine,' bullshit. No, you were not fine, and instead of waiting until tomorrow to have a calm conversation, you just acted a whole fool. Made a fool out of me too. And you know I don't like that." She pushed the bedding off her, sitting up, her eyes bloodshot, her mouth twisted in anger. Fuck, she was gorgeous.

"Listen, I know I fucked up. Please let me explain; I…"

"I know you are going to have an explanation; I get it. But I don't need it. What I do recommend is you take the time to take stock. Create boundaries with your family, and cancel law school. Live your life. Stand up foryourself and what you want. No one else is gonna do that for you. And…" Trinidad sniffled, and my stomach dropped all the way to the ground floor. "And keep opening up, letting people in to help you. You don't have to do any of it alone. Not anymore."

"Trinidad, listen, I get it. I acted wrong, and I shouldn't have, but…don't give up on me. I…we can still be each other's shoulder to lean on. Let me take care of you, and I promise I will let you take care of me."

"No. I need someone who can emote. That can open up, and you aren't there yet. And I have plans; I have a timeline." Her voice cracked, and the sound broke me inside. How had I gotten so close to having everything I wanted and squandered it so soon?

"Are you gonna go to the Poconos?" The bravery it took to ask that question would haunt me forever.

"No. That is not the right thing for me either. I thought… never mind what I thought, but no. I'm not. But I want to get back home to the twins. I've been here long enough." Trinidad stopped crying, and a hardness took over her, muscle by muscle. She put up a barrier between us; if I didn't penetrate it now, I would be shut out.

"Please… Trin, I need you. I… I found Maria, and she is going to bring Maya tomorrow and I… I want you here. I need you here. It's… I need the support." The back of my eyes burned at the hardest words I'd ever utter in my life. This woman…she had my heart. "I love you, and I fucked up, and I don't want to lose you. You have taught me in these few months how to love out loud and how to accept love in a way I never knew possible. With your charisma, your kindness, and your steadfastness, and your cooking, damn your cooking, and that temper of yours that I swear gets me hard every time. And don't get me started with the old sayings. You have me. You have my heart."

Trinidad's eyes watered, and that wall dropped at the same time her face dropped to her hands. A spark of hope ignited in me to die immediately when her head started shaking side to side.

"You need time. You're young and... I knew it, but still, I dreamed. I love you too, Orlando, but sometimes, when you love someone, you know you are not the best for them. I have too much, and you need time to process and—"

"Please don't say it." I held up my hand, attempting to stop her by any means.

"—grow. And I need someone that can commit to all," she finished.

And with those words, she terminated the hope within.

Twenty-Five

Trinidad

Just as I suspected, the wake-up on Sunday felt brutal. Cotton moved into my mouth overnight, and no amount of water in the world would fix it. The constant pounding in my head felt worse than passing by a construction site in Brooklyn, and my body ached in places I didn't even have a name for. Hot Gyal was no longer back to tired, overworked Trinidad Velasquez. But now I sported a broken heart, courtesy of a man-child.

Instincts never failed me until now. Everything felt right with Orlando by my side. The fear and concerns were all minimal to the sense of rightness that filled me anytime we were together. This weekend had been the culmination of the longest flirting I'd ever had, and for a second, I believed it would have an ending worthy of a movie. An ending worthy of what my parents had together, what I had always aspired to.

Instead, the butterflies in my stomach haphazardly flapped

their wings when I sneaked out of my room, hearing Orlando's raised voice in the other room. The urge to stop and listen, to go and comfort him, pulled me, but I resisted. There was nothing to do but to leave. Whatever he was doing, he could manage on his own. After all, that was all he ever did.

The ride took the scenic route, the morning rays not enough to lift the grayness clouding everything. The morning mist clung to the foliage and palms on the way, the streets pristine, as if nothing had ever happened in the town. Bungalows, hotels, and establishments flew by in a combination of colors until we hit the highway.

"Sir, do you mind me making a call?" I pulled out my cell phone, awaiting the verdict. Once the driver agreed, I went to my favorites and dialed Brian's number.

"What's up, Ma, you good?" His husky voice had deepened since the last time I heard it. Damn, I was really hurt if I was this nostalgic by just hearing my baby's voice.

"I… I'm okay; listen, I'm on my way back, currently approaching the airport. I wanted y'all to know I was able to switch to an earlier flight; they had some last-minute openings." Probably a bunch of people got smart at the last minute and switched their travel plans after having too much fun last night.

"What you mean you coming back early?" Brandon's voice popped up. I should have known better—I'd strategically called Brian as he was the most understanding of the two. The boys had invested a lot on this weekend, hoping for a happy ending for their mother. I wasn't naive, the way they talked to me about Orlando had always been more than just care and trust for their mentor. They probably had seen what everyone did when we were in the same room. The attraction and pull that we couldn't fight even at the beginning. I hated to disappoint them, but nothing would happen now.

"Because I am tired, and I need my bed. And more importantly, I miss you both." Even though this was all going on and they had a vested interest, they did not get to know all my thoughts. The boundaries I would set moving forward with them would allow me to have a more fulfilling life. One where I got to be Trinidad and not just Brian and Brandon's mother.

This weekend had been necessary for so many reasons, not only the ones the twins thought of. It was time for some change in my dreams and goals. I could have dreams just for myself nothing related to them. The boys were growing so beautifully, and no matter what they would be okay. So what if I didn't have a husband to be their stepdaddy? I had a village that surrounded us and I hadn't realized the value of it until this weekend.

"We miss you too, but what's up? We thought you had a later flight; I think Orlando was on it too..." Brian dropped the fact so nonchalant I wanted to cackle. These children.

"Really? I wonder how you knew that?" I exited the car while the driver helped me with my luggage. The heat punched me in the face, more concentrated here away from the sea breeze. The relief of the AC welcomed me inside the building, and I found a seat to finish my conversation with the twins.

"Well, you know we be chattin' with Orlando," Brandon explained. I swear they must think I was born yesterday.

"Boys, I wasn't born yesterday; I know what you wanted to happen through this trip. I birthed you. Y'all gone be grounded the whole summer, and we *will* have a big conversation when I'm at home. But for now, hear this. Orlando and I are adults. We do not need anyone's meddling. I'm leaving early and he is staying behind. There is nothing there. And moving forward, I need you to respect that fact. I am the parent here, and you both do not get to dictate my comings and goings. Let this never happen again." The bass in my voice did the trick. The silence on the other side lengthened until a scuffle erupted and then Brian spoke.

"Ma, we are sorry, you right, we…yeah we will see you at home."

"I love you too, more than you can ever imagine."

"Te queremos mucho, Ma," they both replied, contrition finally evident in their tones.

My heart ached for them; this was a lesson that would stay with them for a long time, but it was necessary. I wanted to teach them boundaries, communication, and respect so they would never, ever experience hardships in their personal relationships. Maybe they wouldn't ever be in their airport with a broken heart, yearning for a different ending.

The airport brimmed with travelers going back to their homes, everyone with way less energy than when we arrived a few days ago. As I navigated the crowd, my phone vibrated, and I pulled it to hear Milton's raspy voice.

"Hey, you. You about here yet?" he asked.

This man. Single-minded focus, I would give him that. I hadn't wanted to break up with him via phone, but I had no recourse now. His insistence on me going to the Poconos was feeling more self-serving by the minute. And to be honest, we were never in a relationship to start with. I'd made castles in my mind of what things could be with this man because he was stable and successful, but this wasn't it for me.

I explained everything to him. How I'd come here thinking I was going to the cheerleading tournament and everything that transpired after. I was honest because it wouldn't be fair to break up with him with a lie. And I didn't want there to be any confusion as to where I stood in regard to my feelings and needs moving forward.

"So you can't make it tonight?" he said after everything, after me telling him about Orlando and our escapades, how I had grown to care for him during the time I'd known him. How I realized I didn't want a staid, full-of-responsibility partnership. I wanted that, but I wanted more.

"That's all you can ask me after everything I said?" I responded.

"Well, I know you are not my partner, but I mean, you could do me this last solid before we part ways?" Milton's arrogance dripped all over his words. The passive-aggressiveness was all I needed to say a firm no, goodbye and delete his number from my phone.

All that time I spent building this man up in my brain, and it ended with such a womp womp. I mean, after sex with him, I should have known. I placed my phone back in my purse and let out a sigh of relief for the paths left behind.

Where they needed to be.

By the time I reached the gate, a melancholy had settled on my shoulders. For so long, I had been working toward a goal, and now...

My phone vibrated in my purse, and I pulled it out, expecting to see a text from Miranda or the twins. It wasn't them.

It was Orlando.

A lesser proud woman would admit to palpitations and shortness of breath, mixed with a rush of warmth at the sight of the text message he'd sent me. But they were not like me, proud. Bolstering myself, I read the text message several times, the words eroding my determination and sparking hope for a tomorrow that had disappeared after our conversation last night.

Orlando: I know you left earlier than your flight. I thought we'd have time to chat once more, but... I get it. I just wanted to say... Fuck. My fingers are shaking. I'm nervous.

I do have a lot going on.

But I know what I want.

I want you.

I lost you with my immature move, but I needed you to know. I fell in love this weekend. In a weekend. I never thought that would be possible, but here we are. Is it puppy love? Yeah, maybe, but I know it can grow. You and I can grow together. I heard all you said and damned if you were right, but where you made a mistake is saying I was still a child. I am not. Not anymore because I choose to say what's inside, and I choose to ask for help when I need it, and I choose to set my boundaries and expectations like the grown man that I am. Please give me a chance. Please.

If this boy didn't stop, I would end up crying in this airport. The airline people stood at the counter assisting standby travelers. Changing my flight now might get me some additional money in my credit for a future flight. Changing my flight now would get me back to Ofele and next to Orlando to support him. He'd asked for help last night, and I was so in my feelings about my needs that I missed that. All this time, I wanted him to have the support that he gave other people, and at the first chance, I ran, not because of only him, but because of me too.

But we both deserved another chance, we both deserved the love we've been searching for for so long.

And with that, I made my decision.

It was the easiest decision I'd ever made.

Twenty-Six

Orlando

The ringtone on my phone did not sound like the alarm I'd set before crashing in bed, my head pounding at the turn of events. Not wanting to drive myself wild with thoughts, I let the rum and the day's festivities lull me into a deep, fitful sleep. The sheets were all moist and tangled up around me as I pulled my phone from the nightstand and answered the call.

"I thought you were back today," Melo said with no greeting.

"Call me back when you have some manners." I hung up and went back to bed.

The phone rang less than five minutes later.

"The fuck you hung up on us for? What the hell is wrong with you? You've been MIA most of the weekend. This is not like you. We have needed you; taking care of Mom is not easy, and you just abandoned us to the wolves." Camilo berated me over the phone. His voice was no match to the tension gathering at my temples. Nothing he said bothered me but not because I didn't care, but because they needed to grow the fuck up. And today, they would learn.

"If you and Melo cannot be kind when talking to me, then we have nothing to talk about. If you both are struggling this weekend, it's because it's the first time I have treated you like you are responsible young adults instead of bratty-ass children."

The gasps on the other side of the speaker made my stomach cramp. There was a lot I needed to tell Camilo and Marcelo. There was a lot to heal and growing we all needed to do. But I was done letting them coast through life without responsibilities.

"Today is the first day of our new lives. I am no longer the sole caretaker for my mother. We will take turns. You two got to live your childhood with minimal concerns; that was because of me. I don't fault you either for that. I made a decision, and I stick to it, but what we are not gonna do is act like the two of you are not grown now and can take some of the responsibilities of taking care of Mom. So you both had to care for her a weekend, the fuck you complaining about? That is your mother and she needed you. Man, the fuck up."

"Yooooo, we been trying to help; you are wilin!" Camilo exclaimed.

"Nah, let him speak," Melo said in a quiet tone that gave me hope. Shit, maybe this is what I should have said a long time ago.

"Both of you start thinking of the responsibilities you want to take off my plate because I'm done doing this alone. The questions you both asked this weekend showed me how disconnected you are about Mom's day-to-day. From now on we take turns with the medical appointments, with buying her meds, everything."

The words flowed out of my mouth. The usual calm I sought was still there, but this time, it was combined with utter peace. I'd never felt this peaceful before, not about my family, but with every word I said, I realized this was long overdue.

The slight fear of losing my brothers' love if I didn't provide everything they needed and then some was there, but the peace washed away any of the tools that fear had used to keep me complacent. Now I recognized the fear for what it was.

The silence after was deafening. I sat on my bed, after carving a path on the carpet, pacing back and forth letting my brothers know how I felt.

"Well, you could have told us you were resenting us instead of yelling at us, but I guess we kinda been dicks and deserve it," Camilo said.

"For real, I mean damn, man, that shit hurt but…listen, you right, we…shit. Let's talk when you get back, Orlando; we clearly need a bigger conversation," Marcelo said, and I experienced yet another new emotion with regard to my brothers. Pride.

I could live with that.

"That sounds good; I'll be home later today. Probably late night."

"A'ight. We'll be here, we'll take care of Ma…"

"Actually, is she there?" The nerves hit me as Celo and Milo went in search of our mother. "Let's do a video call," I asked once they were all together.

Marcelo stood next to Mom, who, for once, was dressed in slacks and a blouse, her hair combed and looking more lively than the past few months. Whatever happened this weekend, it seemed it wasn't only good for me.

I smiled at seeing her. Camilo sat next to her and held her hand.

"Ma, I just told Marcelo and Camilo they need to do their part at home moving forward. I need you to do your part too. I know you miss Dad…shit, I miss him too, but we all need to work together to make sure things are better for all of us. And because, well, I have a daughter. A five-year-old daughter, and she doesn't deserve to come into a dysfunctional family on her dad's side. So I need y'all to get it together. For her. For me."

Camilo's and Marcelo's jaws went slack at the news, but Mom? I would never forget her expression. It was as if a light had turned on inside. So much was exchanged between her and me with just our eyes. There was a hope that ignited in her, something I hadn't seen since my father had passed.

I had missed her, this version of her. Even if it was weathered and still dragged down by her cabanga.

The woman on the other side of the screen, that was my mother.

"Bendito, what a blessing, hijito. You're right; we can talk more when you are back, but this weekend, with these two pestering me, I realized I need to do a little better with my meds. But where is this daughter, and when do I get to meet her?" The burning in my eyes threatened to form thug tears. All it took was for Ma to say she would try. That was all I ever needed to hear.

"I'm meeting her later today. She should be here in about an hour or two—remember Maria? She...well, she got pregnant and never told me; Maya is five years old."

"Oh, Maya." Mom sighed with a faraway look. There, I still saw the ghosts that haunted her; expecting her to be right by this good news would be childish of me, but now I realized that seeing her as a burden wasn't fair to her either.

My mom was allowed to have bad and good days. All I needed was for her to try. The rest we would always deal with together.

"Sí, Mama, como tú, Mamá," I said, and we both smiled at each other. The cabanga loomed right over her, and I knew it would always be her companion, but today my family made me feel hopeful. And it all started with me opening up.

Fuck, I wish Trinidad was here to see this. I wish... I wish she'd give me another chance to prove to her that I could and would continue to be the best man I could be because she was worth it all.

The need to let her know my feelings washed over me, drowning me in urgency until I surrendered to the pull.

My phone shook in my hand while I composed one of the most important texts in my life.

Laying it all out to Trinidad would have been torture in the past. To be honest it wouldn't have happened at all. But I wasn't about to let my cowardice to life fully dictate my future.

Trinidad would decide to do whatever she could with the information in my text, with my heart bared completely to her, but I would always have the peace of knowing I put it all out there.

My finger hovered over the send button while I reviewed the text over and over, cleaning it up, deleting some parts and adding new ones.

Agonizing about the words, I pressed Send.

No response. A few minutes passed while I paced back and forth, checking the phone every two seconds. A boulder materialized in my throat when the three dots appeared under my message, but after a few more minutes, I realized no message would come.

Trinidad had made her decision.

I went for a run under the scorching sun. The heat cleared my head and restored my body's well-being, all the rum sweating out of my pores until there was only water left. My heart, though, that shit was hungover, beat up, and aching. There was no run that would fix that.

After a long shower, I got some pastries and cleaned up the living room, finding one of Trinidad's panties underneath the sofa, next to a watermark. Fuck. Everything reminded me of her. I took care of the spill and got everything to rights about an hour before Maria and Maya were set to arrive. Not knowing what to do with myself, I fluffed all the pillows and shams in the living room, then went into the kitchen and fiddled with things until my chest felt ten times bigger than normal.

The front doorbell sang the arrival of Maria and Maya,

and for a second, I froze. Two deep breaths, and my feet were moving.

And there she was.

My daughter.

The pictures did her no justice. She was tall for her age, with a yellow blouse and skirt, her thick coily hair in two adorable buns with yellow bows. As expected, she held her mother's hand with a tight grip, searching her mom's face for reassurance. Maria seemed as nervous as I felt, and for a second, we just all stood there facing each other.

"So…" Maria started.

"Yeah…" I responded, not sure what to say. My heart palpitations were faster than the Flash on his fastest day, and still…

"Maya, baby, this is the man I told you about. This is…. this is your father. He is a very good friend of mine, and he lives in another city, but he came here to meet you!" Maria kneeled next to Maya, bringing the comfort that our daughter needed to go through this new experience.

Our daughter.

Sweet words I didn't know I'd love to say, not so soon in my life, but they felt right as fuck. Meeting Maya now was the right timing; I wouldn't have been able to be the man, the father she needed before. It had taken meeting Trinidad, Brian, and Brandon to evolve outside my everyday point of view. Crouching next to Maria, I extended my hand to Maya.

"Hello, Maya, I am Orlando, your dad. You can call me Dad, or you can call me Orlando, whatever you prefer." Everything stood still. The birds outside and the palm trees completed their dance to the afternoon breeze. In the house, the AC stopped, and silence reigned, and just when I thought my daughter wouldn't respond, she surprised me by putting her little hand in mine and stepping in, enveloping me in a sugar-, shea butter–scented hug that melted every hard corner I'd ever had.

My daughter.

If I could hold on to her and never let her go, I would, but I didn't want to spook her.

"Hello, Daddy," Maya said, timid but with force. She'd squared her little shoulders and gifted me with the brightest, most beautiful smile in the world.

"Hello, sunshine, can I call you sunshine?" I asked her and she giggled, nodding and making her puffs shake.

"Okay, why don't you and Mom come in, huh? I got you some pastries, and I have a gift for you too," I told her, and we all went to the living room.

After a few awkward conversation starters, we all sat in silence, chewing on our pastries. My heart, as full as it was, felt bruised and achy; missing Trinidad would always feel like this.

As if I had conjured her with my yearning, the door swung open, and sunlight and the scent of lemons and warmth walked in through the door, a smiling Trinidad bringing warmth and laughter into the room.

"I am so sorry I'm late! Hi, y'all, I am…" Trinidad's eyes roamed from the top of my head to the bottom of my feet, and with that, the ache in my heart dissipated, washing away all my other worries.

"This is my girl, Trinidad; she wanted to meet you too, sunshine," I explained to Maya, who perked up. Clearly, they were kindred spirits because in less than a minute, Trinidad had Maya giggling, and she showed her the dress I gifted her, which she insisted on putting on right away.

"Damn, Orlando, you did good, my friend; that lady is..." Maria nodded her approval, giving me that "okayyyy" stare.

"I did damn good, and I will never ever take that for granted," I said loud enough for Trinidad to hear. She turned from her very entertaining conversation with Maya and winked at me.

"You better not!" she mouthed, her eyes bright with happiness, her lush lips framing the sexiest smile.

Fuck, I couldn't stop thinking of her, even when she was right here with me.

And I was alright with that.

Twenty-Seven

Orlando

The airport crowd bustled with tired revelers all making their way back home. Trinidad strolled next to me unhurried, knowing we had plenty of time to get to our gate.

"Can you imagine these knuckleheads planned for me to coincide with you on your return flight?" She held my hand and squeezed as I let laughter take over. I hadn't been able to stop grinning since she walked into the rental; the ache in my chest had transferred to my cheeks, and I wasn't mad at it. She'd given me a second chance, and I wasn't one to waste opportunities. She would never regret returning to Ofele. She would never ever have to doubt she made the right decision.

That was my job for the rest of my life if she'd have me. But I wasn't about to spook her with no big declarations; just holding her hand and walking next to her would be enough.

For now.

"You gotta give it to them; they put in the work," I said once the laughter subsided.

"Don't praise those fools; they are in so much trouble." Trinidad shook her head, shaking her locs with her vehemence.

"Listen, I owe them; they saw the vision; all I needed was for you to see it too."

"Oh, I see the vision, alright." She gazed at me, and my skin warmed at the regard. Other things started to warm, too, so I let the distractions of the walk to the gate keep me calm and collected. This woman had me hardening in the middle of an airport with just a look.

Damn, I was in trouble.

"You alright over there?" The deceptive mild tone told me everything I needed to know.

"You trying to torment me, Ms. V?" I asked, winking at her.

"Maybe…" she trailed off as we arrived at our gate and sat to wait for our flight.

"Listen, I don't want you to think I didn't hear what you said today. All that shit was true. I… I was letting my trauma lead my emotions and my actions; that's not very grown up of me. But I want to keep on working at it, and I will; I just want to know how thankful I am for everything you showed me this weekend," I said to her, baring my soul to her.

"Are you kidding, Orlando? We both opened up to each other, and we both learned and taught this weekend. We learned how to love each other, and I'm so grateful for that."

The beat of soca moved into my chest, making my heart skip a few palpitations.

"Love?" I asked, keeping it cool. Then I grinned like a fool, losing all my cool points, but who cared? This woman loved me?

"Yes. Yes. I love you." She rolled her eyes. "I don't know how you did it but… I love you."

She offered her sweet, lush lips to me, and I got lost in the taste of my girl. So sweet and decadent, full of spice and love. Trinidad moaned into my lips, and soon we had to part before we started an R-rated show in the middle of the airport.

"Now, how am I supposed to be calm after you kissed me like that?" She pouted.

"I'm sure you'll be okay." I pressed my lips to her warm forehead and chuckled when she pouted even more.

"I'm going to need more than that, Orlando," she growled, and I had to taste it off her mouth until I converted the growl into a needy mewl.

"Boy…if you don't."

"Don't worry, I got you," I said, faking the calmness because inside, I was as desperate as her to find a spot and put us both out of our misery.

Once we got on the plane, and after some magic from Trinidad we ended up in first class sitting together.

"How did you manage this?" I couldn't hide my excitement.

"Miles, I travel a lot for work and hoard them like *my precious*," she said, Golum voice and all.

I froze. Did my woman just quote *The Lord of the Rings*?

Heart be still.

"You like *The Lord of the Rings*?" I asked, incredulity all over my face.

"Oh yeah, and I love watching anime, and secretly…some hentai too."

Fuck.

I was in trouble.

"When did you get so perfect and why haven't we talked about this??" I asked.

The evil cackle she let out was truly fantastic; she threw her blanket over her and gave me a coy look over her shoulder.

"You never asked." She shrugged and winked.

"Nah, woman, you can't leave it at that and not say more. What type of hentai do you…do you want to watch some together during the flight?" I asked, swiveling my head back and forth to see if anyone was eavesdropping on our conversation.

"Do you have a privacy screen?" I swear I went rock-hard.

"Are we about to become part of the mile-high club?"

"Hentai-style, baby," she said as I pulled up my phone and found a video for us to watch. We shared my headphones, and soon the scene started, the sensual animated display going right to the point with a woman lying on a bed next to a man massaging her massive blessings.

Trinidad's breath increased to the pace of the scene until her warm hand slid below my blanket, searching the waistband of my sweats.

"You sure?" I mouthed at her, the plane already on its way to NY, the darkened cabin hiding all types of mischief.

"Oh, yes, I am," she purred and held on to my length, dragging her hand up and down to a sweet pace.

"Fuck," I groaned. I needed to touch her too. With what I hope was some poise, I ghosted my hand down her belly scrunching up her dress until I found her wet and ready between her legs.

"Sí, right there," she whispered, riding my hand with an undulating motion that I couldn't wait to feel on my dick.

Together, we rode the sky, our hands declaring the love and trust we felt for each other. The passion we created settled in my chest, and tightened my spine, the pace relentless as we both chased our completion.

When Trinidad's soft thighs squeezed my hand until I couldn't move anything but my finger over her softness, she gasped and shuddered, giving me permission to release all the tension she'd created with her magic hand.

We reach our finales together, silently and powerfully, knowing this would be the first of many other times.

"Fuck, I love you, woman, you're one of a kind." I kissed her, tasting that sweet sensuality so unique to her.

"And I love you too. My man." She pressed another velvety kiss on my lips, then proceeded to curl up and fall asleep next to me.

My life couldn't get any better.

Epilogue 1

Brandon

The hallway to our apartment never felt as long as it did right now. It was like walking to our trial, where our mother would determine what would be the end of our summer. I didn't regret anything. My mother worked hard and deserved the world. But I hated disappointing her, so I guess I did regret something. Brian's silence next to me told me all I needed to know. There were no words required between us; at times, it took one look, and we communicated everything we needed to say.

He was pissed at me because I was the one that came up with the plan. Brian had had his doubts, but he went along with everything because that was what brothers did. Now we both were in deep shit with our mother.

Damn.

Brian pulled out his key and opened the door. We both

swung our backpacks off our shoulders, the synchronicity between us a comfort before what awaited us in our living room.

We silently entered the living area, and there she was, with her back to us on the main sofa. Ma was sitting on Orlando's lap, giggling. I don't think I'd ever seen my mom giggling.

"What do you think they'll say?" she asked him.

"I mean, this is what they wanted, right? So they should be cool about it. Now, come here and kiss me again." Orlando's large hand cupped my ma's face, guiding it down to his—

"The fuck?" I mouthed to Brian.

Brian stood stock-still, a look of pure horror on his face. He shook his head and pointed toward the hallway. No need to tell me twice, I followed him as my mother giggled and Orlando's groans grew louder.

We barricaded ourselves in my room and turned on the TV to bury the sounds from outside.

"The fuck was that?"

"I guess that's what we wanted." Brian shrugged and plopped onto my bed.

"Nah, that's, nah, why couldn't they get a room or something?" I said, disturbed, but deep down, I was glad for Ma. She deserved all the happiness in the world. And I had known since I saw Orlando looking at her like the sun shined from her behind that he would be good to her.

So, I guess I had been right all along.

"Man, wipe that smug look off your face. You know she knew we were there, right? They were messing with us."

"For real?"

"Yeah, listen…" Brian brought down the TV.

From outside, I heard Mom's voice.

"Did you see how fast they ran to the room?"

"Serves them right," Orlando answered.

Damn, I thought my dude was on our side.

But whatever, they could get this one. We won the prize.

Our mother finally had her dreams come true.

Epilogue 2

Brian

High school graduation day and our entire family had shown up to support us. All of our friends were standing all over the gymnasium with their families and loved ones, taking pictures and giving them gifts.

I would have never imagined having such a large crowd come to support Brandon and me. That shit was dope.

Surrounding us in a circle of laughter and love were my father and his wife, all dressed up in designer clothes. Pops had taken a turn for the better a little after Mom had started dating Orlando. We never found out what happened, but it seems he and my mother reached some type of better understanding of how to co-parent. At first, I'd been hesitant to trust my father's presence, but day by day, he proved to us he wanted to be a better father.

Orlando's brothers both stood next to two pretty girls who

were their latest girlfriends. The dudes kept a revolving door going, but hey, if it worked for them, that was cool. I, for one, was looking for some deep, lasting love. I might be young, but I wanted something solid like what my ma and Orlando had.

Their relationship wasn't perfect; they disagreed sometimes but always spoke to each other with respect and consideration. They had different goals in life but made it work for each other, supporting each other in everything they did. When Orlando decided not to do law school, my mom stood by him. When mom decided to retire from the event planning business and start an event consulting business for event planners, travel agencies, and hotels instead, Orlando sat by her side on the long nights as she built her business from scratch.

They'd weathered a lot of highs and lows, and still, every day, they showed up for each other.

Ma stood by Orlando's mother, both laughing at something wild Ma probably said. Maya bounced around from person to person, chatting up with anyone who wanted to hear about the latest animation she was working on with her father.

Maya was my favorite; she had wormed her way into Brandon's and my hearts, and we protected her like big brothers, always looking out for her. She ran over and gave Brandon's boyfriend a big hug, then Brandon; then she came to me.

"Hey, sunshine." I smiled at her, crouching to be at eye level.

"Are you happy, Brian? This was a really fun day with all our family, right?" She grinned, her excitement for us so palpable I couldn't help but give her another hug and a squeeze.

"Yeah, it's awesome."

"Look at Mami Trinidad and Daddy. They can't keep from kissing each other. It's gross," Maya confessed.

I stared at our parents. We still called Orlando by his name, but he was a dad through and through. Today, he gifted us and Mom a painting of a woman who looked like her in a superhero cape with two sons who look very like us. Mom, who is badass, something I'd never tell her, started crying when she saw the art. Right now, they were doing too much, though; Maya was right. Orlando had managed to extricate Ma from the circle and had her in a corner, his hands on her ass and his face buried on her neck. Ma's laughter was loud. We could hear her from here.

"Yeah, you're right. They kinda gross sometimes, but you know what? Love is like that sometimes. They are just really, really happy."

Maya sighed the put-upon sigh of a weary eight-year-old, then nodded in agreement.

"I guess you're right. Better to be happy and in love. But I hope I am not gross like them when I grow up." She shuddered.

"Damn, me too, sunshine. Me too."

★ ★ ★ ★ ★

Genevieve Raymond was born an overachiever. After opening a hot new hotel chain location in Panama, she's on track for a major promotion. But first, she desperately needs a break. For two glorious weeks, Gen's giving herself permission to explore—and the attraction she shares with her sexy-as-hell driver, Adrián Nicolas.

To workaholic Gen, Adrián's laid-back devotion to his family's hometown hostel couldn't be more appealing. Their long-term goals might not align, but two weeks in paradise only calls for seductive physical chemistry.

But when their intimate connection flourishes beyond sunsets and spice, Gen finds herself questioning whether a two-week fling might have what it takes to last forever.

Acknowledgments

Gratefulness is a wonderful practice that has kept me grounded during this journey. My cup remains full because of how lucky I am in my author career and life.

Thank you, John Jacobson, for the relentless support of the book. Not everyone will know all you did for Ms. V, but I know and will forever be grateful. You have a fan in me. Thank you to the Harlequin team for trusting my voice and vision.

To my critique ladies, I am so happy to have you in my life. You make me a better author and a more conscious person. Your craft always leaves me in awe. Thank you, Tasha L. Harrison, Katrina Jackson, and Elysabeth Grace.

To my online friends who supported me while I wrote, I made it to the finish line because of you.

To my family, Los Cunninghams, I really couldn't do this without you. "Mi mami/My wife is an author" will always make me smile and expand my heart. The support you give me makes me want to keep trying. Always.

My readers, new and old, your words of encouragement mean the world to me. Thank you for being an integral part of this journey.

Until next time...

A.H.